THE AW
OF LYDIA

CW00928840

THE AWAKENING OF LYDIA

Philippa Masters

This book is a work of fiction.
In real life, make sure you practise safe sex.

First published in 1995 by
Nexus
332 Ladbroke Grove
London W10 5AH

Copyright © Philippa Masters 1995

Typeset by TW Typesetting, Plymouth, Devon
Printed and bound in Great Britain by
Cox & Wyman Ltd, Reading, Berks

ISBN 0 352 33002 3

Foreword

I found the story that follows among the papers left
after the death of my Great Aunt Lydia. It was written in her own hand and, although it came as a great
shock to me, is, so far as my researches can discover,
entirely true.

Great Aunt Lydia was very old when she passed
away – in her late nineties – and was a woman of
immense dignity and presence. Exactly what one
would imagine, in fact, by the phrase 'Victorian spin-
ster lady'. She had lived alone for as long as I had
known her (almost all my life) and had always kept
herself to herself. She attended church every Sunday
and maintained friendly, though distant, relations
with her neighbours. When I was a child she filled me
with the kind of awe children feel in the presence of
very old and very dignified ladies who smell of laven-
der and mint, and even when I grew up I was always
on my best behaviour in her company.

Thus, this story was a great surprise when I found
it, some years after she passed away, in a concealed
drawer of her old desk – which I only discovered
while cleaning the desk ready to send it to auction!
Indeed I found it almost impossible to believe that
the prim lady I remembered could ever have imagined, much less experienced, the astonishing and
highly erotic episodes written out in her own tidy

handwriting. But experience them she did. And never in any way did she give a clue while she lived!

Because the story was so difficult to reconcile with the very 'correct' old lady I remembered, I decided to do what research I could into the family history. Great Aunt Lydia had indeed spent some time with her father in Southern Africa. He had been a civil servant stationed around what is now the Mozambique/Zimbabwe border in the late 1890s, around the time when tension was rising between the British and the South African Dutch which eventually led to the Boer War. Lydia had been just sixteen years old when they left England and around eighteen when, after a long and eventful voyage home, she returned, and although the story shows that Lydia was not entirely naive I must ask the reader to realise that in those days sixteen was much younger in terms of innocence than today's sophisticated and highly developed teenagers.

Surprising as her story is, what for me shines through, and what has caused me to change my mental image of my great aunt, is the strength of character she displays throughout her adventure and the simple candour and honesty with which she describes the events and her innermost feelings and emotions. Though innocent about 'the facts of life' and, as you will see, nervous and confused at the beginning by what was happening, her innate intelligence and strength of character (a faculty she retained throughout her long life) soon enabled her to adjust to and accept it – even to the extent of admitting what in those repressed days was all but inadmissible – that physical pleasure was not just the province of the male.

That she could live through these experiences could absorb them and candidly accept her own physical delight, and then describe it with such simple honesty and insight make her, for me, one of the most admirable women I can imagine.

Lest the reader feel that I have been somewhat disloyal to my great aunt in revealing this story, I hasten to point out that, although there was no note of instruction, the style in which it was written and one or two internal hints made it, in my judgement, obviously intended for eyes other than Aunt Lydia's. I have done very little editing – a few spelling corrections were all that seemed necessary – and so I confidently leave you to judge for yourself whether I was correct.

Philippa M.

THE AWAKENING
OF LYDIA

Chapter 1

All of my new life was exciting. A new land; new sights, sounds, colours; new people; a very different climate. It was the combination of the last two, I suppose, which led to that extraordinary incident with Jonathan. Looking back, I realised that his advances were sparked by my own naiveté – but at the time, knowing as little as I then did about the transactions between men and women, I was utterly surprised and flustered. When he kissed me it was thrilling. What teenage girl in the year of our Lord 1897, or any other year, would not be thrilled to be given her first grown-up kiss by a handsome young officer? It was what followed, the way he became hot and urgent, the way – the *places* – he fondled me, that caused me such agitation. And not least because of the disturbing sensations stirred in me by what transpired.

Being the daughter of the district commissioner newly arrived from England, I had been feted and sought after by many of the folk in the town of P—— where father had his station. Of all those who danced attendance upon me (a heady thing for a girl not yet seventeen, and entirely due, I was sure, to my father's rank) by far the nicest and most solicitous was Lieutenant Jonathan Andrews. He did not treat me, as nearly everybody else did, like a child, but spoke to me almost as though I were a grown-up. I found it very tiresome to be talked down to all the time, as though I still wore pinnies and played with dolls. True, I still wore my hair in ringlets, and did not yet have the full-length skirts of a grown woman, but I did not *feel* like a child. Actually, I was at that very awkward stage between girl and woman, and perhaps it was that which caused me to so thrill to Jonathan's attentions.

When his soldierly duties permitted, Jonathan would walk with me in the garden and talk to me about his adventures, and about the history of this part of the world, quite as if I were an equal. I looked forward very much to his visits, for he was extremely handsome, and his attention thrilled me. Often we would sit under the shade of my favourite tree, near the little stream that runs through our garden, and chat and laugh as relaxed as could be. More relaxed than I should have been, as it transpired, for it was on just such an occasion that it happened.

It was a sappingly hot day. We had walked down to my tree, thinking it would be cooler in the shade and near the stream. Without any thought other than being less sticky, I had left off as many of the bulky European garments as I could. Already, during my brief time in Africa, it had occurred to me as odd, and less than sensible, that we British continued to wear all the layers and petticoats and such we would have worn at home, despite the very different climate here. I was, of course, dressed perfectly properly to all outward appearance; it was just that, beneath a very nice, loose white lawn blouse I was not wearing a bodice, and I only had one petticoat beneath my skirt. It never occurred to me that this was immodest, for how could anyone ever know.

Even so, I had never felt so hot and sticky in the whole of my life. Even fanning myself with my book seemed to drain my energy. I lay back on the grassy bank and closed my eyes, hoping to at least doze away some of the sticky afternoon. After a while, the quiet tinkling of the stream became a splashing. I looked up and found that it was Jonathan. He had removed his tunic and cap, and his boots, and was knee deep in the stream, splashing water over his head with cupped hands. Oh how I envied him at that moment, for the water must have been deliciously cool. I sat up and watched him, the droplets of water sparkling on his hair and moustache and on his chest, for he had undone some of the buttons of his shirt. He looked very casual, and I found myself blushing at the glimpses I got of his smooth, muscular chest. Even an innocent such as I knew it to be immodest for a gentleman to thus expose his torso to a girl. But then, it was very hot, and all he was doing was trying to cool off. If only I might do the same! And then, in a trice, I was pulling off my shoes and stockings, and splashing into the stream to join him.

The running water was wonderfully cold as, holding my skirts about my knees, I waded and splashed, laughing as the coolness spread deliciously from my toes and ankles to suffuse the whole of my body. Oh it was lovely! Then my little heaven was suddenly ended by a sharp pain in my foot. I cried out and staggered. Luckily, Jonathan was close enough to catch me, else I would surely have fallen full-length into the water. He helped me to the bank and examined my foot, anxious lest I had been bitten. There was some blood, he told me, and I lay back while he raised my foot to his lips. He would suck out the wound, he said, in case there was any infection, for although it looked like a cut and not a bite, one could not be too careful.

3

Jonathan knelt, his face all solicitude as I winced with the sting of the cut, and raised my foot to his lips. Had I not been so naive, and so concerned about the stinging, I would have been more aware of the way his raising of my leg necessarily caused my skirt to slide, and expose my underthings to his gaze. As it was, I did nothing, but simply lay there, grateful for his kindness.

He did indeed place his mouth upon the wound, and I confess that, despite his concern, I soon began to feel not a little odd. I have never been especially ticklish in my feet, but the way he was holding me, my bare ankle clasped in one hand, the fingers of the other manipulating my toes, and the way his lips and tongue worked on the sole (seemingly over an area rather larger than the cut can have been), taking in the arch of my foot and moving like a butterfly right up to the joins beneath my toes, caused very strange sensations to tingle through my foot and along my leg. Perhaps it was these, perhaps the shock of cutting myself, perhaps a sudden consciousness that Jonathan's ministrations were rather intimate: whatever it was, I became decidedly hot and flustered.

Jonathan gently released my foot, and hurried to wet his handkerchief in the stream. Its coolness as he dabbed my brow and temples did much to restore me, and I murmured my thanks as he smoothed the damp material about my ears and my neck. I did not demur, though I know I should have, when he undid some of the buttons of my blouse, for the freshly damped kerchief felt very pleasurable as well as being refreshing as he dabbed around my neck and collarbone, and he was, after all, my friend. When he stopped cooling me, and after a moment's pause, I opened my eyes. He was lying close beside me on the

4

grass, resting on one elbow, his face quite close above my own. Something in his expression, a different look in his deep blue eyes perhaps, gave me pause. A lock of his brown hair had fallen over his brow, and his eyes were flicking rapidly over my features.

I lay still, gazing up at him, puzzled to know what might occur yet knowing that something would. I was oddly breathless. When he began to lower his head towards me, I knew in an instant that he was going to kiss me. I had never been kissed by a man, except a goodnight peck from father, and certainly never thus, on my lips. Like, I suppose, all growing girls, I had thought about being kissed, read about it in novels, waited for the day it would happen to me. Now, I did not know what to do! Jonathan's lips touched very lightly on my own, then a little more firmly when I did not turn away. I felt very strange. I knew I should stop him. Knew that good girls did not allow such liberties. But it felt so nice! Warm, and soft, and setting off a delicate tingling such as I had not felt before.

He kissed me for a long time, and it was infinitely more thrilling than they ever suggested in the stories I had read. I kissed him back. The tinglings his lips had sparked off were spreading strangely, and I felt a warmth and tightness in my chest and a fluttering in my tummy. Jonathan was kissing me more ardently now, brushing his mouth over my cheeks and eyes and neck, even slipping his tongue between my lips, which had parted with the quickness of my breathing. He was lying very close to me, his hard body pressing against mine. The sensations in my chest and tummy increased, changed, took on a new form, and through a haze I suddenly realised why. He was touching me. His hand was moving over my bust!

I did not know what to do. Nothing I had heard or read had suggested that a man might touch me thus, nor about the way those touches at once multiplied the tinglings his kisses had aroused! He was still kissing me avidly, and my budding breasts felt distinctly strange and tense as he fondled me very thoroughly. I knew I should stop him. Knew somehow, though I had never been told so, that what he was doing was rude and must not be allowed. But how to manage it?

His kisses were making me weak and hot. I was torn. Jonathan was very handsome, and I liked him very much. I had wanted him to kiss me, and now felt a disturbing desire for his kisses to continue. I felt, too, sparks of electricity course from the hand which fondled my virgin swellings, like arrows of flame, to the pit of my tummy. Yet it was also somewhat frightening, for not only did I know I should not be allowing these impertinences, but the sensations they were stirring within me were startling and took my breath away.

My growing inner turmoil exploded in my mind when Jonathan, murmuring in thick tones that I was beautiful, moved his seeking lips from my neck, and downwards. Somehow, unaware to me, my blouse had come further undone. His hand was inside it. Now, before I could even think, the material parted and his lips were upon my naked breast! He was kissing me, licking my swellings. His lips embraced my nipple! Oh, heavens! I should stop him! Must stop him! Yet I could not, for I was entirely helpless to resist the caresses of his mouth upon my skin; of the tongue which rasped my nipple; of the breath which burned me and sent tingling spasms in waves from my breasts to my tummy, thighs and head.

He was lying even closer to me now, his body as hot as his mouth. His leg had moved onto mine, and he was pressing himself against me most strangely. An atom of panic began to grow in me, for no matter how unprepared I had been for the sensations Jonathan was arousing; how ignorant of the possibilities opened up by a kiss, I knew that soon I would not be in control of myself. Nor, I knew, would Jonathan, for he was very hot and urgent and was muttering broken, incomprehensible words as his hand and mouth moved upon my bosom, now totally exposed by the blouse that had come almost off my shoulders.

And then I was shaken as by a jolt of electricity, for his hand was suddenly upon my private place! I squealed with shock. My skirts had ridden up when he nursed my foot, and his hand was fully upon me, actually between my legs, hot and hard through the thin cotton of my drawers, moving and rubbing in a most lascivious manner. I was shocked to my core! I must stop him! For a moment we struggled, I to get my lips away from his, to rid myself of the marauding hand, he to continue kissing me and molesting my struggling body!

Then, suddenly he was off me. All was confusion. I did not know what to do, where to look! I was trembling and knew not what to say or what to do. Jonathan scrambled to his feet, very red of face and, which puzzled me and made me blush, with an odd distortion at the front of his breeches, which must have been what he had so rubbed against my hip while he was kissing me. He went behind me to sort his shirt and tunic. I was trembling and breathless. Jonathan uttered some strangled sounds, then blurted that he was sorry and that I must forgive him for

7

getting 'carried away', and then positively ran from me.

I kept the incident to myself, as much because of my own confusion as from fear of the trouble its revelation might cause. I knew, somehow, that my own behaviour had caused Jonathan to become so hot, and felt a little ashamed of myself. Worse, though, was the jumble of my own inner feelings. I knew that what Jonathan had done was rude, forbidden; that I myself was at fault for allowing him to kiss me and take the liberties he had. But how strange, how alluring it had seemed!

I could still feel the tingling of his lips on mine, the soft yet commanding way they had caressed my mouth. I knew, from books and journals, that kissing was not entirely forbidden, and was actually supposed to be pleasant. But what of those extraordinary sensations in my breasts; that lurch of electricity when he had thrust his hand between my thighs? It had been shock, yes, that he should touch me there; but it was more. Why had my bosom tingled and tensed so, even before he touched it? Why had the hotness of his hand upon my private place gone so deep into the pit of my tummy, lingered so, made my legs feel so weak? Even now, as I thought about it, an echo of those very sensations caused a buzzing in my nipples!

It was a confusion and a puzzle, and I had no-one to ask about it. I did not dare approach Miss Blake, my governess, for she was a very proper lady, and would, I knew, have castigated me roundly, and revealed all to father. I am sure that had Jonathan visited again I would have got him to enlighten me, but he stayed away. I could understand why, but found his absence disappointing nevertheless. You may be sure that these puzzles, and the new, not entirely comfortable, awareness of myself they had engendered, sent me into a reflective mood. I found myself watching the people around me with a new curiosity. More, I found myself examining my own person. I had a full-length looking glass on the back of my wardrobe door. Without premeditation, as I was about to retire to bed one evening, I caught sight of my reflection, and stopped to regard it.

I had already removed my frock, and stood in just my bodice and drawers. I knew I was quite pretty, for I had been told so, and had often examined my face in the washstand mirror. Now, my eyes travelled over my reflection from head to toe. Suddenly, as if out of nowhere, I felt that selfsame tingling in my chest that Jonathan's kisses had evoked. It was as if my nipples were being chafed by the cotton of my bodice! On a sudden impulse, I grasped the ribbons, loosened them, and tugged the garment off over my head. It had not been the cotton, for my nipples tingled even more when my breasts were exposed to the air and my gaze!

I had only begun to develop towards womanhood during the last half year or so, and my swellings were not large. I stared at myself, and was surprised at the way my chest seemed to become taut, and the little pink nubs of my nipples sparked and actually stiffened! I found myself blushing, not only at the sight, but at the sudden remembrance of Jonathan's hands upon me, and his mouth. As if independent of my will, my own hands rose and I cupped myself. My blushes spread down over my throat and to my collarbone, for I had become strangely excited and breathless. I traced the tips of my thumbs across my nipples, and they sparked and buzzed.

Trembling a little, for I knew that what I was doing was shockingly immodest, but quite unable to stop myself, I fumbled with the ribbon at my waist. Slowly, holding my breath, for I had never actually examined myself there, I lowered my drawers and stepped out of them. The puzzling tension deep in the pit of my tummy I had felt when Jonathan touched me was back, if anything more strongly. My thighs were clamped together, and the place between them, shaded a little by its sparse fuzz of fair curls, was veritably itching and hot. A hand, feeling almost as though it belonged to someone else, slipped from my breast, down over the white swell of my tummy, to my vee of down. The fingers were tense as they cupped the place I had never touched except in bathing. They pressed. I felt such a spasm deep within my body that it shocked me out of my trance, and sent me scurrying away from the mirror, ashamed of myself and trembling hotly. I poured cold water into the bowl, spilling quite a lot onto the washstand in my haste, and splashed it over my burning face and neck. I struggled into my voluminous nightgown, and threw myself into bed, my mind a whirlpool of confusion.

My state did not improve over the next days and weeks. I found myself looking at the world with very different, nervous, curious eyes. Things I had never been conscious of before caught my attention. I became aware of Miss Blake's figure compared to my own. I would notice the set of a man's shoulders, the shape of a brow, the swing of a walk. My eyes seemed unable to avoid glancing at the cut of a man's trousers and especially at the tight breeches of the officers who visited father. I was constantly in a blush of embarrassment. I even found myself searching among the books and journals for some enlightenment as to what was happening to me, but to no avail.

Of course, father noticed that my behaviour had changed. Blessedly, though, he did not infer the real reasons, but simply thought that I might be coming down with something. He decided that I would benefit from a change of air, and arranged for me to visit a colleague's farm in the highlands some days journey away. You may be sure I was delighted with the project, for the visit would distract me, and I would get to see more of this beautiful land.

There were indeed distractions. The country itself, with its tan-coloured rolling hills, which became almost blue in the far distance; its acacia trees and thorn bushes; the myriad forms of animal life, birds, zebra, herds of exotic beasts in the distance. At the farm, though, my earlier confusions soon returned in full force.

Absolutely unlike any farm at home in England, it was a great, sprawling establishment, with many outbuildings, and a number of shed-like huts for the African workers. Mr Ambrose, the owner, was a hearty, striking man of around fifty, deeply tanned from his open air life, tall and broad shouldered, with a deep, ready chuckle. His wife, on the other hand, was a tiny, almost birdlike creature, who hardly came up to his shoulder. But the persons with whom I was to spend the most time, and the persons who so brought back my confusions, were their two sons.

Albert, the eldest, was cut from the same cloth as his father, though not so wide in the shoulders; while Richard, closer to my own age, was like neither of his parents, being of average height. He did, though, have his mother's lustrous black hair and

11

dark, brilliant eyes. From the moment I was introduced to them I was a little nervous, for they both smiled at me rather oddly, almost speculatively.

Perhaps it was that manners in the countryside were less strict than in town, more probably it was a deliberate policy on their part, for I noticed that, whereas they were all deference towards Miss Blake, the two young men adopted a much more familiar, though no less polite, manner with me. At first this was very pleasant after the constrictions of town mannerliness. They took me about the farm, showed me the livestock, chatted and laughed with me about anything and everything. Soon, though, this easiness took on a less comfortable tone, at least for me.

It began when the two young men took me to see my first native village. All the Africans I had seen since arriving in this land had worn European style clothing, and I was absolutely unprepared for the sight of women and girls going about entirely naked to the waist, and with only folds of cloth about their hips, which left their legs exposed even above the knee. I was not a little shocked and embarrassed, as you can imagine, for it is an ingrained part of every girl's upbringing that she must keep herself covered from men's eyes. And now, here were girls and women walking about, or carrying out various tasks, with their breasts naked to the view of the world! I felt myself blushing to my roots, and my embarrassment was only deepened when I saw that Albert and Richard did not hesitate to glance boldly about them, openly enjoying the sight of the semi-naked females.

That I had so recently become aware of my own body, and that at least one man, Jonathan, had made advances upon it, made me acutely conscious that these girls had the same parts as myself, albeit in most

12

cases rather fuller. Even through my embarrassment, I was aware that my own bosom, safely hidden within my blouse and underbodice, had become taut, and that unruly tingling which had so plagued me lately had started afresh – and got worse when I noticed Albert look quite brazenly from one girl's rather full, and completely naked breasts to my own concealed bosom, an impertinent twinkle in his eyes! That nothing was said was a great mercy, but you may be sure that I was in a considerable fluster as we drove back to the farm.

It was as if, encouraged in their impishness by my obvious embarrassment in the native village, the two young men set out deliberately to tease and torment me. Albert took to working about the farm with his shirt quite unbuttoned, and no undervest on, so that I could not avoid the sight of his insolently bared chest, and he would smile saucily when he caught me blushing. Richard was more subtle, for he always kept himself properly dressed. He did, though, frequently compliment me upon my looks and my apparel, and seemed to find many occasions to touch me upon the arm, or shoulder, or the small of my back. The touches were innocent in themselves, and could not be complained of, except that they seemed rather more lingering than strictly necessary. I suspected his motivations to be less than innocent from the way I would frequently catch him glancing at my figure.

I told myself that I was imputing to them intentions which sprang entirely from my own over-sensitive condition, and the confusions caused in me by Jonathan's advances. In terms of manners, both Albert and Richard behaved entirely properly. Surely the fact that the sight of his exposed chest caused me

13

to tingle, and my breath to flutter, could not be blamed upon Albert? Surely, too, the fact that I found Richard distinctly good looking, and his compliments on my appearance quite thrilling, could not be called his fault? The warmth, the sensitivity to his touches upon my arm or shoulder, could only possibly be attributed to my own misunderstandings. Just because Jonathan had kissed me, and fondled my breasts, and put his hand between my legs, did not mean that Albert and Richard would be thus uncouth!

I castigated myself roundly. The two young men were entirely pleasant and unmotivated. The sensations which plagued me were entirely my own fault! That I should tingle so when Richard looked at my bosom was due to my own naughtiness of thought. That my tummy should lurch and flutter at the sight of Albert's chest was my fault, not his. That both sensations were frequent and, if I was honest enough to confess it, alluring, and that I found myself remembering the sensation of Jonathan's lips upon mine, and wondering if Richard's would feel the same, was disconcerting and, I told myself, should be a source of shame. I determined to put my silly thoughts behind me and to return the young men's guileless friendliness with equal innocence. Thus, when Richard invited me to drive to a nearby lake with him for a picnic, I accepted happily.

When he touched me, as we sat beside the lake after our picnic, it suddenly seemed far from innocent and motiveless. True, he had only put his arm about my shoulder, had not said or done anything to suggest more than simple friendliness, but I knew. Somehow I knew that he was going to kiss me, and that I wanted him to kiss me. Already I was a-tremble!

He touched a finger to my chin and turned my face towards his own. His eyes were dark and lustrous; lakes far deeper than the one beside which we sat. When his lips touched mine, it was as if with a soft questioning. Already, butterflies were stirring within me. His kisses were tender, lingering and heady, and I surrendered myself to them as he reclined me upon the grass. I was not thinking at all, only melting into the delicious caress of his mouth upon mine, and savouring the warm tingling which spread from my lips to my breasts and shallowed my breathing.

Echoes of Jonathan stirred within me. Richard's kisses were as sweet, though gentler, with none of the urgency or greediness that had developed with Jonathan's. When Richard's hand, as I had known it would, slipped from my neck to touch almost tentatively upon my breast, I was torn. I knew I should stop him, for this was what had so set Jonathan off, but I could not. His touch was welcome. It was as if my breast were reaching out to greet the hand which gently cupped it, sending sparks and tinglings arrowing down to the pit of my tummy. I told myself I was wrong in allowing him to thus kiss and fondle me, but the sensations were so sweet, so alluring, that I did not want them to stop. Richard was gentle and kind. He would not get carried away as Jonathan had done.

When I felt him fumbling with the buttons of my blouse I did ask him to stop, but I could manage no more than a whisper, and he kissed me into silence. The touch of his warm fingertips inside my blouse, even inside my bodice, made me shiver, but hotly. The slight scratch of his palm across the delicate skin of my breast sent tremors pulsing through me, and I felt a strange pulling tension grow at the base of my stomach, deep within my place. Richard was kissing

15

me more warmly now, and I felt my nipples tense and perk as his hand moved upon my tingling breast. I was becoming carried away myself, and my thighs and insides seemed to have melted around the pulsing warmth that was growing and growing deep in the pit of my tummy.

Somehow, from some well of self-preservation, I dragged up some self-control. The sensations which were sweeping through me were heady, enticing; frighteningly tempting. I would be lost if I let him continue; incapable of forbidding him any liberty, even to putting his hand where Jonathan's had been, unless I stopped him now. I pulled my lips away from his, pushed at him with weak hands, begged him breathlessly to desist. At first he did not, but kissed me again, more hotly, and fondled my aching breast more urgently. Then, at my increased pleas and struggles, he did stop and roll away from me.

The silence was almost solid as I straightened my dishevelled blouse, and it did not lighten all the while we packed away the picnic and drove back to the farm. What were Richard's thoughts I could not know. But for myself, I was in a turmoil. I knew that I had upset him. That in allowing him so much as I had, I had got him excited, only to dash cold water on him with my sudden resistance. It was not his fault, for I had let him, had encouraged him by returning his kisses, by selfishly accepting, relishing even, the sensations he had aroused when caressing my breast. I could not think what to say. I wanted somehow to apologise to him, but could not think of the words.

All the way back to the farm, and even after we reached it, Richard, too, remained silent. Not angrily so, to judge by his expression and posture, but as if withdrawn into himself and guarding a hurt. I did determine to apologise to him, for the more I thought about it the more at fault I felt myself to be. I found him, after supper, tidying some harnesses in one of the barns. He stared at me doubtfully, his posture tense, as I stood before him, shuffling my feet with sudden shyness as I struggled to find appropriate words. At last I managed to blurt them out clumsily.

At my halting apology, he gave an audible sigh. His face became illuminated with a gentle smile as he assured me that, yes, he did forgive me, and indeed should apologise in his turn. It was just that I was so very pretty, and he could not resist the temptation to kiss me. He thought I had enjoyed it, and had no wish at all to upset me. I coloured at the compliments and confessed that I had indeed enjoyed it, but the strange feelings he had evoked had frightened me a little.

We were standing quite close together in the barn. He touched a finger to my chin, and lifted my face so that he was looking into my eyes. His lustrous eyes seemed to reach inside my own, and I felt that surge of unruly tingling suffuse my bosom. He told me that he too had been swept with strong sensations. That in a man they were stronger, more demanding, than in a girl; that I was delicious, and he ached for me. Yes, he told me at my expression of puzzlement, in a man such feelings were powerful indeed, and led to actual physical symptoms.

A delicious girl such as I could cause a man great discomfort, even pain, when those symptoms went unrelieved. You can imagine my concern, for all this was new to me, yet it explained his silence on the journey home, and made me feel even more guilty than I had earlier. Richard was nice. He was a good

17

friend, and I had no wish to cause him discomfort. He stepped closer and gave me a little peck on my cheek. I again told him I was sorry. He kissed my mouth, and whispered that it was not too late if I really did want to help him.

Of course I did, but did not know how. He stepped even closer and took my hand. I *could* help him, he whispered. Thus, for this was where his pain was. I felt him curl my fingers around something strange; something which filled the palm of my hand. I glanced up at his face, puzzled, and he nodded and smiled, and kissed me again. I remembered the odd distortion in Jonathan's breeches and realised that he too must have been in this kind of pain. Richard's hand was covering mine, moving it upon the thing which was obviously part of his body, but none such as I had ever imagined. It was uptilted, and seemed very hard beneath hot skin which moved easily over its core as my hand was slid up and down it. It was quite thick and the end, which reached beyond my wrist, was thicker and hotter.

My hand continued the rubbing motion into which Richard had guided it. Such a stiff, hot, throbbing object must indeed have been uncomfortable, I thought, and if this odd rubbing of it was a help to Richard, I was happy to perform it. I rubbed and rubbed. Richard was very close, breathing quickly, obviously very anxious for whatever relief this strange treatment could bring him. He had one hand upon my shoulder, his hips rocking in time to the rhythm of my pumping hand. Suddenly, his other hand descended and cupped me at the join of my thighs, covering my place as Jonathan's had. His own excitement had already communicated itself to me, and though I knew it to be naughty I did not make him desist. To have done so would only have distracted the poor lad – and actually his hand did not feel obnoxious. When he began to flex his fingers in time to the motions of my own rubbing hand, tweaking actually into the vee of my thighs, the shocks he caused me were not of fright. I myself became as hot as he, and nothing existed except my hand on him and his hand on me, until he gasped and stiffened and jerked, and my forearm was suddenly splashed with hot effusions, which shocked me out of the haze into which I had drifted.

I leapt back in dismay. My arm was covered! I did not know what it was, but rushed to grab some hay and wipe it off. By the time I returned my attention to Richard, he was leaning back against the wall, his face flushed, his eyelids drooping. I did not know what we had done, but knew that it was important. I could think of nothing except to hurry away, flustered, puzzled and, I confess, rather hot and weak in the thighs.

Chapter 2

I did not know what that strange thing Richard had got me to do was, only that he had become very intense and peculiar. And to judge from his contorted features and ragged breathing he was indeed in considerable agony. I did know that – even had his hand not been where it was – those bodily sensations that had so disturbed me of late might well have run away with me! The way he had gasped and jerked; the way whatever it was I had been rubbing more and more rapidly had hardened and pulsed; the way his hand on my place had cupped and tweaked and tormented me, all threw me into a turmoil of confusion. Why did my body plague me thus? To whom, to what source of enlightenment could I turn? What unimaginable things might develop?

Had I stayed at the farm much longer, who knows how my relationship with Richard would have developed. Even my relationship with Albert, who certainly showed signs of liking me in the way Richard did. But it was not to be, for a messenger arrived that very evening from a farm some distance away. There had been some kind of trouble, a skirmish with some people Mr Ambrose called 'those damned Boers'. It was decided there and then that we were to return, Miss Blake and I, to father's station, leaving with the dawn. We were in peril here, and would be safer near the garrison in town.

I had wanted some distraction from the strange new thoughts and sensations which had plagued me lately, and from the turmoil caused in me by my relieving of Richard. I certainly had it now! We packed hurriedly and I hardly slept a wink for nervousness and excitement. Dawn had hardly broken when we set off, our party made up of some of Mr Ambrose's farmworkers, for he could not spare himself or any of the other British in case the farm was raided by the Boers. Our bearers set a rapid pace, and the litters which bore Miss Blake and myself positively bounced rather than swayed. They kept the pace up all day and were obviously exhausted by the time we camped and retired for the night.

The first I knew of the raid, and our kidnapping, was being awakened by a pale and trembling Miss Blake. It was the strangest thing! We had camped last night, safe and content among the bearers who were escorting us, and lo, somehow, as we had slept all unawares, our bearers were gone, and we were in the hands of what Miss Blake called 'naked savages'! Indeed, as I turned my head in fright, I could see through the open flap of the tent, the back and legs of an African, clad only in a sort of flap of cloth which hardly covered him at all! I looked to Miss Blake. As if she read the frightened questions in my eyes, she shook her head and put her finger to her lips. A sharp call startled us, and by gestures the man at the entrance signalled us that we should leave the tent. Miss Blake's eyes told me we should talk later.

There were four men, tall and fierce-looking, clutching spears and wearing only those flapping loincloths back and front. Even in the midst of my fright at our situation, I confess that I was shocked and embarrassed at their skimpy garb, and also by the fact that Miss Blake and I still wore only our cotton nightgowns. At least, though, they covered us far more modestly than these men were dressed! By gestures and words I could not understand, and with some pushing, the men made us know that we were to march with them.

That first day was a maelstrom that made my head spin. We marched, and were then taken in a boat on a river, then marched again. I became more and more exhausted. Worse, though, was the fact that the four men surrounding us were virtually naked, and that the many thorn bushes by which we had to pass seemed actually to reach out for my nightgown. It soon became very tattered, so that I had great difficulty in clutching it about me. Miss Blake had the same problems, and I blushed for her as her legs, and even a hip, became exposed most immodestly.

At last, we came to a village and through a daze of exhaustion I was aware that the villagers about us all seemed to be laughing and solicitous, and that Miss Blake was warning me about keeping my dignity as an Englishwoman whatever things these people did with me. At that moment, dignity was the last thing on my mind! I remember being given some water to drink, and being shown to a trestle bed. I sank upon it, and knew nothing more until I was awakened by a smiling girl.

At once I saw that Miss Blake was not in the hut. I looked about me in a panic. Had she been there last night when I collapsed onto the bed? I could not be sure. What had happened to her? Where could she be? When I found myself being beckoned and gestured to leave the hut, my tummy tightened into a knot of fright. The scene outside only added to my nervousness.

People milled about, men, women and children,

laughing and talking animatedly. They were all virtually naked, as our captors had been. The sun was blinding and I was hard put to adjust my eyes. I was pulled forward by many hands and suddenly found myself in the middle of the mass of people. I stared dumbfounded. There stood our four captors, but more! With them stood Miss Blake. Her hair was loose and dishevelled, and she was dressed, or rather undressed, like the native women, her nakedness hardly defended at all by the skimpy scraps of cloth hanging below her waist! I confess that I was very shocked. How could an Englishwoman appear thus exposed without dying of shame!

I suddenly felt hands upon me! I spun around. Several laughing women were tugging at the torn and dirty cotton of my nightgown! I tried to thrust their hands away; began to struggle. Better the tattered gown than to be naked! Above the noise, I heard Miss Blake calling urgently, 'Miss Lydia! Miss Lydia! Be still! Submit lest they become angry!' I obeyed. I felt I should die of embarrassment as the tattered nightgown was pulled over my head! I tried to hide myself with my hands. Not since I was ten had anyone seen me thus naked, and then only a maid to help me bathe!

I looked to Miss Blake for help. She was standing straight, looking towards me and shaking her head as if to warn me to be still. A girl approached. She tied a sort of cord about my waist, and front and back hung squares of soft cloth like those Miss Blake wore. Even as she did so it entered my head that she was only dressing me as she was dressed. It was not much comfort, but at least part of me was covered. I was led close beside Miss Blake and she held my hand for reassurance, which helped a little.

It became clear from the bundles and water skins on the ground, around the men's feet, that a march was intended. They seemed to be the same four men who had kidnapped us. Bundles were lifted and held out, and I realised that Miss Blake and I were expected to carry our share. I copied Miss Blake and hefted a bundle onto my back and a water bag on a strap onto my shoulder. There were calls and shouts, and the men picked up their spears and bundles. It was clear that we were to be off, but just as the men began to lead us away an old woman came rushing out, calling loudly.

They stopped and there was an animated discussion. The woman held a large gourd and gestured with it in our direction. I looked to Miss Blake, puzzled, but she just shrugged her shoulders and looked down. The woman approached Miss Blake, and using gestures got her to put down her bundles. Then she dipped a hand into the gourd and began to smear some kind of unguent upon Miss Blake's shoulders and arms. I stared transfixed, but was distracted when my own bundles were lifted off me. One of the men stood before me. He was smiling, and holding a gourd similar to the woman's. He began to smear my shoulders with the stuff. It felt cool, and I realised for the first time how hot the sun was on my bare skin. Perhaps the unguent was a protective against its power of burning?

The man smoothed the unguent over my back and arms and shoulders then, oh dear! His hands moved to my ribs, even towards my chest! I shrank back with embarrassment. Images of Jonathan and Richard flashed through my mind. This man, though, seemed entirely unmoved by what his hands were smoothing over. He bent to deal with my legs, and he did not hesitate to cover the whole of them. Right up to, and even under, the loincloth! I felt tears of embarrassment sting my eyes as his hands smeared over my bottom and – horrors – even onto that most private of places! And he did it so casually! As if what was so shocking to me were the most ordinary thing in the world!

My mortification had no chance to be expressed, for we at once set off to calls and waves from the people we were leaving. The men set what was for me a painfully quick pace, their bodies gleaming in the sunlight, their long, muscular legs moving easily through the waving grass. The sun was hot and I had almost to run to keep up, for I was afraid of what would happen if I stumbled. Even so, stumble I did, and often. The man closest to me – we were marching in file, with Miss Blake well ahead – seemed not to get angry, though. Indeed, he helped me to my feet each time, and even took the heavy water bag from me. In fact, had circumstances been different, less outlandish, I might have found him actually friendly. It only added to my confusion that these people, who were our captors, and who had obviously driven off our bearers by fear and even violence (and who were – in Miss Blake's words – 'naked savages') seemed only smiling and relaxed, and not fierce at all!

After about an hour we stopped to rest and drink. This was most welcome indeed, for my feet were bare and, even though we were marching in grassland, they had quickly become grazed and sore. My escort – the same one who had applied the unguent to me earlier – noticed the condition of my feet as I sank gratefully to the ground in the shade of a group of trees. To my surprise, for were these men not supposed to be brutes and animals, his face expressed concern and, lifting each of my feet in turn, he washed them with water from the skin he carried. There followed many words and gestures, but I could not understand what he was trying to say to me. Then, to my astonishment, he reached forward and pulled off the front part of my loincloth! Even as I began to protest, he lifted my foot and bound it with the cloth. I was dumbstruck. He was not stripping me, but protecting my feet! Even as the wonder of this kindness overwhelmed me, he rolled me to one side, pulled off the remaining piece of my loincloth and wrapped my other foot. Only when he began to smear me with the lotion did it occur to me that in thus protecting my feet he had torn away my only covering, and that now, apart from the strand of cord about my waist, I was entirely nude!

It was awfully embarrassing to stand there as he smeared the ointment over my body. Even though he grinned at me, and seemed entirely relaxed and friendly, I felt like to die standing naked, alone and helpless under his ministrations. However, he *had* thought to protect my feet, and his hands were quite gentle, and as he seemed motivated only by kindness, I maintained my dignity and submitted as Miss Blake had told me, while he smoothed the stuff onto me.

His oiling of me this time was much less casual than in the village. Having spread the unguent over my arms and shoulders and back, he seemed to pay especial attention to my bust. He seemed to take considerable pleasure in smoothing the ointment around and over my swellings, which began to feel rather tight and sensitive, for he was very thorough. He glanced at me with a wide smile when, to my surprise and embarrassment, my nipples stiffened and tingled. I felt myself blushing, then blushing deeper as his hand circled down over my tummy.

26

This man was doing what Jonathan and Richard had done, but not with their hotness and urgency. Where they had become excited, he seemed merely engaged in an activity it was necessary to perform – and I was far more helpless under his hands than I had been under theirs! He used both hands to oil my legs, from my ankles upward. I felt myself growing tense as he smoothed above my knees, pulling them a little apart, moving round from back to front, circling slowly higher. I could hardly breathe for the tightness in my chest and tummy, which I knew to be caused by more than just nervousness at what he was doing. When he grinned up at me, it was as if he were toying. I knew what he was going to do. Knew he was going to touch me *there*, and my knees began to tremble.

He spent what seemed an awfully long time smoothing the oil onto my calves and knees and thighs. I felt terribly vulnerable and exposed as his hands began to smooth over my hips, and around to my bottom. I could not stop what he was doing. I understood that it was a strange game he was playing, and hoped that at least it would soon be over! It was not, though, for he seemed to spend even longer oiling my bottom than he had my breasts, circling his hands, squeezing me, sliding his fingers even along the cleft between my buttocks. When he began to slide his fingers over my private place, I trembled indeed, both with embarrassment and with those inevitable sensations his impertinent hands were creating. It was all too clear to me that he was touching me as Jonathan had tried to – but now I had no drawers to protect me! It was awful having to stand there, letting him touch me as he wished. I suddenly wanted to cry, and almost did when I felt him press a fingertip a little into each of my openings.

He stopped when I jerked and gave a little gasp of shock and, as if reading my confusion from my expression, let me go. I felt myself blushing to my ankles as he towered close in front of me. I cared not that he might be irritated, only that he had stopped touching me there, in that way! But he was not angry. He simply gave a low chuckle, patted my bottom gently, stooped to pick up the bundles, and turned to walk off, beckoning me to follow.

I can recall few details of that first day's march, except becoming exhausted, and being frequently oiled. The sun was hot. I was more and more grateful for the stops to rest. I was confused that my escort seemed friendly and caring, rather than cruel as I had been led to expect. He made sure I drank, helped me when I stumbled, he even, at one stage, carried me across his shoulder (though I was sure he did not really need to keep his hand quite so high on my thigh as he did so!). I became very grateful for the unguent, for not only did it protect me from the heat of the sun, but his rubbing it in seemed to ease the aches in my limbs. I even came to accept the way he took that strange pleasure in oiling my bottom and private place, although it was confusing that, each time, he pressed a finger a little into both places. I could not imagine why he wished to oil my insides, but he did, and I had to admit that after the first few times it was not actually unpleasant. I was too exhausted to protest and he did not seem intent on hurting me.

Towards evening we caught up with Miss Blake and the other men, near a small river. They had already begun to make a camp. I was exhausted. Every bone in my body seemed to ache, and my feet were very sore, so I felt a flush of gratitude when my escort

28

gestured towards a pile of furs and put his hands beside his head in a pantomime of sleeping.

I awoke feeling chilly, for the night was surprisingly cool. It was very dark, with only a crescent moon, half-hidden by scudding clouds. I sat up quickly, for a moment at a loss as to where I was. Some yards away I saw the glowing embers of a fire. I pulled one of the furs around my shoulders against the chill, and moved towards it. At first I could not see or hear anyone. Then, beyond the fire, I descried figures, and made towards them, only to stop. Somehow, I do not know why, I felt that I should not make my presence known.

In the pale, interrupted light of the moon I made out a strange tableau. What first caught my eye was a paleness that I soon realised was Miss Blake. She was not alone, for one of the men was lying with her. From the way his hands were moving he might have been smoothing unguent on her – but he could not have been, for there was no sun! However that might have been, he was very definitely running his hand over her bosom as my escort had rubbed his over mine! When the man's hand began to circle down over Miss Blake's tummy, I felt my own grow tense. The hand moved down over her hip, along her thigh, not rubbing but smoothing slowly, down to her knee and then, circling, just as slowly back up her thigh. I caught my breath, for Miss Blake was parting her thighs of her own volition, and his hand was slipping between them!

Visions of Richard's and Jonathan's rude advances upon my body swam before me. The man was touching Miss Blake as they had touched me, only she was naked, and was not protesting; she had actually opened herself for him.

Somehow, without conscious thought, I knew that here could be the answer to the confusions that had plagued me recently. I sneaked closer, anxious not to be noticed by the other men, who I could see sitting close by the fire, seemingly oblivious of what was going on. I moved behind a bush, to a position where I could have a clearer view of what was happening. The man's body gleamed black and silver in the moonlight, the muscles of his back and legs flexing as he moved to press close against her. Miss Blake's knees were wide apart, and the man's hand was moving upon her thighs and her place. He rolled on top of her, though for what reason I could not then imagine. I could see that he was naked and, after a pause during which he seemed to fumble his hand between their bodies, his taut bottom began rising and falling rhythmically. Miss Blake gave an audible gasp. Her legs shone palely on either side of his writhing body, and her heels locked onto the backs of his knees as she began to squirm to his rhythm.

I knew that I should not be watching, but their sinuous movements and quiet gasping noises held an irresistible fascination that caused me to catch my breath – and, all unwonted, that pulsing hotness had grown in my place and my breasts. In a shaft of brighter moonlight I caught sight of her face. For a moment I thought she must be in pain, for her mouth was open and her eyes tight shut. But it was a sort of half-smile; not a grimace of agony, and her eyebrows were raised, so that her expression was of a strange kind of joy.

The man seemed to speed up his movements. Miss Blake's hands went to his shoulders and her whole body began to writhe to match his more and more forceful rhythm. She started to emit sort of sobbing gasps in time to his movements. It flashed into my head that, whatever was happening, whatever the man was doing to her, she was more than simply submitting. She was, indeed, sharing in some strange excitement! I stared, amazed and puzzled, as the man suddenly began to jerk and writhe even more furiously, and to grunt, and then, with a low shout, to stiffen dramatically, his spine arching. Miss Blake, too, seemed galvanised, and her legs clamped around the man as her hips writhed and circled against him.

I felt hot, with a squirming tension between my legs. It was as if the ghost of Richard's hand had found me. After a breathless interval, both the man and Miss Blake seemed to collapse as though punctured. Her legs fell away from him, and after a long moment he rolled away. Miss Blake's pale body curled into a ball as he got up, and moved towards the fire. I stared at her, not knowing what on earth had been happening, but knowing somehow that it was strange and secret.

The spell was broken when one of the other men said something with a laugh, and got up to move towards Miss Blake. I was startled, and began to creep away, only for him to turn his head and laugh again. I hurried back to my bed of skins, blushing, for I knew he had seen me and must have guessed that I had been watching. For a long while I lay trembling, wondering what on earth my governess could be up to, hearing renewed gasps and knowing that, whatever it was, she was doing it again!

I must have dozed off at last despite the chill, for the next I knew was that someone came and lay close beside me. I was lying on my side, and I felt grateful for the warmth as whoever it was snuggled close behind me, put an arm around me, and tucked the fur close about us. I know not how long it was before I realised that it was not Miss Blake. I know I dozed, and awakened to the odd feeling of a hand moving over me – slowly, very gently, warm, and definitely moving! For an instant I was about to protest, then I recognised the touch as that of my escort of the march, and dared not.

I lay very still. The hand was concentrating on my breasts, exploring my swellings and my nipples, just as it had done when he oiled me, but more so. It felt most peculiar; a strange sort of tingling, as if his fingers were sparking. Butterflies started in my tummy as the hand began to move down, describing little circles, dipping a fingertip into my bellybutton. What on earth could he be thinking of? Was he going to do to me what that other man had been doing to Miss Blake?

I grew very nervous as the hand slid further, exploring the tops of my thighs, then – oh heavens – moving towards my private place! My head whirled. I should stop him! Touching me thus while oiling me was one thing, I could not avoid that, but this was surely different! He was lying close, the pressure of his legs warm against the backs of my own. Perhaps he thought I was asleep? My legs were together, and I pressed them closer as his fingers sought me.

The hand moved again, running up my body to touch my chest, then down. This time he grasped my hip. I felt pressure, soft but firm. He was pulling me towards him. I could not help but move as he wished, rolling half onto my back. His hand returned to my stomach. Slid down. Found its target! He had touched me there each time he had smoothed the unguent on me, but now, as I lay pretending to be asleep, his hand lingered, explored!

He moved slowly, softly, sliding along my legs, pulling them apart a little. Then to my belly again, and down. His whole hand smoothed over the insides of my thighs. I felt myself trembling, so he must have guessed I was awake, but he did not desist. I trembled afresh as a fingertip explored the cleft of my bottom, then moved up, to slip between the folds of my place and slide along my crease. I again felt those strange shocks that seemed to come whenever a man touched me thus, Now, though, he did not simply touch and move away. The shocks continued, grew, as he stroked back and forth. It was scary now, for it was as if my place was growing moist and more and more sensitive to his touches.

It was awfully confusing, for although what he was doing was rude and forbidden, it was strangely tantalising! Visions of Miss Blake and the man just now, flooded my mind. I began to feel hot, and very aware of every movement of his fingers. Low down inside my stomach that ball of tension was growing, my chest was tight, and I began to become breathless. I wanted to stop him, but could not think how. He was touching every part of my place now. He found a spot near the top, and it was as though I had received an electric shock. I could not help but gasp. I heard him give a low chuckle, and felt him slide his free arm around my neck, cuddling me to him, his hand sliding onto my breast. He began to rub his fingers around the spot he'd found, then down along my crease, even pressing a little against my opening, and the electricity surged.

I found myself breathing more quickly, aware of a warm, musky scent in my nostrils. His fingers were moving even more boldly now, exploring every part of me, and as he did so I felt an almost irresistible urge to part my legs further, to press against him. The hand upon my breast was rolling and tugging my nipple, and my chest ached with a strange tightness. He was holding me so close! A shock went through me when I felt his fingertip press against the tight opening in my place, then slip in a little! He was rubbing his whole hand upon me. His palm pressed that sensitive spot; his fingertip pushed in; his other hand caressed my breast; his body was hot against me. It was as if I had been wound up inside, and there was a glowing ache growing deep in my stomach. I felt a small pain inside, then it was not a pain as my place of its own accord seemed to push itself against the finger that was now fully inside me; against the palm that was pressing and rolling that aching sensitive spot; against the whole hand that made my place, my stomach, my chest, tense and churn, and drove my breath from me! It was awful, overwhelming, frightening, and I did not want it to stop!

It did stop. At least, the churnings began to die away after he slipped his finger out of me and moved his hand away from my seeping place. I felt like crying, though I knew not why. I heard him give a quiet chuckle, and he squeezed me close as if with satisfaction. For a long, long time I could only lie still, the tension in my body slowly easing. Even after his breathing told me he slept, I remained awake, acutely aware of his hand lying hot upon my stomach, confused and puzzled about what he had done to me, about the sensations that had overcome me, far more powerfully than those aroused by Richard and Jonathan.

Chapter 3

By the next morning I had determined to ask Miss Blake for answers to my puzzles. Having seen what I did last night, I guessed that her 'properness' was at least in abeyance. I could not, though, find a chance to speak to her, and so remained in frustrated ignorance as we prepared to move off for the day's march. I was soon distracted by the attentions of the man I had already begun to think of as my escort, for inevitably he chose to oil me before our departure. I found it difficult to even look at him, knowing that it was he who had lain with me and stirred those unwonted sensations last night, and I found myself blushing furiously as his hands roamed over my body.

The fact that he smiled at me, for all the world as if we were sharing some secret, only served to increase my embarrassment. Everything in my society and upbringing insisted that modesty was all important. Young ladies must be chaste; why, to show even an ankle was reprehensible. Now here was I, my scraps of loincloth concealing little, standing trembling while a man ran his hands over every part of me. Even telling myself that it was to protect my skin from the heat of the sun could not help me hide from the fact it was his hands, rather than the unguent, to which my senses were reacting. Miss Blake's instructions in the village, whispered with such an intensity, had filled me with nervousness about the things the men would do to me. But she had not named the 'things', nor warned me of the dizzying sensations I would experience when those tormenting hands roved over, and into, my body.

I knew my escort would do things; would fondle me, even slip his fingers into me, again soon, and images of last night flashed into my head. I would have to let him, for I was his captive and he was bigger and stronger than I. But surely, last night, I had more than just let him? Visions of Miss Blake's moonlit writhings, and of my own meltings under this man's hands, made me feel hot again, though I did not know why. I sneaked glances at him as he walked ahead of me, his long legs easy over the ground. He *looked* for all the world like a naked savage; bundles across his shoulders, spear in hand, skin gleaming in the sunlight. Yet when, every once in a while, he turned and smiled back at me, with the same smile he gave when oiling me, he seemed so friendly!

And then, sure enough, within the hour, when the others were a long way ahead, and we were alone, he signalled a halt.

Yesterday and last night, had shown me what to expect. I was already tense when, smiling, he took the gourd from his bundle. There was a sureness in the smile with which he beckoned me across to him. I knew what he was going to do, and my unruly bodily sensations, even before he touched me, made me blush to my roots. I stood still. He hummed in a deep bass tone as he oiled my shoulderes and arms. Before he reached them, while he was still smoothing the ointment along my spine and around to my lower ribs, my nipples tensed. He moved round to begin oiling my front, and I found myself watching his face,

36

fascinated. He did not resemble the natives I was used to at father's station. His nose was narrow, with flared nostrils. Under a high forehead, his eyebrows were slender curves. His cheekbones were sharp and his mouth wide, with slender, clearly outlined lips, across which a pink tongue-tip flickered.

He looked me full in the eyes, smiling, as his hands circled towards my breasts. I had been expecting it, but even so could not prevent a gasp as his hard hand cupped me. He smiled more broadly as his hands smoothed over my swellings, and I tensed, and felt helpless. That strange tightness and tingling returned. The unguent had become an excuse, for he was now very obviously more intent on fondling me than on a simple oiling. He clearly knew exactly what he was doing, what sensations he was causing in me, for he gave a low chuckle and moved very close behind me, pulling me to him with a hand around my waist as he began to tease my nipples. It was as if his fingertips were afire as he cupped and touched and teased me, and my nipples got harder and my breasts felt as though they were actually swelling!

The arm about my waist held me very close. His hot, musky scent and the hardness of his chest against my shoulder, added to the dizziness the sensations in my breasts were causing. He seemed to spend a long time fondling me, and his breath on my neck was lambent, like tiny flames touching without burning. I knew his hand would move downwards, and when it did it was as if my nerve ends were anticipating his touches as he circled slowly down, smoothing over my tummy, dipping for moments in my navel then sliding over my hip and easing aside my loincloth.

I was trembling and my legs felt as if they would hardly support me. Even though I knew I was helpless to prevent him doing whatever he wished, I somehow did not want to. I was leaning against him. I felt a flush of shame that I did not want him to stop but actually wanted his hand to go further, to touch and release the tension which had grown deep within me; to stop the torment. His arm moved from around my waist then descended. He began to caress my buttocks and the backs of my thighs. I tensed as his fingertips began to trace the cleft of my bottom, to find my opening, to press in! At the same moment, his other hand moved to cup my place, and it was as if the breath was forced out of me by a slow, inner paralysing of my lungs!

How long it lasted I know not. For an eternity his fingertips explored me, smoothing, pressing and teasing, as the very lips of my place seemed to seek to open to them. He found that specially sensitive spot, and I gasped and shuddered as he circled it, tormenting it into life and sending shocks of bewitching sensation to my nerve ends. I did not feel his finger enter me, just became aware that it had, and was moving in the same way as the finger in my bottom. I knew that the flat of his hand was pressing my burning folds, and that with each press-and-release, each probe of those fingers, it was as though my very body was melting and a giant spring were winding itself tighter and even tighter in my loins.

And then he stopped! Just stopped! There was no warning, no signal. One moment he was holding me, his scent drowning my breath, his hands electrifying me; the next he was gone. It was as if I had been drenched with cold water! I staggered on liquid legs, and fought to control my breathing. I looked at him for some sign, some explanation for his sudden change, but he was calmly picking up the bundles.

My head spun to try to understand. I must have been staring open-mouthed at him, for when he straightened up with the bundles, he laughed. Not cruelly, but seemingly with genuine amusement. Then he approached, handed me the water skin, smilingly traced the shape of my left breast with a fingertip, and started to walk away.

If I had been confused before, I was now in a turmoil! Why had he stopped? Why had he worked me up so, then left me thus gasping and bereft? Everything seemed to spin in my mind as I followed him, as acutely aware of the cooling dampness between my legs as I was of the tension in my chest and the sunlight gleaming on the muscles of his back. Blessedly, the mind refuses to keep spinning around seeking to explain the unexplainable, and soon everything was driven from my head except the effort of keeping up with him.

The next time we stopped to drink and rest, I found the puzzles welling up again. I found myself watching him as he sat lounging against a tree trunk, gazing at the horizon, and chewing a stem of grass. A change had come over me. Had he not been an African, and naked save for the pale loincloth which emphasised the gleaming darkness of his long legs, he might have seemed actually handsome, resting there in the sunlight. Or was it that the way I saw him now was coloured by the way my senses anticipated how he would touch me again soon?

He had been so relaxed and friendly as we walked, pointing things out as we journeyed, smiling, talking to me even though I could not understand his words. He had even told me his name, tapping his chest and saying, 'Talesi' several times until I understood and repeated it, then pointing to me and, when I said my name, repeating, 'Ridja, Ridja,' in a soft, bass voice, smiling and clapping his hands. He had carried my water bag and taken my hand when we came to difficult bits of the march, helped me over gullies and up steep banks. In fact he had shown every sign of friendliness. A 'savage' who seemed so far from savagery!

And now he smiled and chatted as we rested in the mottled shade of the trees. When he stretched, and stood, and rummaged in his bundle for the gourd, I caught my breath. I already felt the tightness begin in my place as he beckoned me towards him, and a sort of melting in my stomach. To my surprise, he simply handed me the gourd! I had to oil myself! Would this strange man never do the expected? I actually felt a flush of disappointment as I took the gourd and turned to smear the unguent on myself, and reproved myself inwardly for such shocking sentiments!

I was left to oil myself at each of the rest stops for the rest of the day, and had quite decided that he had chosen not to touch me again, when we caught up with Miss Blake and the others making camp among some trees and bushes not far from a small stream. At least, Miss Blake was making camp, for she was alone, breaking branches for the fire from the surrounding shrubs, while, to judge from the noises, the men were splashing in the nearby stream. I came to know that this was quite normal. For among the tribe to which we were being led it was the womenfolk who did the work while the men only hunted or worked on their weapons.

On seeing Miss Blake my first urge was to run to her but Talesi stopped me, and by means of gestures told me I was to take the water bags to the stream and fill them. Disappointed, for of course I had no choice but to comply, I took the two bags he offered me, picked up the others from where they lay upon the ground, and made my way through the bushes towards the stream. I would surely have an opportunity to talk to her later on.

The first of my lessons that evening came when I was kneeling at the stream filling the bags. I had chosen a spot a little way off from where I could hear the men splashing and laughing, concealed by some shrubbery. I had filled two of the bags when I felt a tap on my shoulder. It was one of the men. He was gesturing to me and shaking his head and talking rapidly, but what shocked me most was that he was utterly naked. I felt myself blush to my roots, and tried to look away, but he tapped me again, and I had to turn back to him as he continued to gesture and speak to me. It took me some moments to understand what he wanted, for my head was spinning with embarrassment. But when I did I grabbed up the unfilled bags and scurried along the bank with relief. He had only been telling me that I should fill the bags upstream from where the men were bathing, but what was burned into my mind's eye was the image of him towering above me, his body wet from the stream, the dark columns of his legs rearing before my eyes, and that strange apparatus bobbing and swinging so close to my eyes at the join of his thighs.

For obvious reasons, I had never seen a man naked before. I had seen little children, of course, in the village we'd stayed at, and knew that little boys were different from girls, but this! I had to pass the spot where the other men were bathing, and tried hard to avert my eyes. They took no notice of me whatsoever as they bathed and splashed, for of course to them nakedness was entirely natural, but for me the embarrassment was intense. Even so, I confess that I was not entirely able to prevent myself sneaking glances. I had to return past the men to retrieve the filled bags I'd left behind in my hurry, and my efforts to avoid looking were destroyed when Talesi walked out from the bushes towards the stream, and waved and smiled to me while calmly pulling off his loincloth! For an awful instant I could only stand frozen, staring at the thing which dangled where his private place should have been. His chuckle shook me from my daze, and I was able to scamper off, feeling myself burning with blushes.

More and more I longed to get to Miss Blake; to pour out my questions upon her. Trembling, out of sight of the men, I filled the water bags as quickly as I could, frustrated that it seemed to take so long. At last it was done. There were too many to carry all at once, so I heaved four onto my shoulders and began to make my way back through the bushes towards the campsite. As I neared the edge of the clearing where the fire was, I became aware that one of the men had just emerged from the bushes further along. Something, some presentiment, made me stop.

He was still naked, his loincloth dangling from his hand. He strolled over to where Miss Blake was kneeling near the fire, breaking sticks. He stopped beside her, his back to me, said something, and ruffled his hand in her hair, which hung loose and dishevelled. Miss Blake looked quickly up, as though startled, then down again, then all around. I crouched down behind the bush, not knowing why, but knowing that I wanted to see and not be seen. The man spoke again, and moved to stand in front of Miss Blake, very close to where she knelt, stroking her hair and tracing the line of her cheek with a fingertip. I crouched down, not knowing what to expect, but knowing somehow that I was about to witness one of the things men did with women. Miss Blake glanced around again, then reached up with both hands and took hold of the thing atop his legs.

I stared, hardly able to breathe. My governess shuffled forward a little on her knees, her face very close to the sausage thing her hands were holding. Stroking. Then I could not believe my eyes, for, as the thing seemed to grow in her hands, she moved her head forward and took the end of it into her mouth! My mind spun. Into my stunned head came the realisation that this thing, this rod that Miss Blake was even now taking into her mouth, was the same as that which I had rubbed to give Richard relief! I stared at the unimaginable sight of my tutor kneeling at the feet of this naked man and, yes, as her movements showed all too clearly, actively sucking his sausage, which now seemed to stand out straight and thick! I watched, astonished, as her hands kneaded and her head moved back and forth, her lips sliding along him.

His hand was resting upon the top of her head, but he was not constraining her. Miss Blake's movements were of her own doing. For long minutes I could only stare at the amazing tableau, aware of my own mounting tension as Miss Blake knelt as if in supplication at the feet of the tall African she was so avidly sucking. At last, hardly able to breathe, I managed to force myself to creep away from this disturbing scene.

How much later it was that Talesi came to find me where I sat huddled on the bank of the stream I cannot say, for I had been lost in a whirlpool of confusions. Not the least of these was the pulsing tension which had grown unbidden in the base of my tummy at what Miss Blake had been doing. At the sudden sound of his voice the tension seemed to lurch and grow hard. He was standing close to where I sat, and when I turned towards him he placed his hand upon my head. Oh, Lord, did he want me to do what Miss Blake had done? But no, to my intense relief he gestured that he wished me to go with him, and I gratefully scrambled up and followed when he beckoned.

I found my chance to question Miss Blake when we were set to tend the fire and watch the meat cooking on sticks above it. Her quietness, her downcast eyes as if she did not wish to look at me, put me off more than my inability to find words for the things that puzzled me, but at last I was able to blurt out, 'Things, Miss Blake. You said they would do things! What thi . . .?'

At once she looked up at me, her eyes urgent. 'Have they . . . has one of them . . .?' she said, in a voice almost a hiss.

It was difficult, embarrassing, but I managed to describe to her the way Talesi had touched me when he oiled me, and when he had lain with me last night. I wanted also to ask her about what I had seen her doing, but could not bring myself to do so, for I did not know the words. Since none of our captors was able to speak English there was no danger of them understanding what we were saying, but even so I was nervous and kept glancing at them, speaking in whispers, as did Miss Blake when she began her astonishing revelations. I could hardly believe what she was telling me, and had I not seen what she had done last night and then this evening, and felt the strange sensations of Talesi's hands, it would have been entirely impossible to do so!

As it was, the truth of what she said was driven home when, after we had served the men their meal and the sun was beginning to set, one of the men stood and called to Miss Blake. She glanced at me, blushed deeply, and rose to follow him. I saw his hand slip beneath her loincloth and begin to fondle her bottom even as they moved through a gap between the bushes. The tension returned to my tummy. Nervously, I glanced to where the other men lounged, but to my relief they were ignoring both me and the couple behind the bushes. As I crept beneath the bed skins my head spun with the things Miss Blake had said, and images of what must be happening behind those bushes.

Did men really put those sausage things inside us? Were females really meant to submit to men's pleasures thus? How could such a thing fit inside something so small as my private place, which even Talesi's finger filled so? Would I really have to suck a, what had she called it? A member? Was a member inside Miss Blake at this moment, behind the bushes? Was she really being shagged right now? My spinning thoughts froze in my head as I felt Talesi slide under the skins beside me.

I knew what to expect, but the touch of his hand upon my shoulder made me tense nevertheless. I was hardly able to breathe as he began his familiar caressings. What Miss Blake had not explained was why those strange tinglings began in me at his touch; why his fingertips felt so electric; why my skin seemed to anticipate his movements and welcome them. He stroked my neck and shoulder, his breath caressing my cheek as he lay close against me. His knees were warmly tucked behind mine. I found myself tingling and growing hot as his hand moved along my side and across my ribs in tiny circlings, and then up to cup my breast. The warmth and tightness grew as he fondled me, and I felt my nipples stiffen as he gently squeezed and rolled them.

Talesi moved, pulling me so that I lay on my back, and slid his arm about my shoulder as his other hand circled down over my stomach. My skin seemed so alive with sensitivity that I could feel the scratch of the hard callouses on his palm as it eased across me. I knew where his hand was going to move; how it was going to caress me. Miss Blake's words about what men did were drumming in my head, and those images and the very knowledge that I must submit seemed to make me more helpless before the sensations I could not prevent him arousing in me. The warm scent of his body so close beside me, his soft breath upon my face, the tingling in my bosom, the growing heat in my stomach, the insidious caresses upon my flank, my hip, my thighs. All combined to drive coherent thought from my head.

As if of their own accord, my legs had parted a little as his fingertips crept up from my knee, along my inner thigh. He stroked me gently on my thighs and hips and belly. I was trembling and tense even before his hand slipped down and cupped my place. He seemed to take a long time, as if deliberately delaying, building up the burning tension which was overwhelming me. I felt his finger slide into me, and I shuddered almost with relief as its penetration pushed my breath from me. When he moved above me, his thighs hard between mine, I became nervous, but his breath was upon my neck, and his hands were cupping my breasts. There was a knot of dragging tension deep in the pit of my stomach.

I felt his member press against me, sliding along my

folds, seeking for my entrance. He was so hot! So big! Then he found me, and I felt him push in, stretching me. I had tensed with nervousness, and he held his position, pressing gently, only inside me a little, pushing and easing in that slow rhythm his finger had made me so familiar with. I was very confused, for my mind was flicking backwards and forwards between the knowledge that he was going to shag me, which Miss Blake had described as so awful, and the tantalising, melting sensations his movements were stirring between my thighs, and in my chest.

Then he began to push, and I was staggered at how stiff and powerful he was; at how he eased me open so easily and overwhelmingly. And then it hurt a little, and I was too full. Surely too full! He seemed to overfill me, and I felt his very shape stretching and moving my insides. I was lost, yet stunned at the way my rebellious body seemed to be easing his penetration by its own hot moistenings! And then he began to move in me, and it did not hurt at all. He began a breathtaking motion that set fire to my lungs and my place and drove everything from me save this shaft overwhelming me; sending spasms to my very nerve ends and back again to churn my loins and my thighs. How long it lasted I know not, for I was swept out of myself by the dizzying confusions of what was happening – confusions which only increased when he began to move deeper. He was not pumping now, but holding his place, deep, pressing, circling, and my mind was swamped by the pulsing of my flesh about the hardness pushing for my soul! My head spun, and my body churned and seemed to cling to his filling of me, and I could only gasp for breath as his body jerked and liquid heat flooded me.

When I began to come to myself again, he was

lying still, his weight pressing upon my chest, but somehow more comforting than uncomfortable. He was still inside me, but smaller, less hard. His head was lying beside my cheek, his breath soft and warm on my neck, and I felt a strange wave of gentleness overtake me. When at last he moved, and slipped out of me, I felt empty and oddly lost. I found myself snuggling against him for warmth, and drifting off into a soft languor that banished thought.

When I awoke with the first glimmer of dawn, thoughts and sensations again swept over me. My place felt stretched and sensitive, though, I was surprised to realise, not sore. I felt amazingly relaxed and well. I knew (and felt myself blush at the memory) that Talesi had done what Miss Blake had said, that he had shagged me, and that it had been strange and overwhelming. But she had made it sound so nasty, and it hadn't been! I found myself looking down at where Talesi still slept, the early sun lighting his face. He seemed so relaxed, with a little smile on his lips, that it was hard to think of him as my ravisher!

He was lying on his back, only half-covered by the skins in which we slept. His chest was smooth and muscular, and gleamed in the sunlight as it moved to his breathing. His arm was thrown up above his head, and his feet protruded from beneath the skins. I was suddenly overpoweringly tempted. I did not dare, yet could not stop myself. Gingerly, not even breathing, I found myself reaching down to lift the edge of the skin beneath which he lay.

Could this be the thing that had so stretched and transported me last night? Surely not! That had been big, and hard, and overwhelming! What now filled my breathless gaze, lying limp against Talesi's thigh, looked too small and, yes, even sweet, to so fill and dominate me! A sleeping sausage, growing from a nest of tight black curls on the vee at the top of his thighs; a plump, wrinkled-bag arrangement lolling beneath, it looked more vulnerable than fearsome. It certainly did not shock me as it had when I first saw the men naked yesterday. Indeed, to my surprise I found it actually quite charming. What had Miss Blake called it, a member? It seemed a nice name. Greatly daring, I reached out and touched it tentatively with my fingertip. I was startled when it twitched at my touch, then horrified when I heard Talesi give a low chuckle. He was awake! He was looking at me and was grinning with amusement! He had seen what I was doing! I leapt up and ran off hot with embarrassment, his chuckles burning my ears.

I was stopped short by the sight of Miss Blake lying asleep between two of the other men. She was on her side, her head resting upon the chest of one of them, her hand lying across his waist. The other man was close against her back, his arm around her as hers was around his companion. Their coverings had slipped down, and the entwining of their muscular, glistening brown bodies and her pale softness told me clearly that they had been very close sleeping companions at the very least!

As I stood, transfixed by the sight of the sleeping group, I was startled by the touch of Talesi's hand upon my shoulder. He had his finger to his lips in that unmistakable gesture that signifies silence, and nodded in the direction of the stream, beckoning me to follow him. I obeyed with strangely mixed emotions. Of course I had to obey, for was he not my captor, and had I not been told my Miss Blake to submit? And yet as I did, I found myself watching the movement of his back and shoulders, his long muscular legs and his tight buttocks, with what I had to confess was admiration. For his movements, and the early morning light, and the flexing of his muscles under the glistening skin, seemed to fascinate my eyes. It was with surprise that I found the word 'graceful' dancing in my mind!

It was a shock, too, to realise (when we reached the bank of the stream and he had indicated by gestures that we should bathe) that it had not even entered my head that we were both entirely naked! But it was too late to be embarrassed, and in any case the water was deliciously cool, and Talesi was behaving in such a casual manner, that I found myself enjoying kneeling in the crystal water, and splashing and cleansing myself.

It was only when we returned to the bank and Talesi began to dry himself with tufts of soft grass, indicating that I should do the same, that his nakedness, and my own, and his nearness struck me again. I had begun to walk back to the campsite when Talesi touched my arm. I stopped and turned to him. The moment I saw that soft smile in his eyes, I knew. Holding my hand, he pulled me gently towards him. My nipples were already sparking as I stepped close, and I felt myself blush hotly.

He was not oiling me. We were not beneath the skins in the dark of night. Instead, in the bright of morning, he was standing before me, softly, knowingly cupping and caressing my breasts. And all I could do was tear my eyes from his and stare at the ground as that breathless, tingling warmth I was beginning to know only too well began to grow. He rolled my nipples with his thumbs, and they grew hard and tense and oh-so-sensitive under his touch. He lifted and rolled and squeezed my swellings, and as my breasts began almost to ache, that ball of heat throbbed in the pit of my stomach. I knew, without consciously seeing, that his member had begun to change, to fatten, to stand out more from his thighs.

I knew what was going to happen. I even wanted it to. With his free arm about my waist, Talesi pulled me even closer. I felt his breath warm upon my neck, the heat of his body so close to mine. The hand on my breast moved down, circling and caressing my side, my stomach, my hip. Between my legs I was already tingling and moist by the time his fingers found me. My own hand was holding his member, hard and erect now. Without command, without conscious volition, I found myself sinking down with him onto the smooth grass of the river bank.

Chapter 4

When he began to shag me that second time there was not the slightest pain. And as he stretched and pressed and slipped deeper and deeper into me I knew that, whatever impressions Miss Blake had given me about what happened when men 'did things', my body was open to him. I welcomed these caresses; this awesome penetration.

He fondled me for a long time as we lay there on the grass beside the stream, his hands moving knowingly over me, seeking and finding the places which sent those shivers of sensation through me, so that it seemed as though nothing existed except his hands upon me; his closeness; the burning in my chest, and the ache within my loins. When he moved above me, his knee parting my own willing thighs, his member seemed like a pole looming over me, or like a rod to plough me, and one which my body longed to receive!

His shoulder was close to my face, his quick breathing hot on my ear, as he found my place. He slid the tip of his member along me, easing my swollen folds apart, moving back and forth before at last finding the opening which now seemed to squirm to receive him. When I felt him press and begin to enter me, a shuddering breath filled my lungs with air, only for it to be driven from me as he surged into my depths, and seemed to cram all my insides up into my chest.

And when he began to move in me, thrusting for my depths, crushing and releasing my hips, in an overpowering, impossible rhythm, I was lost. If I were to try to describe to you in any coherent way the thoughts and sensations which surged through me, I would be committing a falsehood. All was a gasping, surging confusion. My breasts burned and felt fit to burst as his hard body crushed them. My legs wrapped themselves about his of their own accord, and my hips could not help but move to his movements. Spasms of electricity shot through me before surging back to churn in the centre of my being; to swirl and cling around the shaft which filled me and speared my very soul! And then he began to move more quickly, deeper and harder, and he jerked and pumped and hotness flooded me. My lungs exploded and light burst in my head, and my thighs and stomach cramped and dragged and churned, and all I wanted in the world was to wrap myself around him, to cling to him, to enfold his hardness within my heart, and to cry.

I tumbled back to a kind of reality when Talesi rose from me. The sudden chill, the sudden feeling of loss as he moved to stand up, made me almost want to sob. I felt weak as I struggled to my feet in obedience to his beckoning. I had entered a new world as, like an automaton, I went through the motions of helping to break camp and we began the day's march. Although a deep languor seemed to suffuse my body, and my place felt so sensitive, my mind was swimming with contradictions as I walked behind Talesi.

I was his captive and he was a 'savage', yet now he was walking beside me at a gentle pace, chatting to me and pointing to animals in the distance, showing me the birds and trees, for all the world as though we were old friends! He had decidedly 'done things' to me as Miss Blake had warned, yet although what he had done had been astonishing and overpowering, it had been entrancing rather than terrible as she had suggested. And then there was Miss Blake herself. She it was who said these men were like beasts, yet had I not seen her shagging with one of them, and even taking one into her mouth! And she had not looked especially terrified when lying cuddled between two of them this morning! Had her sensations been like mine when Talesi shagged me? Did her body respond like mine when they touched her? Why then had she made it sound so awful?

Then it struck me. She had said 'they' would do things! They! I had been with Talesi, but she had been with the other three men. Did that mean that all three had shagged her? That they would shag me? What Talesi had done with me this morning had left me stunned and weak and achingly sensitive. How much more so would it be if they all did it! A shiver ran over me, and my chest tightened at the very thought. Miss Blake had told me I must submit. Did that mean to all and any of them? Did she thus submit?

My questions were answered that very evening and night. As yesterday, we camped near a stream well before evening, and the meal and sleeping places were ready well before sunset.

I was anxious to speak to Miss Blake, to find some sort of answers to the questions which had filled my head all day. I would have spoken to her as soon as the fire was lit, but I was sent by Talesi to fill the waterskins. Upon my return I was met with the sight of Miss Blake moving to where Talesi leaned against the trunk of a tree and kneeling at his feet. The image of what I had seen the previous day flashed into my mind as she reached forward with both her hands and pulled aside his loincloth. With one hand she cupped the bag-like apparatus that lay tight beneath his member, and with the other she grasped and began to stroke the thing itself, which immediately grew and stiffened.

I was transfixed, astonished to find that I actually felt a twinge of envy at what I was seeing. I do not know what I would have done or said had not a touch fallen upon my shoulder. I spun round, startled, to find one of the other men smiling at me, and nodding his head towards the pile of skins already laid out on the ground. What could I do? I turned back, but Miss Blake and Talesi were oblivious. The man took my arm. It was as though all will left me, and I allowed myself to be guided towards the pile of bedding. So: it was to be 'they' and not only Talesi.

With a smile and a nod, the man motioned me to lie down. He knelt down beside me. He did not move to caress me as Talesi had, but simply reached for my knees and nudged them apart. He flicked up my loincloth, and smoothed his hand only briefly between my legs before pulling off his own. At the sight of his member standing stiff I shut my eyes. I felt his weight descend, felt him seeking my entrance. He had not prepared me as Talesi had done, and I was tense. He had to push his way in, even though I tried consciously to relax myself there. He was not rough, but even so he hurt me a little, for he seemed so big and my place was tight and dry. My head was swimming with images of Miss Blake sucking Talesi, and of this man's member as it had loomed above me and now thrust into me. He took his time, moving deeply and powerfully. And even though my head was filled with the realisation that I was being taken, that I had no choice – would not have any choice – but to submit to this man's will, and surely the others' too, my rebellious body began to respond to him. Even before he finished and flooded me with his heat, I was breathless and trembling, and my insides clung to the organ that was filling me.

Somehow, though, there was part of my mind which was strangely detached, which seemed to seek to reassure me. Had the others been agog at the spectacle, for I was being shagged in full sight of them, I might have died of embarrassment, but they were not. Indeed, for all the attention they seemed to be paying us, we might as well have been drawing pictures in the dust! And had not Miss Blake shagged? Had she not taken at least two of them into her mouth, in full view? 'Submit', she had said. Had I any choice but to do so?

I found myself oddly resigned, even relaxed, as I got to my feet and went to fetch the remaining water bags. If this was the way it was to be, then so be it. Being shagged was overwhelming, it was true, but one soon recovered. And, really, it was not actually unpleasant. I even found myself wondering whether I too would have to take their members into my mouth, and what it would be like when I did! My speculations were very soon resolved.

I was sticky between my legs, and decided to wash myself. I had finished bathing and was drying myself, when I heard a slight noise, felt a touch upon my shoulder, and turned. I had thought to see Talesi, but it was in fact one of the other men. At once, guessing from the look on his face and, I confess, from the way his loincloth was raised at the front, I turned, spotted a flat, grassy spot, and began to lie down. He said something, shook his head, then took his member in one hand and pointed with the other to his open mouth. With a surge of shyness, I understood what he wanted of me.

Nervously, I moved to kneel at his feet. His loins were almost exactly level with my face. This was the very first time I had closely examined a member in its pride, and it was a very different proposition from the pretty thing I had peeped at on the sleeping Talesi. At the very top of the cleft of his legs was an area of thick, tightly curled hair. From it stood his member, part way between that soft sausage condition and the upright rod that had poised between my parted thighs a little while ago. Below was that crinkly, bag-like affair which, when I cupped it, seemed to tighten and within which my fingers detected two softish, pebble-like objects.

My mind raced to remember what I had seen Miss Blake doing. I reached forward nervously, the bag cupped in one hand, encircling the shaft of the member with the fingers of the other. Even as I touched it, it seemed to jerk and become more erect. The shaft was glossy and not much smaller in circumference than my wrist. At the end was a sort of plum-like swelling, thicker than the shaft, satiny, and with a hint of purple to it, in the middle of which was a tiny opening almost like an eye.

The man adjusted his stance and grunted something, which I took to mean that I should stop delaying. Taking a deep breath, I advanced my face towards him, opened my mouth wide and placed my lips upon him. His member was surprisingly warm, and at the touch of my tongue it twitched and grew even stiffer, so that I had to open my mouth wide to

57

accommodate it. The plum-like end seemed to entirely fill my mouth and I panicked a little as he began to push forward, so that I almost gagged. In my mind's eye I saw Miss Blake sliding her mouth deep onto the members I'd seen her sucking, seeming to engulf almost the whole length, and for a moment I felt nervous that I would be unable to do it and might thus risk displeasing him.

With tears in my eyes caused by his size almost choking me, I tried several times to suck him properly, but could not help retching. Then I discovered that by flattening my tongue, angling my head so that he thrust along my tongue rather than the roof of my mouth, and at the same time consciously relaxing my throat and breathing out, I could slide my lips along his member until I could accept fully half its length. Pleased with my discovery and with the thought that I would be able to do it properly and thus avoid irritating the man, I began to slide my mouth as deeply onto him as I could, sucking hard as I withdrew until the rim of his plum was against my lips, whereupon I would lick all around it with rapid flicks of my tongue, as I had seen Miss Blake do, adapting to his rhythm as he moved just a little back and forth.

He became very stiff and hard, angling upwards so that instead of moving in and out I was now moving my head up and down. His member was very warm, and the shiny skin slid easily over the almost bone-hard shaft. It tasted a little salty, and the slight mustiness of both the taste and the aroma this part of his body exuded was strangely heady.

In fact, the relief I felt that I was able to accommodate him in this way, and thus avoid failure to please, gradually became overlain by a feeling of pleasure at my success in managing the act itself. I found to my surprise that I was enjoying what I was doing and that it was not nearly so distasteful as I had imagined!

Soon, he began to move quicker and more jerkily. Recognising the signs I had first felt when Talesi shagged me, and when I had rubbed Richard, I realised that he was nearing his spasm, and so I slid and sucked harder. Then, with a gasp, he spurted hot fluid onto the back of my tongue so suddenly and in such volume that I almost choked and nearly bit him in my frantic efforts to swallow.

But swallow I did, and soon after that, although he continued to move gently and I continued sucking, his member began to soften. He withdrew from my mouth and, for no reason other than that I felt an urge, I gave his plum some final licks and kisses. He reached down and helped me to my feet. He was smiling broadly, so I knew I had pleased him. He looked me over, patted my bottom, and left me to gather up the water skins.

As I did so, I could not help reflecting (and not without blushing) upon the amazing changes in my circumstances and attitudes. Only a few days earlier I had been a typical English girl, dressed in frocks and petticoats, doing nothing more strenuous than carrying school books, regarding native Africans as no more than servants when I bothered to think of them at all. Now I was captive of just such natives, and was naked save for the little loincloth. I was carrying *their* water skins. I had also learned that men – Miss Blake had implied all men – had strange requirements of women. Had not Talesi felt me all over, and slipped his fingers into parts of me I had thought inviolable? And had he and the other man not shagged me, and had I not taken that man's member into my mouth and sucked it, and swallowed what he spurted? And what was most amazing of all was that I now found myself admitting to myself that I had derived a strange and alluring kind of pleasure from what they did! As I lugged the heavy water skins back towards the campsite, I even found myself visualising (and not without a certain tingling in my place) the member I had just sucked, and being shagged beside the campfire, and I wondered which of our four captors would have me next.

At the campsite, some joints were cooking over the fire, tended by Miss Blake, and all four of the men were lounging a little way off, talking quietly. I dumped the water skins and went to assist Miss Blake, regarding her closely for the first time as she knelt to turn the wooden spit upon which the meat was impaled. Her hair was loose, and though it was tangled and knotted I could not but admire the thick, brown tresses that tumbled halfway down her back. She had only glanced at me before returning her eyes to the cooking, and so I was able to look at her without dissembling. Her breasts were large; much fuller than my own swellings, and they trembled as she moved. Her tip-tilted nipples pointed up from areolas much larger and darker than my own little pink things. She was altogether plumper than I, her hips full and round, her thighs and calves squashing together as she knelt, firm and white. Such a huge contrast to the soberly dressed, neatly coiffured, and very proper woman I had known as my governess since just before the sea journey out to this country only a few months ago!

Although I had many questions buzzing around my brain, I was not able to ask them yet for, deciding that the meal was ready, she pulled the spit from above the fire, and carried it across to where the men sat. Even when she returned with my own portion, she seemed concerned to avoid my eyes, and certainly unwilling to talk to me, so I was obliged once again to contain myself in silence. Perhaps, I thought, she was constrained by the fact that she knew I had seen her with Talesi, and was embarrassed. She had certainly seen the man shagging me at the same time. Perhaps that was what caused her to avoid my eyes. Whatever it was, I resolved to let my questions rest for the while, but also determined that I would find, or force, an opportunity to speak to her on the morrow.

Then, from the corner of my eye, I noticed that all the bedrolls were in the same place, and the significance hit me in a rush. Although it had been only two nights, I had come to assume that I would be set to lie on one side of the campfire, where Talesi would inevitably join me, while Miss Blake would go to the other. The import of seeing that we were all to lie together struck me at once.

Instantly nervous, for the prospect of sleeping as a group daunted me greatly, I tried to find things to do; ways of postponing lying down. I snatched up a water skin that had been half-emptied and hurried to the stream to fill it. I tidied together the other skins. I threw some sticks onto the fire, then scurried off to gather more. I did everything I could until at last, when it was almost fully dark, smiling as if he knew what was on my mind, Talesi came and took my hand, and led me towards where Miss Blake was already lying. It was obvious what was going to happen, for already one of the men was beside her and a second was sliding under the skins. As Talesi handed me .towards the bed place I became very aware that the front of his loincloth was bulging, and as I slipped beneath the covers, my own unruly body was already tingling in anticipation.

Had I puzzled earlier whether all the men would want to shag me? Foolish girl! I lay between Talesi and the fourth man. At once four hands were upon me, and instantly, it seemed, that pit of heat lurched awake in my stomach. My own hand was pulled down, and I found myself grasping a hard member. My loincloth was pulled off and tossed aside. The hands were everywhere, fondling my breasts, sliding over my hips and tummy, parting my thighs, caressing my bottom and my place. A mouth descended upon mine; the lips demanding, the tongue seeking my own.

I could barely breathe. Could not think. Could do nothing to resist the voluptuous sensations they were already arousing in me. I felt myself being pulled, turned. Hands grasped my head and I was pulled down towards where my hand still grasped the member. It bumped against my cheek. Hands were sliding between my legs, exploring the cleft of my bottom, the folds of my place. Fingers slid into me. My head was moved again, and the member touched against my lips. I was helpless to resist. In truth, I did not wish to! As I opened my mouth to receive the hot plum, I felt another begin to press between my thighs. My body was bent double. The man behind me – was it Talesi? I knew not! – moved his stiffness along my cleft and my folds, pressed, found my opening, then pushed.

The man in my mouth was no longer holding my head, and without even thinking I began to move my mouth upon him. I tried to concentrate upon sucking him properly, breathing, and flattening my tongue, and licking around his plum, but the member thrusting into the depths of me drove the breath from me. I drifted away from myself, giving up any attempt at coherent thought, becoming little more than a willing receptacle for the men's thrustings; the inexorable, overpowering rhythm of their ploughing. Yet I felt everything with exaggerated sensations, so that the hands on my hips, pulling me rhythmically onto the rod which seemed to be cramming me to my waist, the hot, silk-on-iron shaft in my hands, the plum about which my tongue writhed, the pressure against my buttocks as the man shagging me thrust in, all, all, seemed fire and electricity and confusion, and fulfilment. My insides churned. My breasts burned and ached. The very lining of my place, so stretched and filled and tormented, seemed to be melting and clinging to the hardness moving within me.

I became no more than a churning of reactions, a ball of red tensions which dragged at my pelvis, and exploded, and burst in my chest and head, and contracted again into a writhing ache in my place, to explode again in delirious spasms through every muscle and sinew of my being. I thought I was going to die; wanted to die; wanted to expire of the sensations which were so driving me from myself!

I did not die, though when the man shagging me jerked and crammed and filled me with hot spurtings, and the other flooded my mouth, I longed to. For these shattering sensations were surely too voluptuous to survive! When it stopped I did not return quite to myself, for I was in a swirling languor, at a distance from myself as it were. Aware, through a glowing mist, of what was happening, yet incoherent, compliant to how they moved me; turned me; filled me. Time after time, those shattering, pulsing cramps swept over me, condensing in painless fire in my breasts and vulva before bursting outwards to suffuse my whole being with wave after wave of delirious sensation. I was on my back, my legs held high, a rod ploughing me. I was on my side, my mouth seeking. I was lying on a hard body, my thighs clinging to his as my pelvis writhed upon his shaft. Even when, at some point in the whirl of lascivious sensations, I became aware that someone was pressing from behind me, parting my buttocks, I felt only a sort of surprised petulance that he was trying for the wrong place, before acquiescing to yet another sensation, and I concentrated as best I could on the member in my mouth.

How many times, how many ways, even whether all four of the men had me or not, I cannot say, only that at some stage I lapsed into a dream, and was awakened in the full light of a new morning. I felt weak and stiff. It all rushed back into my mind the moment I sat up, or rather a whirl of half-coherent impressions did. I looked around me. The men were up, and were laughing and chatting as they gathered their spears and bundles. Miss Blake, too, was moving about. That her night had been like mine showed in the downcast of her eyes and the stiffness with which she moved.

Not wanting to think, nor yet to face anybody, I made my way down to the stream to bathe, for between my legs I was sticky, and my bosom and jaw ached, and my bottom felt sore. I hoped the cool water would revive me. It seemed that we were in a hurry, for the moment I returned from the stream the party set off, walking quickly, and I had to struggle to keep up with Talesi's long strides. Though hard, the quickness of our pace was a blessing, too, for the stiffness in my hips soon wore off, and Talesi did not try to talk to me, so I was able to reflect upon the night and my sensations.

All Miss Blake's predictions, part stated, mostly hinted at, had been true. The men had indeed done things, and such things! Yet here I was, unhurt, seemingly undamaged, albeit my private place felt oversensitive and my bottom a little uncomfortable. I had received them into every part of me. I had writhed and sweated wantonly beneath, above and between their hard bodies. I could even still taste them in the back of my throat and feel the echoes of their hands upon my breasts and thighs. Yet had I not also felt like to drown in such sensations as I could never have dreamt? If this was to be my fate until, as would surely happen, we were rescued; if, as Miss Blake had enjoined, I was obliged to submit, was it so terrible as she had made it seem? True, I had no choice in the matter, for they could do with me as they wished. But then, was it not also true that the voluptuous sensations I had experienced were a kind of compensation? I knew I would have to ask Miss Blake, to seek some kind of reassurance, but in the back of my mind I was already beginning to believe that our fate might not be as awful as I had at first dreaded.

The reason for our hurry became clear around the middle of the day. And hurry it had been, for Talesi, who seemed to have some authority over the other men, hardly let us pause even to drink. We had been climbing steadily, and topped a high crest, and the men all shouted and pointed and slapped each other's backs. The cause of their joy was a village, which could just be discerned, away off at the end of the long valley which descended from the ridge. Now at last, Talesi allowed us to rest. How gratefully I dropped the water skin which had been dragging at my shoulder. How good it felt to sink to my knees in the thick grass and rub my aching back! How delicious the water and the piece of cold meat one of the men gave me tasted! Somehow, I knew that the village in the distance was our destination, and I felt eager to reach it and to rest, and even sleep in a bed! What would actually befall us when we got there I could not guess and did not care.

Despite the fact that the village was within sight, that last part of our journey took several hours. Talesi set a much gentler pace now, and for the first time I was able to walk with Miss Blake. Now was my opportunity to question her, and I did so eagerly, pressing her, even though she answered only in monosyllables and with obvious reluctance, until I eventually dragged out of her the answers I needed. Somehow, they did not seem so fantastic as had her earlier cryptic utterances.

Despite her reluctance, I badgered out of her that men's greatest pleasure was to 'come' or 'spend', which were terms for the spasms and spurtings they had when thrusting themselves into our bodies. I learned that my place was really called my quim; that shagging was also called fucking; and that pleasuring a man with one's mouth was called fellating, which some men liked most of all. When I asked her about when the men had used my bottom she looked askance and shook her head. She said that, yes, they would use even that place for their pleasure, and that it was called buggering.

I found it more difficult to ask her about the sensations I myself had felt, and when at last I managed it she looked shocked, and turned her head away from me. For a moment I was chastened, but I was determined to know, and I nagged at her and even got a little irritated. At last, but in tones which showed only distaste, she told me that sometimes women, too, had comes, for there was an element inside us which responded to men's demands even against our wills, but that it was shameful and beastly, and no lady would admit to it.

This puzzled and subdued me. Should I feel shame? I had not been able to prevent what they had done; had been told by Miss Blake herself to submit to it. I had not been prepared for the feelings they aroused in me. Was I a beast to have surrendered thus to those sensations? My mind flashed to the scene of Miss Blake writhing beneath that man on the first night of our march. If I was shameful, than so was she! Suddenly I felt a surge of irritation, anger even. Why on earth should Miss Blake be so disapproving when, as I had seen only too clearly, she herself experienced the same arousals as I did! It was I who now looked askance at her, for of all things I detest hypocrisy. I stopped and let her walk alone, whilst I waited for Talesi.

He did not scowl at me as she had done. He smiled a broad, cheerful welcome, put his arm about my shoulder, and we walked together towards his village.

Chapter 5

The village was like that which Albert and Richard had shown me: a deep thorn fence surrounding huts with high, conical roofs and mud walls. What surprised me was the horde of people who came running out of the wide entry gap in the fence as soon as our party was spotted. They were mostly women and children, laughing and calling as they ran towards us, and we were soon surrounded by a chattering mob. Instinctively, for although the faces were not unfriendly their numbers made me nervous, I drew close to Talesi.

We were taken across a wide expanse of trampled earth, which I was to learn was the heart and meeting place of the village, towards a large hut close by the only tree within the fence. As we neared it, the crowd in front of us thinned and opened out to reveal a group of men sitting on a semicircle of stools. In the middle, on what I was startled to see was a real wooden chair with back and arms, sat an imposing figure clutching a long, heavy stick with a great knob at the end. He was wearing what looked to be a lion pelt around his shoulders. I guessed he must be the chief, and it was towards him that Talesi now led Miss Blake and me.

I grew acutely embarrassed to find that we were the object of all eyes, and could feel myself blushing as a loud conversation ensued between Talesi and the chief, of which Miss Blake and I were clearly the subject. It was quite excruciating to have to stand there thus, the objects of talk we could not understand, and subject to the close scrutiny of so many eyes! If my status as a captive had begun to slip from my mind during the last few days, I grew very conscious of it now!

After a lot of talking the chief gave a signal. Talesi stepped back, and some women ran forward and ushered us noisily towards a hut off to one side. Slowly, my eyes adjusted to the gloom and I began to be able to perceive some details of the place to which we had been brought. It was a large hut, longer than it was broad, with a high, pitched roof of wooden poles supporting some kind of thatching. Stout posts supported the roof, and here and there partitions of woven sticks divided the hut into various alcoves. It was in one of these that Miss Blake and I sat on a sort of wooden camp bed or divan, on which a layer of grasses and skins was strewn for a mattress.

Outside our alcove any number of women and girls were gathered, all chattering, some hurrying to and fro. For a while Miss Blake and I were left alone as some sort of preparation seemed to be in progress. Then, without warning, four young women came and, taking our arms and gesturing, took us out into the middle of the hut. The place seemed crammed with women, but there was a space in the middle into which we were thrust. The women chattered and stared at us and pressed close, as if we were some strange kind of creature on display, which, I suppose, we were.

An older woman, tall and bearing herself with great dignity, stepped out of the crush. Compared to the other women she seemed very proud and self-assured, and she clearly possessed some authority for the others made way for her as she moved forward. She looked around the crowd commandingly and said some· words, at which the circle around Miss Blake and I widened as the women backed away. The older woman, whom I later learned was called Mitia, and who was sister to the chief, stepped forward and regarded Miss Blake and I closely, looking us over from head to foot slowly and imperiously. I felt myself reddening under her gaze but, when she reached forward and lifted my chin to stare into my eyes, even though I quailed, I managed to meet her gaze before she turned to Miss Blake. Unlike me, she was staring at the floor, her head low and her shoulders hunched. I had thought her so brave, and now it seemed that I was braver than she!

Then Mitia gave some sort of command, and another woman stepped out from the circle. They spoke together, then the new women turned and spoke to us, and in English!

'My name Tala,' she said. 'Me have some English words. I tell you things Mitia say, tell Mitia things you say.'

Open-mouthed with astonishment, I listened while Tala told us in rather awkward English that we now belonged to the village of Ngossi, the local chief, and brother to Mitia. We would be presented to him later, and must obey his every wish. Ngossi was a mighty chief, but not cruel, and if we were good women we would be treated well. Tala talked for a long time, occasionally turning to explain something to Mitia in their own tongue or to answer a question, and we too were able to ask questions.

It seemed that we were the property of this Ngossi,

and that by virtue of that fact we were also the property of the whole village. Tala used the word 'slave', and a chill went through me. I had read about the slave trade in my school books, and had awful visions of shackles and whips. Images of Miss Blake and I being treated the same way sent a shudder of dread through me, and I found myself clinging to her in fright.

My dread did not lessen when Tala told us that we were to be presented to Ngossi that very night, and I trembled as the women stripped and bathed us. How far away now seemed Talesi's friendliness! Even the gentleness and smiles of the women who bathed us and combed our hair with wooden combs did nothing to ease me. I sat dumbly, and could not look at the girls who brought us food and drink, nor partake of it, but just sat staring at the ground, knowing that the worst had happened.

When they came to lead us out of the hut, I went like an automaton – aware that it was dusk, aware of drumming, a crowd and flickering firelight – the word 'slave' echoing in my head. Thus I was amazed and confused when an arm was thrown around my shoulders, a hand lifted my chin, and I found myself looking into Talesi's smiling face! He seemed jubilant, delighted, as he hurried me towards where I saw Ngossi sitting, surrounded by laughing men. Mitia and Tala were standing behind him. Had I not been so distracted by the dread engendered by the word 'slave', I might have recognised this as the first indication of the difference between what I understood by the word and the tribe's attitude.

What followed was as confusing as anything I had experienced in my life. Whereas I had dreaded shouts and blows, I was met with smiles and strange ceremony. Through Tala, I was told to kneel before Ngossi. I was touched, but gently; my hair was held out and allowed to fall; paint of some kind was streaked across my forehead and chin by a smiling, nodding Mitia, then I was told to stand and turn around. I became acutely conscious that I had been left entirely naked when the women had prepared me earlier, and could almost feel the scores of eyes crawling over me. Then I was told to kneel again and wait as the confusing ceremony continued.

Then it was Miss Blake's turn. She was brought up by a man I recognised as being from the group we had marched with. She, too, was made to kneel. Her hair was lifted and displayed, then dropped, and I was aware of noises betokening approval from the crowd. Her chin was lifted as mine had been, and Mitia marked her forehead and chin with lines of red paint. She was told to stand, to turn, to raise her arms above her head. There came more murmurs of approval from the crowd, and I found myself fascinated by how striking, how statuesque, she looked with the firelight flickering upon her pale body, her breasts high, her hips full and round. Only the expression on her face detracted from the lovely image, for it was closed and downcast, and I felt a sudden pang of pity for her obvious unhappiness.

By means of snatched whispers, Tala told me that this ceremony was the presentation of Miss Blake and I to Ngossi, and that if he approved us, which he surely would, we would be accepted into the tribe, and a ceremony of welcome would take place. The idea of a welcoming ceremony did not sound much like my notion of slavery, but I was still nervous and confused as I stared around at the crowd of faces. When I espied Talesi among the throng of men, I felt a surge of relief, and somehow his smile and wave were hugely comforting.

When Miss Blake's turning and posing had finished, she was made to come and kneel beside me, and we waited while loud conversation ensued between Ngossi, Talesi, the man who had presented Miss Blake, and any number of others. Then, with a suddenness which made me jump, drums started up, people began to chant and dance, and the ceremony of welcome began. Miss Blake and I were made to stand and face out towards the crowd, which had moved back to leave a clear space before us. Ngossi stepped between us and spoke in a loud voice to the crowd, which clapped and ululated. Then, moving in time to the drums, Tala came forward carrying a pot of the red paint.

Ngossi moved first to stand before Miss Blake. Tala was kneeling beside him holding up the pot. He dipped his fingers into the paint, and added to the marks Mitia had already made on her face by drawing a single line down the centre of her forehead and to the tip of her nose. Then he drew a line from shoulder to shoulder along her collarbone, and another down between her breasts to her belly button, and further, to the edge of the bush of black curls about her place. He then called something, and the man who had presented her stepped up. He smeared paint upon the palms of both hands, and Miss Blake flinched and blushed as he smoothed both hands over her breasts, then slid a hand between her legs, leaving three large smears of redness. The man then moved to stand behind her, grasped her by her shoulders, and turned her this way and that as if to show her to the crowd, which once again clapped and called loudly.

Ngossi then came to stand in front of me, and I felt

very small and helpless as he towered over me. I, too, trembled as he painted the lines on me, and could hardly bring myself to look up at him. When I did, as he called Talesi's name, I was surprised to see that he was smiling broadly, as was Talesi when he approached. Ngossi said something to Talesi, including the word *mantolla* which was to become such an important part of my life among the tribe, and Talesi nodded and grinned even more widely as he smoothed the paint lingeringly between my thighs and upon my breasts and displayed me to the laughing, clapping crowd.

A girl approached, bearing a bowl and cup. Ngossi took the cup and drank from it ceremoniously, before refilling it and passing it to Talesi and the other man in turn. Then he dipped the cup into the bowl again, and handed it to Miss Blake. She hesitated, then took a deep breath, and drank the contents. Then the cup was refilled and given to me. The liquid was clear and brownish, and tasted very sweet when I drank. I was nervous as to what it might be, but made myself swallow it. I was astonished at the heat it seemed to spread instantly through me even as I drank, and for a foolish moment I was afraid I had been poisoned!

That it was some kind of strong spirit very soon became clear, for the drumming seemed to grow more insistent and to take on an echo, and the voices from the crowd became muted and less distinct. A feeling of deep languor suffused my limbs. When Talesi grasped my arm I jumped, for his touch seemed intense on my skin. My vision, too, seemed affected, for although I could see his face with startling clarity, things around him, things more than a very short distance away, were misty and swirling. I felt Talesi pulling my arm, knew he wanted me to go somewhere

74

with him, but I seemed to be moving through treacle as I followed, and had no consciousness about where he was leading me.

Somehow, we seemed to come to a bed, and I sank upon it gratefully, longing to drift off on the tide of relaxation the drink had filled me with. Then I became aware, through my haze, that Talesi was touching me; touching me as he had during our march, his hands running softly over my neck, my arms, my breasts. It was as though his hands were inside my skin, touching directly onto my very nerve endings. Oh, he knew so well how to touch me! I could feel my breasts swell and harden under his knowing caresses. I struggled to open my eyes. Talesi was very close to me, his eyes smiling. He kissed me on my forehead oh, so gently, then on my eyes. When his lips brushed then pressed on mine, it was as if an electric charge paralysed my lungs! Talesi's mouth upon mine dizzied me and seemed to draw my very essence from my lips, and to fill me with his.

Every sensation seemed to become one. The mouth, moving from my lips to my neck, my shoulder, my breasts; the hands caressing my arms, my flanks, my hips, my knees, my thighs; all became one trembling heat, urging me to unfold and enfold, to spread myself so that he could touch more of me, and to curl about him and enclose the touches within my heart. When he began to caress between my legs it was as if the whole universe became centred on his fingers; on the folds he parted and explored; on the sensitive spot which strained to be excited even more; on the opening which seemed to weep for him.

He entered me, and I think I moaned with awe and gratitude. He was wonderful! He filled me with glorious heat and power, and I spun up and up in a spiral of churning, pulsating, helpless ecstasy, which exploded into gasping spasms as he jerked, and thrust for my soul, and filled me with his flood of heat.

He seemed to become insatiable, and in my woozy, sensitised state, I slid into a maelstrom of touches and caresses. He was in my mouth, and I drank him greedily. He was between my legs again, and I wanted to cry with gratitude. He was in my bottom, and it felt full and delicious. On and on he went, as I drowned in a burning fog of swirling sensation, filling every grateful part of me. He seemed many-handed, seeming even to inflame my mouth and my quim and my bottom at the same time!

When I came to myself there was sunlight streaming through the entrance to the hut I found myself in. I felt such a suffusing weariness that for some minutes I lacked the strength to sit up, but just slumped where I was, growing more and more aware of a stiffness and tenderness in every part of my body. Vague memories of last night filled my head, and I found myself smiling deliciously at how transported I had been. When, at last, I managed to sit up and look about me I was astonished to see half-a-dozen or more men sprawled asleep about the hut, and it struck me as curious that they seemed all to have red paint smeared upon their thighs and torsos. Then I saw that the paint on my own body was smeared and smudged, and I blushed when I realised how the paint must have got onto the men. It had not been just Talesi who had transported me! Had *all* these men . . .?

A tremor ran down my spine and settled in my loins as the connotations struck me. Almost against my will, my eyes began to flick from body to body, gazing in fascinated wonder at the painted thighs, the sleek, muscular bodies, that lay all about me. Yes, it must be so! Had I really accommodated so many men? If only my mind were not so fogged. Even so, I felt a flush of warmth deep in my quim as vague images flitted through my mind.

This hut, like the others I had been in, was partitioned, and I crept off the bed and began to search, for I discovered I was very thirsty. To my joy, in a small alcove near the doorway, I found a large clay ewer containing water, and by it some wooden cups. I drank thirstily, even splashing some of the liquid down myself in my haste. While I was drinking I heard stirring among the men in the other room, and crouched still as I heard them apparently leaving the hut. Although I could hear noises outside, the hut itself seemed silent. Had they all gone? I crept out of the alcove to find out.

The men had not all left. Talesi remained, yawning and rubbing his face to get rid of the remains of sleepiness. He looked up and smiled broadly as I came into view. I still had the wooden cup in my hand, and when Talesi pointed and lifted his hand to his mouth, miming drinking, I straight away hurried to bring him some water.

Talesi drank, and stood and stretched. He towered over me, and my cheeks grew hot at the sight of the red paint smeared on his body – paint he could have acquired in only one way! I looked down at my own body. The lines of paint Ngossi had drawn on me, and the three patches Talesi had placed upon me, were liberally smudged, so that my whole torso was a cloud of red, pink and white. Talesi, too, was looking me over, and a shiver, though not of cold, ran over me as he reached out and traced the shape of my breast with a fingertip. We were both entirely naked, and my eyes widened when I saw his member twitch and move. Surely he could not want to . . . ? Again? Already?

I glanced up, already blushing, to find him smiling down at me. He took his member in his hand and gestured with the other hand, and I knew at once what he wanted. I knelt, and he moved close. His member was already half stiff, and I felt a strange sense of gratification that 'my' Talesi seemed somehow more impressive in that department than the others had been. His stomach and thighs were muscular and glistening. From the tight bush of curls below his navel stood a member which seemed indeed prouder than the others, and which twitched and grew, even as I curled my fingers around its shaft – which they could only just encircle. At the base of his member, his bag (which Miss Blake had told me was called his balls) was large and tight, and as I cupped it I could feel the two spheres inside move and tighten further. His plum glistened and seemed to stare at me with its single eye as I moved towards it. As I gazed at it the new knowledge given me by Miss Blake's revelations and my own fresh experiences came together in my mind with my realisation of men's weaknesses and women's strength (for had I not served fully half-a-dozen men last night and woken less exhausted than they?), and I determined that my small mouth and my weak hands would conquer this powerful man by the skill with which I reduced him to his quivering spasm.

And then a strange thing happened. As my lips slid over the bulb of his member and my tongue swirled around the ridge between his plum and shaft, I suddenly felt that it was beautiful! Suddenly longed to engulf its power; to taste and smell; to pleasure it in order to receive pleasure in turn. All at once, I ached simply to excite this beautiful organ with my lips and tongue and hands, and to be excited in turn by the gift of his surrender.

Unashamedly carried away by this sweet excitement, I squeezed and sucked and licked with all my heart, lost in the act, cramming my mouth onto him until he touched my throat, sucking back until only the plum remained within my lips. My own body was tingling and hot; my breasts felt tight, my tummy burned. Each time I slid my mouth down along his shaft it was as if another, ghostly shaft was moving inside me, between my legs. Oh, strange power! As I increased the speed and strength of my sucking my own sensations grew. It was as if, in pleasuring Talesi, I was in fact working my own self into an excitement. Which was indeed the case, for I began those awful, delicious pulsings in my tummy even before he began his come, and when he did I found myself gasping and licking and squeezing and sucking as if the hot fluid spurting onto my tongue was the very ambrosia of the gods! I continued sucking avidly long after he had ceased to throb and spurt, and even felt a twinge of regret when at last he eased my head back and withdrew from my lips.

He pulled me to my feet then lifted my chin to look me fully in the face, and smiled so gently I felt an urge to hug him. I felt hot and weak and astonished at my own reactions. Talesi left, and I sat weakly on the bed, pressing my hand upon my quim, which was hot and oozing. I sat for a long time, my tension slowly easing, the taste of Talesi dry in my throat. I was startled out of my reverie by the noise of someone outside the hut. Into my mind instantly flashed the thought that it was another man, that I was to be pressed into service again, and so soon! I stood up and took a deep breath.

The person who entered was so far from what I had expected that I almost laughed aloud. All the men I had seen in the tribe had been tall and well-muscled, even the older ones, so this man was such a shock that I found myself openly staring. If the other men were like trees, this one was some kind of scrawny bush! Thin, spindly legs seemed only just able to support an almost entirely round body; arms like twigs waved as he seemed to teeter, rather than walk, towards me. He had an oversized and entirely bald head which rose hardly higher than my own, and his face wore an enormous grin showing many creamy teeth, above which sparkled eyes like black cherries. The figure was made to seem even more ludicrous by the fact that his loincloth was like a pinafore, at least twice the size of the other men's, and hung down to his knees. Instinctively I covered my grinning mouth with my hand lest I annoy him, but my mirth instantly turned to a gasp of shock when he spoke to me, and in English!

'I am Motallo!' he said in a high-pitched voice, and struck himself upon the chest as if he were the greatest person on earth.

Whether it was nerves or shock I know not, but the sight and the sound of his piping voice, struck me as so ludicrous that I burst into an uncontrollable fit of giggles. Through the tears streaming from my eyes I saw him fold his arms across his chest and plant his feet apart. The more I tried to control myself the worse my giggles became. I turned away, gasping as my ribs began to ache, but when I turned back his posture and his serious gaze set me off again and at last I could only sit on the bed clutching my ribs and snorting, tears streaming down my face. Even the thought that my behaviour might be considered rude could not stop me. At last though, aching and breathless, my giggling eased.

Then Motallo surprised me again. Far from becoming irritated, as I had every reason to expect, he said, 'Ah! You laugh! Good! Good!' and sat down beside me on the bed. He looked pointedly at the paint smeared on my body, patted my thigh, and said, 'So! You have good welcome to tribe, eh! Good girl! Give men good time!' I blushed, knowing exactly what he meant! 'Now, you come with me, we sort you out!'

I followed his comic figure out of the hut, aware suddenly how stiff my hips felt, how weak my legs were. I was aware too, of the glances and calls of the people we passed among, but was too tired and disorientated to even consider the fact that I was walking among them entirely naked, the paint smeared over my torso giving ample evidence of my night's activities!

Motallo led me to his hut, set a little aside from the main body of the village. There, to my astonishment and delight, he showed me a large tub, like a sort of flattened barrel, filled with steaming water, and told me to bathe. Ah, bliss! The water was too deep for me to sit, so I knelt, the heat of the water instantly reaching to my core. Motallo pottered around, handing me a yellow, waxy block which lathered just like soap, and a tied bunch of grasses which served as both flannel and brush. While I soaped and scrubbed and wallowed in the delight of the hot water, Motallo chatted to me, telling me he learned his English during years he had spent as a cook for an English farmer, and that now he was the triber's healer, although not himself of the tribe (which explained his different appearance). I felt an instant liking for him, and he did indeed become one of my best friends among the tribespeople.

When I had climbed out of the bath and dried myself, Motallo inspected me closely, which somehow did not seem at all embarrassing. He tutted over some reddened patches on my hips, and shook his head about some slight bruising on my breasts and shoulders where, I supposed, the men had gripped me during the night. He led me into his hut and told me to lie face down on the bed. For an instant I thought he was going to engage in what Miss Blake had called buggering, and with a sigh I parted my legs. Instead, he began my first ever massage, and wonderful it was, too! Using some kind of cream or oil, which gave off a subtle, sour-sweet perfume, he smoothed and kneaded the muscles of my shoulders and back, and almost at once I began to feel a deep relaxation and easing of stiffness. He massaged the soles of my feet and my toes and my calves and the backs of my thighs, and by the time he reached my bottom so relaxed was I that his voice seemed to come from a great distance when I heard him mutter something about a ring that looked a bit red, and would need sorting.

At his signal I turned over, and he massaged my front, easing my flanks and tummy and thighs, surprising me a little by paying scant attention to my breasts – which seemed to have been a main target for all the other men who had touched me. He did pay more attention to my quim, spreading my thighs wide to massage their inner surfaces, then parting my folds to inspect me.

'Hmm! Pretty, pretty!' he said, and I opened my

eyes in surprise. He was bending over me, his head between my raised knees, and his face bore a broad smile. He ran a fingertip between my folds, and I twitched at how sensitive they were. 'Good girl!' he said. 'Healthy! Lots of men, and still ready!' He patted me full on my quim with the flat of his hand, and bade me stand. He rummaged in a sort of chest and brought out a small wooden box. He sat on the bed and told me to stand before him and part my knees. Dipping his fingers into the box, he approached me with a cream covered hand.

'This good for you!' he said. 'Pretty cunny must not get sore. This make you feel nice, keep cunny tight. Arse too. Good for men, and you feel the cocks better!'

I was rather puzzled by the odd words he was using, and especially at the notion that I should want to feel the cocks better – as if I had not felt them very thoroughly already! Then all such thought left me as his hand smoothed over what he called my 'cunny', and my cleft, and into both entrances. The cream was freezing, and I yelped. Then I yelped louder, and began to dance about, for it straight away turned warm, then hot! I was on fire and clutched myself front and back, my eyes starting as Motallo swayed back on the bed and roared with laughter. I leapt about like a dervish, my insides on fire, gasping and yelping as Motallo, tears streaming down his face, chuckled and flapped his hands in quieting gestures.

The burning in my loins and bottom soon began to ease, and when I was able to control my dance, and Motallo his chuckles, he told me he was sorry for not warning me, but that the cream would cure any soreness and, 'Keep you tight. Feel more! Feel better!'

I was still feeling shock, and would have berated

83

him had not his grin and the merry light in his eyes set me off, so that I found myself beginning to giggle, too. And he was right, at least in so far as the cream had made me more sensitive, for when I obeyed his gesture and sat down beside him it was as if my folds and bottom could feel every distinct hair of the fur upon which I sat.

Motallo brought a jug and poured us both drinks. It was a golden, slightly frothy liquid, which he told me was called *changa*, and which was delightfully refreshing. Again, he chatted away to me, telling me about Ngossi, the chief, and his sister, Mitia, in whose charge, it seemed, I would principally be. To my nervous, halting question about being a slave he laughed, and pooh-poohed any thoughts of burdens and shackles. Oh, yes, I was a slave, in that I belonged to the tribe, but the tribe was good, would treat me well. I would have to work, of course, but only the normal women's work.

'And then, little Ridja,' he said, rubbing his hand along my thigh, and making me blush to my roots at his next words. 'You be very popular with the men. Nice cunny! Good fuck! Maybe even *mantolla*!'

It seemed that cunny was another name for my place, what Miss Blake had called my quim, as were, I was to learn, cunt, pussy and minge. So many unpretty names for such a pleasant place! Fuck meant the same as shag, and *mantolla* was the tribal name for a girl who was a good fuck. At my instant blushes, Motallo hastened to assure me that *mantolla* was a title of honour among the tribe, to which every girl aspired. I was not sure it was such an honour, but since I was likely to be popular with the men anyway, perhaps being titled *mantolla* might ease my time until rescue. Besides, an impish voice in the back of my mind urged, shagging was rather nice!

The jug having been emptied, Motallo told me that we must now go to Mitia. He asked how I felt, and my stiffness had indeed gone. When I made to rise, he held my shoulder and stood himself.

'Motallo has made you feel better?' he asked. When I nodded yes, he said 'Then Ridja must be polite, say thank you!'

For a moment I was puzzled, then, as he stepped close and began to pull aside his loincloth, I realised what he meant. I was to learn that every time I left Motallo's company (and I usually at least ate my evening meal with him) he liked me to say thank you in the same way – by sucking him.

Motallo stroked my hair and smiled broadly down at me as I finished and sat back. 'Ha! Maybe *mantolla*,' he said. 'Maybe *bassawiti* too! Yes, maybe *bassawiti*. We see!'

He did not enlighten me as to what *bassawiti* meant, but handed me a length of cord and some squares of cloth. I thought ruefully, as I tied the loincloth about me, that I seemed to be getting into the habit of forgetting that I was completely naked! Then Motallo led me out of the hut, and took me to find Mitia, who would introduce me to the work of a tribeswoman.

Chapter 6

And so began my life among the tribe. I worked mainly with the girls and women, tending the vegetable plots, fetching water from the river, grinding corn, any of a hundred tasks. I was accepted by the womenfolk with such easy, good-humoured sisterliness that the notion that I was a slave seemed entirely ignored. Of course, my main duties were towards the menfolk. Even that first morning, as I clumsily attempted to aid a group of girls grinding corn, I encountered my first example of what was to become my primary activity.

There, perhaps ten yards off from the group, stood three men, leaning on their spears and glancing mock-casually at us. One of them beckoned. I looked around at the women, embarrassed that I was being summoned right in front of them, but the women were simply smiling and nodding, obviously amused rather than offended. Even so, I know I was blushing furiously, and that tightness in my breasts had already begun, as I put down my pestle and went towards the men, acutely conscious of the renewed giggles and whispers behind me, and the way the men's eyes roamed over me.

And I confess that my eyes were moving over them, too! Like pretty well all the men I met among the tribe, they were tall and slender, though well-muscled, with broad chests, flat tummies and long legs, which seemed to drag my gaze towards the loincloths that topped them. I was still very much the prudish English girl, and scolded myself for looking thus openly at that part of a man, but could not prevent myself imagining what the scraps of cloth hid, and what I was very soon to see and accommodate!

Already, as they led me around some huts and to a grassy space, hands were exploring my breasts and bottom, and I could see that at least one loincloth had lifted somewhat at the front. I had expected them to lie me down and leap upon me straight away, but they did not. Rather, they seemed fascinated by the paleness of my skin, and the length and straightness of my hair, and they ran their hands slowly over every inch of me, from the top of my head to the soles of my feet, neglecting nothing in between, least of all my bosom and between my thighs. Whether it was the knowledge of my situation or that the cream Motallo had put on me had indeed made me more sensitive I know not, but I do know that before the first touch of a hand at the top of my thigh I felt that by-now-familiar moistening within my folds.

My knees were drawn apart; hands caressed my inner thighs; others cupped my breasts and teased my nipples. Lips touched as lightly as a moth along the curve of my neck and shoulder, a spot which I find especially sensitive. I gasped as a hand slid beneath my bottom, exploring the cleft between my buttocks, pressing a fingertip against my puckered opening, then slid up to smooth and press against my cunny. I gasped again as fingers parted my folds and slipped along the length of my burning quim, only touching fleetingly on my entrance before moving to circle that pulsing nub of sensation I later learned to call my cherry. My eyes were closed and I was breathing rapidly as the half-dozen knowing hands fondled me. A fingertip found my entrance, pressed, then slid in as a thumb rolled my cherry. My thighs parted further of their own accord. I felt a movement, and opened my eyes to see the first man poised above me, his weight held on straight arms, his rod poised above my oozing quim, which the hand had now left.

When he entered me it was as if my very being were drawing him on, stretching to accommodate; clinging to retain the rod which sought my very self. When he began to move my breath shuddered from me. I longed to spread myself to the corners of the world to take more of him, and at the same time to curl myself into the smallest ball so that he touched every atom of my being.

I felt a touch on my face, and opened my eyes to see a proud plum nudging towards me. With a surge of what I can only call gratitude, I welcomed him. I did not care that I had given up any semblance of control as the two men dizzied me. All was a swirling, pulsating mass of overwhelming, voluptuous sensation. When both thrust quick and deep, and had their comes at the same moment, I welcomed the floodings of delirious heat which filled me.

When they pulled out of me I groaned, then gasped aloud as my knees were lifted high and the third man eased into me, hooking my knees on his arms, sinking even more deeply and powerfully than the first, holding his place, and not pumping but circling. He got the full benefit of his companion's efforts, for even as he plumbed my depths I churned into such a come as I felt would burst me asunder, and I writhed and sobbed and pumped my hips in an uncontrollable effort to cram myself onto him.

Oh! Lydia! How far had I come in such a short time! No more the prim, even haughty, daughter of the British commissioner, parading with my frocks and parasols and ordering cold drinks from quiet servants. Instead I was writhing naked and transported on the grass, my body pulsing helplessly under the men's ministrations, for all the world like a wanton!

When the men had finished with me I was like a dishrag, and my legs buckled beneath me as they helped me to my feet. I found a pot of water beside one of the huts, and rinsed myself, for I was awash with perspiration, and between my legs was moist and sticky from my effusions. The cold water refreshed me greatly, and when I went to rejoin the women I no longer felt weakness, but that suffusing inner languor which I was learning was so pleasant.

I felt a little trepidation as I approached the group still grinding flour, with the rhythmic thuds of their pestles setting the time for their singing. How would they react towards me, knowing as they must what I had just been engaged upon, and with their own menfolk? In the light of Miss Blake's disapproval during the march, I was prepared for coldness, even scorn. Instead, it was as if nothing unusual at all had occurred. Indeed, the women were, if anything, more friendly then before!

I quickly learned that this open and, I think, more healthy attitude towards relations between the sexes than that of my own society, was normal among the tribe. Not for them the secretiveness, the hypocrisy, the prurience even, that I was to become familiar with when back among my own people. That men and women enjoyed each other was accepted as a normal, and pleasant, part of everyday life, to be got on with like any other. Thus there was a perfect balance and harmony within the tribe, with no jealousy or competition among the menfolk of whatever age or standing, and very little among the women.

Status within the tribe was visibly signalled by dress, and it is surprising what differences can be marked even with only loincloths and armlets. Men, and especially successful hunters, would wear proudly the pelts of beasts they had slain, and especially the lion, whose tail they would use as a fly whisk. Married women wore wide loincloths which wrapped around them almost like skirts, the richness and decoration of which reflected their husband's status. Unmarried girls, too, wore loincloths decorated to reflect their father's standing, but briefer than the married women's and designed to show them off. The younger boys and girls, who had not yet been initiated into adulthood, wore nothing, but ran about as happily naked as the day they were born.

These younger girls looked forward eagerly to the time when they would be initiated and paid close attention to all the work of their mothers and older sisters. While still quite small they would be adept at basket-making, and would help with the preparation and cooking of food, and although not strong enough to carry full sized water pots, would accompany us older ones on our morning trips to the river, even carrying smaller pots on their heads in imitation of their elders. Perhaps it was this early experience of carrying pots upon their heads that gave the women of the tribe their graceful, high-bosomed posture, for I noticed, after only a few weeks, that I myself felt more lithe and that my breasts were fuller and more prominent.

The young girls, especially as they grew close to the time of their initiation, paid close attention to the ways their older sisters comported themselves in relation to the menfolk. One would notice them sitting just by a group of older girls and watching very closely, for all the world as if they were at lessons, learning the smiles and giggles and secret signals with which their elders would court a chosen man. One would even see them peeping into the huts where the couple had gone to conduct their exchange. I myself was often conscious of being studied closely, as if they were keen to learn exactly what was involved in the ways of pleasuring men.

One girl, Tiliu, who was to become my best friend in the whole world, was bolder or perhaps just more curious than the rest, and made no bones about watching me closely. She began to follow me everywhere, and despite my initial embarrassment I soon became accustomed to seeing her hovering nearby when I was taken aside and spread or bent over. She seemed especially keen to witness me using my mouth, and from the corner of my eye I would often espy her elfin face, wide-eyed and serious with curiosity, only a short distance away from my own. One or two of the younger men found this annoying and shooed her away, but others ignored her and one, a lovely cheerful old man called Doluttu, found her eagerness positively amusing and actually welcomed her. For myself, I soon ceased to find her attention distracting, and we became almost constant companions.

As well as Ngossi, the chief, the tribe was governed by a council of senior warriors. It was the councillors who determined a girl's status and decided her bride price, so you can well imagine that the young girls all vied for their attention. Not many days after I joined the tribe I learned how important this was when, having spent the night with Ngossi, I was awarded my titles.

Whether I was tired or in an odd mood when Ngossi took me to his hut for the night, or whether it was that he did not attempt to gentle me into warmth before starting I know not, but I seemed to take little pleasure from the event. He was surprisingly small in the cock, and I was just lying there, getting little from his pumping of me, when I suddenly noticed an expression of irritation on the face that hovered above mine. For a moment I was puzzled, then nervous, for this was the chief himself, the very last man I should irritate! It flashed into my mind that the men all seemed to take great pride in the way their shagging of a girl sent her into transports, and here I was, with the chief himself, lying like a log!

I found myself remembering the sensations other men had given me and pretending they were happening to me now. I wrapped my legs around Ngossi's hips, gripped him with my arms, rolled my head and made loud groans of pretended pleasure. My efforts seemed to please him and he pumped more vigorously. On and on he went, his eyes screwed shut, on his face that grimace of pleasure-pain they seemed all to adopt when shagging.

I felt strangely detached. Even though his weight was squashing me, even though his hands mauled quite harshly at my breasts, even though I was clearly helpless against his use of me, I actually felt that it was I and not him who was in control. I even found myself consciously adjusting my position and movements and assessing their effect.

Talesi liked to have my legs high: I raised my knees up and clasped my ankles around Ngossi's back. He grunted, gripped my shoulders and pulled me harder onto himself. I moved my hips in time to his thrusts, pushing when he pushed, relaxing when he pulled back, circling my pelvis to his rhythm. He lengthened his thrusts. I moaned loudly, and he laughed proudly, pumping hard.

I found to my surprise that in behaving thus I was actually increasing my own pleasure, and indeed began to experience a mental pleasure at my own control as well as the physical pleasure that was inevitably growing. When he began to come, laughing aloud as his hotness flooded me, I pumped my hips rapidly against him, consciously clenching my cunny sheath to bring him off more quickly, and cried aloud as if I too was coming. He groaned, stiffened into a final spasm then, with a great shudder, collapsed onto me.

For a long time he lay still, and despite the fact that I could hardly breathe because of his weight I was able to reflect, as I felt his member shrinking and slipping out of me, that I had been right. By responding I had averted the irritation he had shown. The importance a man gave to his cock and its activities was indeed a source of strength for women! By pretence I had pleased Ngossi. By co-operation I had satisfied Talesi and our other men. By accommodating their need to pleasure themselves I had ensured that they treated me well. Surely this new knowledge and my earlier realisation that I could take and surmount their demands would be a powerful weapon in my survival until our rescue.

With my new-found understanding, I became more active, took control, if you will. Unbidden, as Ngossi lay beside me, I squirmed around and took him into my mouth. He was soft and small, and I could taste myself upon him. It was delightful to feel him arousing under my ministrations, swelling and stiffening, and beginning to squirm a little. Even when at his fullest, I could still take almost all of him onto my tongue, and I felt a heady sense of power as I licked and sucked, and squeezed his shaft and balls in my hands. He groaned aloud when he had his second come, and I took delight in milking him of every drop. I kept going even after he had begun to soften again, revelling in my control over him. I even, before releasing him, gave his shrinking plum a really hard suck and lick, and almost laughed aloud when he groaned and shuddered!

Some kind of imp was in me, and I gave the poor man little rest. When not shagging or sucking him, I held his member and caressed him as it lay like a helpless little sausage in my palms. At the merest twitch of life, I would clamp my mouth upon him and suck him to erection. I even learned how to vary my ministrations so as to bring him off quickly or maintain him in a state of tension.

We did sleep, of course and, in the fresh light of the morning, Ngossi had the stength to shag me again. This time I was much more in the mood and, actively pumping and writhing as I had last night, I did indeed have a delicious come, the more so because, drained by my night's ministrations, Ngossi took a long time to come off himself!

The result of my efforts became known to me later that day, when Motallo came rushing up to me as I swept out Mitia's hut, and, laughing but not explaining, dragged me off to where the council sat under the tree. I had no idea what was happening as Motallo stood me in front of the seated councillors and went to stand behind them with every appearance of glee. The seated men were all talking quietly among themselves, and nodding and gesturing in my direction. I began to feel very self-conscious. Then Ngossi stood up, and in the ensuing silence made a long speech with much gesturing and clapping of hands and pointing at me. Of course, I understood hardly a word, and it was only when he stopped and sat down, and Motallo translated for me that I understood the full import.

Ngossi had proposed, and the council had accepted, that I should be awarded the coveted status of *mantolla*, and more than that, of *bassawiti* too! Although at the time I did not really understand what these titles signified, the nods and smiles of the assembly, and the gasps and applause of several girls who had come up to watch, told me that I should feel honoured. Only later, when Motallo explained, did I realise that the honour could be viewed askance in other circumstances!

It seemed that *mantolla* meant 'she in heat', and betokened that I was a willing partner in shagging; what Motallo called 'a good fuck'! The other title, *bassawiti*, literally meant 'tongue' (bassa) and 'lips' (witi) and signified that I was skilled with my mouth. Both these titles were soon given visible expression, for the moment the council dismissed me I was taken by a group of giggling, evidently delighted women and girls, and bathed and combed and decked out in what I came to think of as my uniform.

The sign of my status as *mantolla* was a short, white cloth, perhaps six inches deep and fringed with beads, which took the place of my earlier loincloth, and which I wore at the back. The effect of this skimpy garb, which left my front entirely exposed and came only half way down over my buttocks, so that my cleft was clearly visible, made me feel more naked

95

than had I actually been so, and clearly distinguished me from almost all the other females, who wore a variety of loincloths but none so distinctive or skimpy as mine. And so, by title and by physical presentation, it was signified to anyone who cared to look that I was 'a good fuck' – a signal of which men took full advantage, you can be sure!

My status as *bassawiti* was also given a visible sign, for my hair was dressed into a sort of topknot held with a leather band so that it stood fully three inches up from the crown of my head, the rest of my long hair flowing out from the band like a tail. And not only was the topknot a signal; it was sometimes used to hold my head still while a man employed my mouth. This could be rather awkward for, holding me thus, the men would often push deeper than was comfortable, and I would have to struggle hard not to gag. This was yet another reason for me to fellate them well, for if I pleasured them by my own efforts they would not feel the need to hold my head.

But I am getting ahead of my story.

As you can imagine, after I was awarded my new titles I was kept very busy by way of celebration. It began when, through the throng of girls and women who had rushed up to congratulate me, I saw Talesi beckoning. He seemed to be standing more proudly than ever (for was it not he who had presented me to the tribe?) and grinned broadly, his head high, as he took my hand and led me towards his hut.

You can be sure that I did not have the chance to rejoin the women at their work that afternoon. And by the time Motallo came to fetch me away for a blessed bath and massage as dusk was falling, I had begun to re-assess my judgement as to the ability of a woman to outlast many men, for I am sure there was actually a queue of warriors wanting to celebrate my new status. I know it was with trembling legs and aching jaw that I followed Motallo to his hut.

The bath had already been prepared by my friend, and I wallowed long and luxuriously before lying down for his delicious massage. Even his creaming of my bottom and cunny was a joy, for by the time the now familiar freeze-burn had eased, the slight soreness caused by the many cocks I had accepted into both places that afternoon had quite worn off.

Motallo was a true friend and a delight, and chatted away quietly to me, knowing how weary I was, as he prepared some food. He introduced me to a new drink, which he called *dissna*, which had a subtle, rather sweet taste, and seemed to spread warmth and relaxation even as I swallowed it. It was good to sit there with this lovely little man, chatting in my own language, for I had seen very little of Miss Blake since we reached the village. I told him somewhat about myself, and he responded with a little about himself, and the tribe, and what with the food and the *dissna* and my weariness from the afternoon's activities, I was soon lying back on the bed in a pleasant half-drowse.

Then, for the very first time, Motallo began to touch me in a non-massaging manner, in the way my other lovers did. He ran his hands over my tummy and thighs very gently, seeming hardly to touch me. He moved up and began to fondle my breasts.

'Nice, yes?' he said after a while. I nodded drowsily, for it did indeed feel very soothing. 'These called in English, titties,' he said. 'Feel nice when man caress them.' He moved, scratching lightly with his fingernails around my armpits and ribs, near but not now touching my breasts, which had already grown taut

97

and very sensitive. Instinctively, I moved to try to get his hands back on my breasts, which felt deserted. Motallo chuckled. 'Ha! Ridja want her titties felt, yes!'

And I did. I did!

His hands cupped and caressed and squeezed my tingling bosom and I became breathless. It felt wonderful! Then, his fingernails scratching gently, but oh, so commandingly, he moved down over my ribs and tummy. My hips rose to meet him, but his touch curved away from my cunny and continued down, to scratch with agonising gentleness, no heavier than a moth, the length of my thighs and around the backs of my knees and calves, to the soles of my feet, before moving along the insides of my legs, which parted wide of their own accord. Slowly, tormentingly, his hands slid up my thighs. I rose to meet him, but again his fingers avoided the place that now so wanted them. I moaned as his fingers moved away, circling near but never touching the lips that seemed to pout for his caress; moving over my thighs and tummy; sliding quickly up to fondle my breasts, then down again.

My legs raised themselves and parted even further. The teasing fingers moved over my tummy and waist and hips and the backs of my knees and my thighs and my bottom, but never, never onto the place that now trembled for them. I heard him say, 'Ridja want fuck? Want Motallo fuck her, eh?'

I could not, at that moment, remember what fuck meant and, frankly, was incapable of asking. But, pressing a finger into my burning quim, Motallo went on, 'You want Motallo up here?'

And I heard my own voice whisper, 'Oh, please! Yes please!'

Suddenly a soft, beautiful warmth descended upon me. Ahh! My breathing quickened and I began to tremble. But I had felt no weight upon me, no penetration, and opened my eyes. Motallo's head was between my legs! He was kissing me, licking me! I was startled and moved to sit up, but he placed a hand on my chest and pushed me back.

'Be still!' he said, his voice muffled. 'Motallo make you feel good. Make you come!'

My legs rested upon his shoulders. His arms reached around me and his fingers parted the lips of my quim. The heat of his mouth upon me sent shudders through my whole being. His tongue rasped across the insides of my folds. He licked and nibbled avidly at my cherry, and I squirmed and moaned. His tongue explored every crevice, even slipping into my opening, moving more and more rapidly. My mind spiralled away from me as churning, surging waves swept over me. A finger slid into my bottom and I welcomed it. A hand touched my breast and I gasped my pleasure. His teeth rasped upon me. I yearned to engulf all of him and crammed my oozing folds against him. His lips and his tongue and his teeth drove all control from me. Even when he nipped me I only wanted more. And more, and more!

Afterwards, while my body spiralled down from the heights he had driven me to, we drank more *dissna*. At his prompting I told him that, yes, I enjoyed what he had done (as if it were not obvious!) and liked sucking his cock. He kept caressing me and urging me and, to please him, I said aloud what he wanted me to say, using all the words – cunt and arse and fuck and prick and tits, and all the others he seemed so delighted to hear – and telling him how much I liked what he and the other men did to me.

(I realised later that, perhaps because of some quirk in their nature, men seemed to derive great pleasure from women talking that way. Odd!)

Night had fully fallen and wick lamps had been lit to illuminate the hut when Motallo suddenly announced that he was going to fuck me. Said thus, baldly – 'Now Motallo fuck you!' – his words were quite shocking. But he had been feeling and fondling me, and the cream between my legs had had its usual effect, and I had drunk quite a lot of *dissna*, and I have to admit that I actually wanted to be fucked! I lay back and spread my legs. To my surprise, this was not what he wanted.

Instead, he motioned me to stand up. I was puzzled, for so far I had always been shagged lying down, and I became more puzzled when Motallo lay down in my place. Seeing my expression, he chuckled. 'Not to worry Ridja! You on top! My belly too fat!'

He slapped himself on his tummy, which was indeed very round, making me laugh along with him. He pulled up his loincloth and, as we both giggled like children, I obeyed his instruction to climb astride his hips, and grasp and rub his half-soft cock, and move myself over it, and lower myself upon it.

It was, I confess, a strange and delicious experience. Because I was on top I was able to choose the depth to which I sank upon him, and to set my own rhythm. His hands roamed over my breasts and thighs and buttocks. I circled up and down, revelling in the delight of his cock filling me, setting my own time, moving to my own sensations; in fact, shagging him rather than the other way around. Only after a long while, by which time I could hardly breathe and the churning in my cunny had become dizzying, did he exert any control, pressing his hands upon the tops

100

of my thighs and pushing with his hips, and suddenly I was coming helplessly – and this time it was me who cried out.

Whereas a man's spending is a quick thing, soon over even though vehement, a woman's come is wondrous. A delicous tension, a tingling of pins and needles in breasts and tummy, spreading and building to an ache and then to a pulsing glory of overwhelming tautness and surging, ecstatic release. All her body coils into a glorious kernel of tension to surge out in staggering waves of surrender and greed and joy; her mind bursts with light; her very toe-tips feel the effects of the lance piercing her being. And more wonderful still, it goes on and on, receding only to surge and burst again; but gentler and fuller and deeper, until she is lost upon a sea of radiance and sensation. Such was my case now as Motallo held back, and held back, and at last jerked and spurted, and I writhed and then drooped over him, entirely spent as if my very being had melted away!

Chapter 7

The routine of my days among the tribe was gentle and pleasant. Most nights (unless there were visitors from another tribe) I ended up sleeping in Motallo's hut, and at dawn would hurry down to the river with the rest of the women and girls to bathe and fetch water. I became adept at many of the women's tasks, and enjoyed working with the laughing, singing girls.

Of course, I would be called away pretty often by some man or other, and so was not as useful to the women as I might have been. One man who invariably came for me, usually early in the afternoon, was my Talesi, and I always felt a thrill of pleasure when I saw his smiling face and beckoning hand. He usually took me down by the river, where he would gentle and caress me into that pellucid, enkindled state he knew so well how to arouse in me, and then he would spread me and slowly, oh, so knowingly, shag me into a pulsating delirium of joy. None of the other men, except perhaps Motallo when he used his mouth on me, could take me to such heights of rapture, or sound the depths of my senses so.

Talesi rarely let me fellate him, although he was obviously proud that I was *bassawiti*. Among the other men though, my mouth was the most popular source of pleasure, and over the months I grew familiar with the sight and taste of pretty well every man in the tribe. What it is in men that makes them prefer a girl to suck them when there is such a snug and welcoming place as her cunny waiting warm for them I know not, but such seems indeed the case. For the girl it has obvious advantages, for she it is who is in control and, if she is skilful, she can bring her man off at more or less any speed she wishes. Another advantage of a knowing mouth is that it can stiffen up a flaccid cock with remarkable efficiency. And besides, it is delicious!

Of course, it was not only my mouth the men enjoyed, for my other parts received a generous share of visitors. Not many of the men who took me aside were as wonderful lovers as Talesi, but few were rough, and infrequent were the occasions when I had to pretend excitement, as I so usually did with Ngossi. Perhaps the cream Motallo put on me every night really did make me tighter and more sensitive; perhaps it was the frequency with which I was pleasured by one cock or another. Whatever it was, I know my title *mantolla* was richly deserved, for my body delighted in theirs!

An occasion which showed how highly the tribe regarded a girl's potentiality to give and receive pleasure was the initiation ceremony I witnessed. Those girls who were to take part in the ceremony; girls whose bosoms had now developed and who had grown a little fuzz between their legs (eight of them on this occasion), were taken by their mothers into a special ceremonial hut, where they spent the night and the day before the actual ceremony. I do not know what transpired there, for entry was strictly forbidden to all save the girls and their mothers.

As the day of the ceremony unfolded there was much activity around the cooking fires. The meeting ground was cleared and swept and any number of woodpiles for fires were prepared. As evening approached the whole tribe gathered and there was much beating of drums, chanting, dancing and drinking of *changa*. Even during the afternoon the men and boys seemed to become very excited, and I found myself in great demand.

With the dusk, everybody gathered in a great circle around the meeting ground. The drums began a steady beat, and more *changa* was drunk. The drums rose in a crescendo and stopped with a final crash just as the sun finally sank below the horizon. A silence fell over the crowd as a large wooden statue was dragged out of the hut where the girls were, and was set in the middle of the meeting ground. This statue was of a grotesque and stylised man-figure, with a huge, erect member sticking up and out leeringly.

After a silence some minutes long, a single drum began to beat insistently and from the ceremonial hut the initiates emerged, dancing in a line. Each was entirely naked save for a rope of many beads about her waist. The girls looked utterly lovely as they danced, swaying sensuously, leading first with the left hip, now with the right, in a motion which turned their slender bodies into liquid. They formed a circle around the statue, their hands moving over their painted bodies as if to draw attention to their budding breasts; their firm, round bottoms; their slender thighs and their virgin cunnies, the lips of which had been painted pink for emphasis.

The girls' dance was designed to emphasise that they were now ready to be introduced to the glories of womanhood, and its effect upon the males was instant and obvious, for all around us cocks grew rigid. I half expected to be leapt upon there and then, but the men were spellbound by the sight of the young virgins and did not grab us until later.

As the drumbeat became more insistent one girl broke from the dancing circle and moved lithely towards the statue. Grasping the great wooden cock with both hands, she writhed her hips suggestively as she slid her hands along its length. She rubbed her small breasts against the body of the statue, then slid slowly up and down it, her arms around it, her legs on either side. Again she grasped the cock and rubbed it with both hands, even approaching it with her quim several times so that I held my breath at the thought that she was going to impale herself upon it. Instead, moving more quickly now, her eyes tight shut, she straddled the huge wooden phallus and rubbed herself against it in exact simulation of the helpless movements my own quim made when I was being fucked or fingered. After a while of this very erotic movement, the girl stopped, moved back, rubbed the wooden phallus lingeringly for a while with her hands as if to make it come, bent to kiss it upon its great plum, then whirled away to fling herself to her knees before her mother, who was standing forward a little from the circle. She remained kneeling there, her forehead on the ground, her pert bottom towards the statue, while the next girl repeated the performance.

As I watched each of the girls, who seemingly tried to outdo each other in the wantonness of their dance, I suddenly realised that one of them was Tiliu. I found myself watching in fascination, for she no longer looked like my innocent little friend, but had become a sinuous, almost ethereal image of eroticism. The firelight flickered on her slender curves, causing warmth to stir even in me, let alone the watching men!

When the last of the eight girls had finished her dance and was kneeling before her mother, more drums joined the single one to which the girls had danced. Now the eight older women began to move, dancing slowly around the still forms of their daughters, touching them with their feet to show possession, pumping their hips and lifting their breasts in suggestion of what was about to happen. Then, with a great crash, the drums stopped.

In the silence which followed, each woman reached down and helped her daughter to her feet. The girls stood motionless as the women ran their hands all over them. The women were each given a rolled animal skin, which they in turn handed to their daughters. The girls spread the skin onto the ground so that they formed a circle around the statue. They then lay down on them upon their backs and spread their knees wide and lifted them high, their plump little painted quims facing out to the crowd.

Murmurs of appreciation rose at the truly delicious sight they made, and these grew in volume as the eight women moved to stand above the girls. Each of the mothers bent, smoothing an object, which I could not see clearly, over their daughter's torso and thighs. Then it was held to her face so that she could kiss it. They then turned and held the objects out towards the crowd, and I was able to see that they were oddly shaped carvings: smooth and shiny, with a large bulge at one end, from which protruded a sort of rod. Only when the carvings were handed to the girls, who holding them by the bulges, approached them to their opened cunnies, did I realise with a gasp of shock what they were for!

My eyes were glued upon Tiliu as she brought the rod down to the parting of her thighs. I found myself holding my breath as she slowly traced the length of her folds with the rounded top, sliding it from end to end, even down to the cleft of her bottom, before moving up again in a caressing motion over her pink-red cunny lips and cherry. Slowly, the rod descended again, poised over her little entrance. She moved the bulb in a circle, the rod-tip now pressing a little into her. She paused, shuffled her hips as if readying herself, then pressed. Perhaps I imagined the slight wince which flickered across her face. I must have imagined her gasp, for all the crowd about me was murmuring noisily, but gasp I am sure she did as the rod pressed and pressed, and began to slide into her.

All the girls were in the same case, and the audience became silent as the initiates pressed the rods into their maidenheads, pulling back a little, to press deeper and deeper still, until the bulge itself was against their plump folds. Once the rods were fully embedded, the girls, as one, arched their backs, and lifted their bottoms from the ground, splaying their knees wide, so that the crowd could see clearly that the rods were firmly implanted. A great shout went up and the drums beat wildly. The crowd clapped and laughed as the girls lowered themselves, then they carefully removed the rods, which they handed to their mothers, before standing to smile triumphantly towards the watching circle.

At this point I lost track of the ceremony for a while, for my shoulder was tapped, and a man next to me indicated that he would enjoy the attentions of my mouth. Fortunately, he was already very excited by the ceremony, and I was able to bring him off very quickly.

By the time I could look back at the ceremony, the

girls were moving proudly, if a little haltingly for they must have been somewhat sore, across to where Ngossi and Mitia sat near the council tree. Kneeling before them, their foreheads to the ground, the row of pert bottoms reflected the firelight like so many glossy peaches. The drums settled to a steady throb. The many fires flickered around us, highlighting the lovely, glowing bodies of the eight naked initiates. Mitia stood and stepped forward, looking positively regal in the firelight. In her hand she held a long slender rod with many tassles hanging from it. The girls knelt very still in a half-circle at her feet, and one by one she touched the pole on their bottoms and shoulders, whereupon the girls stood, their heads bowed. In her other hand Mitia held a sort of baton, shaped to resemble a rigid cock, and she smoothed this over each girl's bosom and between her legs before holding it up for the girl to kiss.

The circle at once broke as people rushed to congratulate the girls, and to dance and shout and drink *changa* in a celebration which lasted all through the night and into the dawn. I was at once approached by the nearest man. As he shagged me I was able to see that I was not the only one, for all around me bodies, Miss Blake's among them, were already writhing on the ground or lurching off to refill *changa* cups. It seemed that on the night of an initiation the normal rules lapsed, for even married women were shagging men who were not their husbands. Some of the younger girls were also trying to join in, and looked disappointed when they were invariably turned away.

It was, I can assure you, a very busy night and I did not see Miss Blake again until after the dawn. Seeing her sitting, her head on her knees, beside a hut, I ran to her eagerly, for somehow we seldom had the opportunity to talk together these days. My joyful greeting died on my lips when, at my first call, she looked up at me. Far from the smile of welcome I had expected, her face bore a blank, dispirited look which stopped me short in my tracks. I hurried over and sat down beside her, putting my arm about her shoulders, which seemed to shrink at my touch.

'We are lost!' she whispered after a long silence. I stared at her in surprise. 'These people, with their licentious, immoral ways! They have turned us into their whores, their playthings!'

I was stunned. Whores? What could she mean? I stammered a protest. What had we done wrong? Their ways were not ours, but had she not said we should submit; should rise above by maintaining ourselves as Englishwomen should? What choice had we had? And, really, was it so bad? She looked at me almost listlessly.

'Come,' I said, hugging her shoulders a little tighter. 'They are not cruel to us. Our state could be much worse. We could be real slaves!' I meant the kind I had read about in my school books.

'But we *are* slaves!' Her voice was low and thick with emotion. 'Slaves to their lusts! To shameful bodily sensations. We will never be accepted back to civilisation! And you are worse than I, for have I not seen you playing up to these . . . these beasts!'

I tried, I really tried to talk her out of her black mood, reassuring her, cajoling her, but to no avail. Indeed, it seemed that the more I pointed to the brighter aspects of our situation, the blacker she became, and I slowly discerned that it was not *what we did* that she so hated, but *that it gave pleasure*! That we experienced comes was what made us whores! Yet how could we help it? And how could she say I was worse than her? She responded to the men as much as I. She had comes. I had seen her. Suddenly I felt a wave of irritation at the unfairness of what she had said. How could she? How dare she be so . . . so horrible to me. And was it true we would be cast off, be spurned even if we were rescued? I ran off, tears stinging my eyes.

How much later it was that the young woman I came to know as Malanni found me, I know not. I was sitting clutching my knees and staring unhappily at the river when suddenly she was there beside me, her arms around me, pressing my face into her shoulder. Miss Blake's words had made me miserable, and when Malanni smiled and asked me what was wrong, I burst into tears. At once, she stooped and picked me up and carried me off to her hut for all the world as if I were a tiny child. And indeed I felt like a child as she dried my eyes, put me on her bed, then lay beside me and enfolded me in her arms.

My sobs soon eased to an occasional hiccup of exhaustion. Malanni's strong arms comforted me and her warmth and kindness enveloped me as she pressed my damp face to her bosom. I was weary after my night of sex and my unhappiness at Miss Blake's horrid words. Somehow, in Malanni's arms, I felt just as I had so long ago when, as a little girl, my mother had cuddled away my tears at some hurt or upset, and even though Malanni was only a little older than me I found myself snuggling into her for warmth and comfort. Her hands gently stroked my hair and shoulders and her soft, cooing voice and her warm, deep breathing, all soothed me towards a gentle, comforted doze. The contentment was only deepened when, through a glow of warmth, I felt her press my face to her breast and I found myself sucking her sweet, warm nipple as I dropped into sleep.

I awoke to such a feeling of bliss that for a long while it was as if I was not awake at all but was floating in a dream of gentleness. Warm perfumes caressed my breath, strong arms cradled me, gentle hands smoothed over me. My mind unable or unwilling to register thought of any kind, I flowed with, and opened to, the gentle caresses of hands on my body, to the soft kisses which brushed my forehead and cheeks. The kisses moved to my lips. The hand stroked down across my tummy, and over my thighs, and between them. My body opened to the welcome touches and my mouth responded to the seeking kisses. I floated, eyes closed, on a dream of muted colours and music. The gentle lips left mine then descended, kissing my throat, my shoulder, my breasts, ribs, tummy, thighs. I sighed blissfully as the mouth moved between my legs. Ah, Motallo!

But this was not Motallo! My mind swam weakly from dream to consciousness. I was with Malanni! This was my friend Malanni kissing and now licking me! Startled, I gasped and made to sit up. At once she enfolded me again in her strong arms and hugged and soothed. Her hand descended to my quim, which at once grew warm as my legs pressed together. She pressed my face to her neck and rocked and cooed. My surprise at what she had been doing to me eased. This was my friend Malanni, who had comforted me and looked after me. She was kind and warm. Surely there was no harm?

The hand between my legs moved gently. Malanni relaxed the arm about my shoulders and I looked up at her, still a little nervous. She smiled down at me, her eyes flicking all over my face, then bent her head

111

and again kissed me on the lips. She held the kiss. It was warm and inviting, and I was kissing her back. My thighs relaxed. The hand moved gently. I slipped back into my warm dream state.

Perhaps because I was so exhausted from my tears, perhaps from gratitude, perhaps simply from instinct; I knew not, nor cared as Malanni began again to kiss and nuzzle my folds. So delicious was it that when she turned and moved around, I welcomed the warm, musky scent and rested my head contentedly upon her thigh. Her hands caressed my bottom, pulling me onto her lips and tongue which, with infinite knowledge and patience, sought out my nerve ends and set me aflame. As if of its own accord, my mouth moved to seek her. I nuzzled into her warm, moist folds, her scent filling my veins, her flavour and softness drawing me on. Nothing existed save my body and hers, her mouth seeking out my soul, her quim pressing onto my face, my tongue lapping gently, her delicious tulip-folds oozing sweet honey lotion onto my face.

Afterwards, after I had spiralled slowly down from the orange and gold delirium of the comes that began as almost tentative spasms and grew and grew under Malanni's wonderful mouth until I felt my very heart ould burst with the ecstasy of them, I felt overwhelmed with a sort of shy gratitude. Malanni had risen before me and now came into the hut carrying a bowl and some grasses, with which she proceeded to wash between my legs and my face, all the time smiling and looking softly into my eyes. Her own eyes were so deep and warm I wanted to drown in them. What strange feelings engulfed me. That a man could arouse me to transports I now knew well, but that a woman could desire another? That the caresses of another woman's hands and mouth; the sensations of

112

another woman upon my own mouth, could arouse in me such emotions, drive me to such long, gentle, awesome climaxes, was a profound revelation to me! So too was the strange yearning I now felt to reach out to her, to touch her, to feel her arms about me, to be rocked and sheltered in her embrace.

Perhaps the episode was an aberration. It never happened again, indeed was never refered to or hinted at. Nevertheless, always afterwards Malanni behaved gently and protectively towards me, and for my part I felt a shyness, almost a meekness when with her. And I am sure I would have gone willingly to her bed again had she invited me!

Ceremony was important to the tribe, and one I witnessed, a few months after the initiation, was Malanni's wedding. I was given the honour of serving as her bridesmaid – a very different proposition from that of a bridesmaid among our own society.

The wedding was very lavish since the groom was the son of one of the council elders and Malanni was the granddaughter of another. The preparations took well over a week, for the main requirements were that a new hut be built for the couple, a bridal bed constructed, and a whole set of new baskets and pots made for when they set up together. All of these activities were shared by the women and girls of the tribe and were performed with great good humour and, to judge by the gestures and the smattering of the language I had mastered, many lewd jokes and comments were made concerning the bed and its uses!

At last the great day arrived. Malanni and I had been hidden away in her mother's hut since the night before. I had been bathing and oiling Malanni, and had decked her in her wedding jewellery, and fed her the special marriage foods which had ritual and

113

magic properties. Now, as the sun began to descend and the menfolk of each family went through their ceremony of bargaining the bride price, I sat with Malanni waiting for the signal that agreement had been reached. At the signal Malanni, naked save for masses of chain jewellery around her waist and throat and wrists and ankles, and I proceeded out of her mother's hut to join the groom outside the new hut. I felt my throat catch at how lovely Malanni looked, her shoulders erect, her oiled skin outshining even her jewellery. The bride and groom stood on opposite sides of the portal, not looking at each other; he tall and gleaming in the low sunlight, his head high, haughty and remote; she looking demurely to the ground. For Malanni to look demure almost gave me the giggles, for she was a big, full-breasted girl who I knew to be very bold, outgoing, and thoroughly familiar with the pleasures of the body.

Torches were lit and held high in a circle. The groom was brought forward by his father to stand in the doorway of what was now his hut. Malanni was brought forward by her mother and father and stopped in front of him, still looking to the ground. Now came the culmination of the ceremony. As Malanni stood, her mother marked her forehead with zigzags of white paint. She then spread smears of bright yellow paint onto her buttocks and, as Malanni parted her knees, smeared a fistful of bright orange paint around her cunny. Then, to a great ululation from the women and girls, the groom turned and went into the hut.

Now came my real part in the ceremony. Taking her by both hands, I tugged the protesting (for she was supposed to be reluctant) Malanni through the door of the hut. Lamps had already been lit inside and Tunku, the groom, splendid in the flickering

114

light, stood waiting by the bed. Malanni stood before him, eyes down, while I removed all her jewellery, and presented her hand to his. The sight of these two, both, to judge from her straining nipples and the rearing evidence of his excitement, eager to conclude with each other, sent a delicious shiver down my spine, and I felt my own nipples stir.

My task now was to kneel beside the bed and witness their consummation – and such a consummation! The couple were both very ready, and the joy on Malanni's face as she lay back and parted her magnificent thighs was a delight to behold. I caught my breath as Tunku moved to poise between her knees, for he was very large! I need not have been nervous though, for Malanni was well able to accept the thrust with which he buried himself in her depths. At once, her legs clamped about him, and she gave a cry of delight as their bodies bucked and writhed as one. Perhaps, though, Tunku had been overexcited, for the bout was a very quick one, and I confess that I felt a pang of disappointment as he jerked into a very obvious come.

If Malanni shared my disappointment she gave no sign and only smiled at the patch of orange paint upon his loins. The first sign of consummation had been affixed. As required by my role as bridesmaid, I gave them both cups of *changa* and returned to my kneeling place. They sat side by side on the edge of the bed, arms about each other's waists, then kissed with all the halting gentleness of new and tentative lovers. I found myself moved, a lump in my throat, as their lips tenderly explored each other's brow and cheeks and neck, returning again and again to join mouths in such tender demonstrations of love it almost brought tears to my eyes.

To be witness to such a gentle scene was a privilege indeed, and I was hardly able to breathe as Tunku moved to kiss and nuzzle Malanni's glorious breasts. His hands cupped their fullness and her eyes closed in the rapture I knew she was feeling – indeed, was beginning to feel myself. She was kissing him now: her lips exploring his broad chest; her teeth and fingers exciting his nipples; her tongue lapping over his hard muscles, dipping into his navel, moving to his thigh. The second sign of consummation was transferred when her gentle lips parted to draw his slumbering member in, and the white zig-zag from her forehead was imprinted upon his hard belly.

I was myself in a state of considerable arousal, my hand pressed instinctively between my legs, as Malanni gently, oh so tenderly, paid homage to her new husband's manhood, and I had to snatch my hand away to prevent a come as the memory of that same mouth upon my own body flashed across my mind!

Although she took a long time rousing him to full erection with her sensuous mouth and fingers, she did not bring him to a finish. Instead, she pulled back and, planting a kiss upon his swollen plum, moved to lie face down upon the bed. Now it was Tunku's turn to pleasure her, and I was held spellbound. His fingers and lips and tongue were no less gentle than hers had been when Tunku caressed his new wife from toes to neck, and I could see, reflected in the face she turned towards me, the success with which his kisses were arousing her as he moved from the soles of her feet, to the backs of her knees, to her neck and the small of her back, and to the insides of the thighs she now slowly parted for him.

The transference of the third (yellow) mark from

Malanni's body to Tunku's was accomplished with such sinuous movements, such expressions of delight upon both faces, such sensuous joy in each other's bodies, that when Tunku writhed and gasped into his second come, I confess that I, too, came off between clamped and trembling thighs!

After a brief rest and another cup of *changa*, Tunku and I completed the final part of the wedding ceremony by going out of the hut, and displaying to the tribe the white and yellow and orange proofs that he had taken possession of his wife. At the sight of the paint upon his loins, to which it was my task to point and indicate success, a great shout went up, drums crashed, and the party began.

As usual during a tribal celebration I was kept rather busy, and I confess that I was very eager for my first encounter, for the sight of my friend's nuptials had got me very aroused! The party went on far into the night. As an 'official' at the wedding, I was very popular, and so was very grateful to at last make my way to Motallo's hut.

All in all, the easy rhythm of life with the tribe, my friendships, my growing skill at the women's work (although I never did conquer the skills of basket-making!) and, yes, I confess it, the dalliances with the menfolk, all engendered in me a sense of comfort and belonging. I even found that I was thinking less often about my father and the station and had stopped wondering when he would come for me. And then, out of the blue, after half a year or more, came rescue!

It was sudden and shocking. Tiliu, another girl and I were accompanying a group of hunters on a hunt several days journey away from the village (it was usual for some girls to go on longer hunting trips, to

117

help carry the catch as well as for the more obvious reasons of night-time comforts). The menfolk had left us early in the morning, and we girls were cutting strips of meat from an eland they had killed, and were hanging them on rods above the fire to dry. Suddenly, the peace of the afternoon was shattered by loud drumming and crashing noises, and a group of horse-men burst from out of the bushes. In instant panic, we screamed and ran away as fast as we could in all directions at once. I grabbed Tiliu's hand and we ran towards the bushes. The drumming got louder and louder. Suddenly, I was snatched up, and found myself flung across the shoulders of a galloping horse.

The jolting of the horse knocked the breath out of me, and I lost consciousness and collapsed in a faint. When I regained my senses I was lying on some kind of bed within what appeared to be a tiny room that was rocking. For a while I was confused. Every part of me ached from the pummelling of the horse. I thought the movement was in my head rather than the little room, and then I realised that I must be on a boat. I stirred and tried to sit up. As I did so a voice startled me. I turned my head to find, to my aston-ishment, a European! He spoke, but in a language strange to me. He spoke again, then realising that I did not comprehend, changed to English which he spoke with a thick accent. I realised that he must be one of the Dutch farmers who had settled themselves in Southern Africa and who called themselves Boers.

Chapter 8

I should have been delighted at being rescued from the tribe, but somehow felt only a strange sense that this man disliked me. He sat in a wood and canvas chair and stared at me. He was wearing a shirt and trousers of a thick, brownish material, heavy, badly-scuffed boots, and a floppy, wide-brimmed hat which shadowed his face so that I could discern little save a close-trimmed beard. He seemed to be avoiding my eyes even as he wordlessly handed me a brown bundle. When I shook it out I found that it was a man's shirt. Suddenly blushing that I was naked except for my tribal garb, I hurried to pull the shirt over my head.

Gathering myself together now that I was covered, I began to tell him who I was and to thank him for rescuing me. He sat in silence, staring at the floor in a way I found more and more disconcerting. Earlier, during my time in the village, I had imagined that my rescue would be a time of delight, of joy and relief. Now, as this strange man sat in silence, not seeming to react in any way to my words, I felt a sinking sensation. This was not what I had expected. Not what it should be like. And when I told him of Miss Blake, still captive with the tribe, his reaction was shocking indeed. He refused point blank to even consider attempting to rescue her!

At first I was upset, and hated him for his callousness. Later though, as he explained more during the time I was with him, I saw some sense in his argument that it would take something like a military raid to effect her rescue from the village itself – for my own rescue had only chanced because I was away from the body of the tribe. Perhaps, though, something might be arranged at a later date? I was not too discouraged by his rather neutral shrug at my suggestion.

During the journey by boat, which lasted a day and a night, and the wagon trip to his home, I came to know how strange this man really was. His name was Hendrick, and I learned that, as well as running his small farmstead, he served as some kind of preacher in the Boer church. Most confusing at first were the strange swings of behaviour which seemed to overtake him. For much of the time he was coldly polite, asking about my background and the story of my capture, talking to me about religion and (which annoyed me greatly) criticising the British as landgrabbers and imperialists. At other times, though, he seemed nervous, even shy of me.

He left me alone for most of the time during the river journey, and I found myself puzzling over my situation, and his increasingly baffling behaviour. On the several occasions he brought me food and water, he would enter the cabin very quietly, as though seeking to catch me unawares. While I ate, he would stand to one side and I noticed, from the corner of my eye, that he would look at me intently, his eyes flicking rapidly over every part of me. But if I looked up at him, he would at once become stiff and distant and cold.

Once, when he told me that his party, which had come across us by accident, had also taken the other girls, I grabbed his hand in delight at the knowledge that I had not lost Tiliu, but he snatched it away as though stung, and stared at me with every appearance of fright.

His oddness continued after we reached his farm. I had been given some clothes – a blouse of blue cotton, a thick cotton skirt, and a pair of drawers with a two-inch frill below the knees – and was assigned a small room at the back of the house, which had a narrow bed, a chair, and little else. While I had been clad in only the shirt, Hendrick had been odd and erratic, as I have described. Now, from the first moment I appeared before him in European garb, he became all politeness and courtesy.

He talked much more freely now, indeed seeming anxious to pour out information about his farm and the chapel he preached at, almost as though afraid to allow either silence or response from me. At the same time, he was still anxious to avoid my eyes, although I still often caught him looking surreptitiously at me. And then I was suddenly vouchsafed the answer to the puzzle. I had cause to reach up to a high shelf to fetch down a picture he wanted to show me. In doing so the blouse, which was a little tight anyway, clung tightly to my breasts and, hearing a stifled gasp and glancing around, I saw that he was staring at them. When he realised that I was looking at him, a deep blush suffused his features, and I had my answer. He fancied me!

I felt at once that I was on firmer ground, for surely I knew much better how to handle this than his religious and farming talk. Had not my time with the tribe taught me how to flirt? How to tease and attract a man? And to be sure, for though he was Dutch, and a preacher, and disliked the British, Hendrick was only a man! I softened my manner towards him: hung upon his words; fluttered my eyelashes; found ways to stretch and turn and lean so that he could look at my figure. And look he did, with the effect I desired, for I espied a telltale bulge in his trousers!

For the rest, though, the result of my flirtatiousness was the reverse of what I had expected. Had he been one of my friends in the tribe, we would have been engaged in a nice shag within minutes. As it was, he grew more and more red-faced, he coughed and stammered, and then he leapt up and veritably scampered from the room! I stared after him amazed. That I had had my effect was clear from the erection he tried to hide, yet he had run off! And then in a flash I understood. My time with the tribe had made me forget the very different ways of European society. Ladies did not openly flirt. Nothing was direct. Of a certainty, exchanges between the sexes were bound and buried by circumspection and mannerliness, and my coquettishness had shocked and scared him. What a puzzle.

That evening, when I retired to my room, I gained a fresh insight into this strange man. I had noticed that there was a large knot-hole in one of the planks of the door. I closed the single curtain over the little window and began to undress. As I unbuttoned the blouse and shrugged it from my shoulders, I noticed, from the corner of my eye, that the light which had been shining through the knot-hole seemed to have been cut off. At first I was not sure, but when it gleamed then died again, I knew. Hendrick was peeping through it! He was trying to watch me take my clothes off!

For an instant – ridiculously in the light of the months I had spent naked among the tribe – I was embarrassed that a gentleman should be so rude as to peep at a girl undressing. How much worse that it should be a supposed upholder of morals such as a preacher! And then I felt only amusement, for had I not tried to flirt with him earlier? Had I not already planned out my strategy of using my wiles to make him help me get back to father? Well. If he wanted to peep, let him enjoy it, for it would surely help me bend him to my will.

I untied the skirt, dropped it to the floor, and bent straight-legged to pick it up, ensuring that my bottom was towards the door. I stretched and yawned, giving my watcher a fine view of my figure as I moved and turned. To my delight, I heard the hiss of an indrawn breath as I moved to face the door, giving him a clear sight of my breasts.

So, despite his preachiness, and the way he had run off earlier, Hendrick was just another man in so far as lust for a woman was concerned, and surely I could turn that to my advantage. I was beginning to enjoy my new sense of power, and gave him a good show as I stripped off the drawers, and moved about naked, folding the discarded clothes, turning and moving to allow him as good a view as he could wish for, bending, bottom to the door, to blow out the candle before climbing into the little bed and hugging myself in delight at my little game, and the hope it gave me.

From the first moment I saw him next morning, I played up to Hendrick, watching to see if there was any change in his manner towards me, praising the breakfast he prepared, insisting on washing up the dishes. If anything, he seemed even more stiff and reserved than before, which puzzled me until I realised that he must be feeling guilty, was perhaps ashamed of what he had done.

Despite his rather unevenly trimmed beard, Hendrick was really quite a handsome man, and now that I had my clue as to his behaviour I actually began to find him quite appealing. Or was it my own little scheme that appealed?

His hair was dark brown and rather unkempt, and from a complexion deep-tanned by the sun, there shone eyes of almost Wedgewood blue – so blue that, on the rare occasions he could summon the nerve to meet my gaze, they were quite startlingly attractive. Slim of build, though tall, he lacked the lithe grace of Talesi and my other erstwhile lovers, but nevertheless his movements betokened an underlying strength. It was, though, his shyness, and his very obvious fancy for me, that I found most appealing of all.

All through breakfast, and again at our evening meal, I delighted in the sidelong glances he frequently cast upon me, staring at the swellings in my blouse or the swing of my skirt when he thought I was not watching. I decided to put more pressure on him by asking, very meekly – for was cleanliness not next to godliness – whether I might bathe myself, for the hot day had made me perspire. I had to hold back a smile when his eyes lit up and his face grew crimson at the thought. And again at the sudden awkwardness with which, unable even to look at me, he showed me to a sort of scullery at the back of the house.

There was a stone sink, and a wood-fired boiler in which I might heat water, which could be drawn from a well just outside. I noticed, too, that there was no curtain at the tall, low-silled window. I was left to draw water and light the fire in the boiler myself, while Hendrick clumped off, ostensibly to check something about the farm. In reality, I was sure, to take up a vantage point from which to observe the scullery window!

The water took a while to heat, and was not ready until nearly dusk, so I took an oil-lamp with me when I went to wash. I stripped naked before scooping the water from the copper to the sink, determined that Hendrick should be wound up as much as possible by the sight of me. I soaped myself thoroughly all over, wiping the flannel slowly around my breasts, and my bottom, and between my legs. As I raised first one foot and then the other to the sink, I found myself almost giggling at the thought of the forbidden excitement poor Hendrick must be suffering.

As I rinsed and dried myself I was struck with such an inspiration as made me almost laugh aloud with pleasure. What a way to force matters! Ah, well. In for a penny, in for a pound! I picked up the clothes which were lying where I had placed them on a little stool, and dumped them in the water that remained in the copper, and began to wash them. Only when I was half way through did I jump back and pantomime shock and dismay, my gestures broad for the benefit of the man I was sure had his eyes glued on my every movement. Snatching up a towel and holding it in front of me, I opened the door a crack, and called, in the most dismayed tones I could muster, for Hendrick. I had to call again and again, for naturally he had to rush all the way around the house to get to me, but at last he came hurrying up to the door.

I had opened the door just enough so that he could glimpse my bare shoulder and a knee and the way I clutched the towel to my bosom, while still seeming to be trying to hide from him. He was red-faced and panting, and could hardly drag his eyes up to look in my face. I stared at him all wide-eyed, and in my most innocent, pleading voice, told him I had been a silly girl, and had gone and got my clothes all wet, and had absolutely nothing to put on, and I was sorry, and could he please, please be kind to a silly girl and let me have a shirt or something to put on! I was gazing up at him imploringly, all innocence and pleading, and I let the towel slip just a little. He went very red in the face, and coughed and swallowed, and his eyes skipped down along the gap in the door before, with an obvious effort, he turned away.

He returned very quickly, carrying one of his shirts. Naturally, as I reached to take it my towel slipped, and he had a quick glimpse of my exposed breast before I shut the door to, calling out my thanks and apologies. I grinned to myself as I shrugged the shirt over my head, for I had detected that familiar lump in his trousers, and was sure I was well on my way to victory.

I was wrong in my presumption, though. I had forgotten, or rather had never needed to know, the strangled conventionality which so besets European society, and which is only deepened by the piety of people such as Hendrick. Had he felt the honest easiness of Talesi, or any of the other tribesmen, we would have already been on intimate terms, and all would have been settled. As it was, Hendrick's behaviour towards me took on a new tension, which frustrated me greatly, and when I went into his parlour to thank him for the shirt he actually ordered me to go to my room with every sign of anger! Obviously, if my plan was to succeed, I would need to find another tack.

For the first few days, I had remained inside the farmhouse and so had not seen my dear Tiliu. When I did, on my first venture out into the farmyard, she gave me the inspiration for the breakthrough I so badly needed. We greeted each other with delight, and relief that neither of us had been badly treated – though Tiliu complained about the European clothes she had been made to wear, and the fact that she had been obliged to serve as cleaner and laundress for the other farm workers. More important, though, she asked me about 'that strange, pretty man' who had burst into her sleeping cubicle last night and shagged her wildly.

So! After watching me bathe, and angrily sending me to my room, Hendrick had straightaway gone and relieved his frustration with Tiliu! What a hypocrite! And he had actually castigated me for having consorted with kaffirs (such an ugly word for such lovely people!) as if it were a sin beneath contempt! I made sure that Tiliu had not been hurt in the encounter (she told me it had been very quick and rather frantic) and I determined to use his own hypocrisy to undermine him.

That evening, as Hendrick sat in his armchair reading his Dutch Bible, I broached the subject.

'Please, sir,' I said, looking as coy and humble as I could manage, and calling him sir to show respect. 'Please, sir, may I speak to you?'

He looked up, surprised and obviously as uncomfortable as he always was when alone with me.

'Please, sir,' I said again. 'I am very conscious of how kind you have been to me, and how unworthy I am of your concern. You have rescued me from a terrible fate, and brought me here to your home. And you are so very kind to me, teaching me the error of my ways and to strive to reach those higher moral standards you yourself, sir, so clearly cleave to.'

I had rehearsed my speech all afternoon, but now, even to me, it was beginning to sound po-faced and artificial. Hendrick had put down his Bible and was openly staring at me for the first time.

127

'Sir,' I went on. 'You have been so kind, and I am so grateful, and have been seeking a way to show my gratitude.' He hurrumped and shifted a little in his chair. I took the bull by the horns. 'Forgive me for saying it, sir, but you have rightly castigated me for consorting with na . . . with kaffirs.' I made myself use his ugly word. 'Even though I was a captive and had no choice in the matter. But, sir, please forgive me, I have noticed that you . . . Oh, sir! It seems so wrong that an honourable man such as yourself should be forced to visit that native girl!'

Hendrick's face was very red, and he was half out of his chair.

'Oh, please, sir, do not be angry with me! I know that I am far below you, but it seems such a shame that a man as upright as you should need to consort with a kaffir girl when I . . . when you could . . .'

Here I lowered my eyes and tried hard to make myself blush. Hendrick leapt from his seat, spluttering and gesticulating. For a moment I thought he was going to strike me. Instead, he pushed past me and stomped from the house. All was not lost, though, for as he rushed out I saw that he had a very obvious erection!

I was in my little room, clad in the shirt I had adopted as a nightgown, when I heard him return and go into his own room. I waited, determined to make at least one more attempt. When I was sure enough time had passed for him to have got to bed, I took my candle and approached his door. He answered my knock and I went in, looking shy and penitent. He was indeed in his bed, his thick nightshirt and floppy nightcap making him look faintly ridiculous. I stood at the side of the bed, my head bowed, and apologised to him for being so impertinent, and begged him to forgive me, and teach me better.

The expression in his eyes told me what his thoughts were, and I knew that if I was cunning this facade of rectitude would crumble. Until then, I had to keep up the charade, and so did he. He cleared his throat and told me that it was hardly my fault, for how could I have known better. I thanked him for his kindness. He talked of morals, and proper behaviour. I sat on the edge of his bed, looking at him with wide-eyed admiration, having made sure that the shirt rode up a little so he could glimpse my legs. He talked of the hard life of a farmer. I praised his strength of character. He spoke of loneliness, of missing the care of his own kind since he had been widowed. I leant upon the eiderdown, all innocent of the fact that my hand was on his thigh. I commiserated with his loneliness, and wished there was some way a grateful girl like me could help him.

However I had expected the moment of breakthrough to occur, I could not possibly have predicted the suddenness with which he changed! One moment he was sitting back against his pillows, not looking at me, shifting a little beneath the bedclothes. The next, he had leapt forward, grabbed me, and was kissing me wildly! It was so sudden that my squeal was quite genuine as I found myself dragged onto the bed. In a trice, my shirt was about my neck, and his hands were all over me.

It was as though, in breaking down his resistance, I had burst a dam! He was panting, kissing me clumsily, running his hands over me so frantically that he even hurt me a little. I co-operated, of course, squirming to help him get above me, pulling up his nightshirt, splaying my thighs, but he was so pent, so eager that he nearly came off before he was even in me! And even then, he only had time for a couple of thrusts before he burst into his come!

Then I learned another strange thing about this peculiar man. It seemed that, for him, sex was a guilty thing, and now he rolled off me and turned his back, lying tense and stiff, for all the world as though consumed by shame. For a long while I just lay beside him, unsure what to do, for I had never known a man behave thus. Should I lie still and wait? Should I creep away? Should I break the silence? I determined to wait, and snuggled myself against him as if preparing to sleep. He tensed even further, but did not move away.

It was a long wait. Hendrick lay perfectly still, his tension and quick breathing showing that he was wide awake. I pretended to sleep. I waited. I shifted and snuggled closer. He held his breath. As if I was in a dream, I snuffled, and rubbed my face against his back, and slipped my arm across his waist. He did not throw me off. The waiting was interminable! What a frustrating man, to be lying thus with a girl in his bed and doing nothing! At last, giving up, I did indeed drift into sleep.

I was awakened by the creaking of the mattress. I had the presence of mind to keep my eyes closed. Hendrick had shifted and turned. Through my eyelashes I discerned that he was leaning on his elbow, looking down at me as I lay revealed by my disarranged shirt, his eyes gleaming in the faint light of the moon through the window. Ah, the game was afoot again!

Haltingly, as though he might receive a shock, Hendrick reached out and touched his fingertips to my flank. I remained still, breathing slowly as though still asleep. Softly, with no more weight than a butterfly, Hendrick's fingers drifted over my hip, along the curve of my waist, to the edge of my shirt. Then beneath it. As his tentative hand traced the under-swell of my breast, I sighed 'in my sleep' and turned a little more onto my back. Instantly, the hand was snatched away, and Hendrick held his breath. Relieved that I had not awakened, and emboldened by the easier access my change of position had given, the hand returned. Gently, so as not to wake me, Hendrick pulled the hem of the shirt higher, exposing my breasts to his eyes as well as his touch.

I was hard put to it to maintain my pretence of sleep as he gazed down at my swellings. His breathing was quick and shallow as his hand reached out again. With a single fingertip, he circled around and over each breast, tracing around my areolas, his touch so light and teasing I could not prevent my nipples stiffening. The tantalising hand moved down, smoothing over my tummy, exploring the crease where my thigh was bent against my hip, slipping down to measure along the valley of my closed legs before moving up to touch oh, so tentatively against the curls below my navel.

Again, I feigned to move in my sleep, snuffling, and throwing my arm up, and rolling onto my back, raising a knee as I did so. Again, the hand was snatched away, but soon returned to explore the insides of the thighs which were now opened to him. He did not caress them for long, for by now I knew him to be at boiling point. Gently, still anxious not to wake me, Hendrick nudged my raised knee so that it fell away, spreading my thighs and exposing my intimate parts to whatever he desired. He hesitated, held his breath, pulled off his nightshirt, crept between my legs. Through my eyelashes I saw his face above me, a mask of tension, his eyes burning. He lowered himself, and I felt him touch against the lips of my cunny.

131

I mumbled 'in my sleep' and wriggled a little, 'accidentally' giving him easier access. He pressed, found me, pushed. I 'awoke' as he thrust into me, to the hilt in a single surge!

'Oh! Oh, what? Oh, Hendriiick!'

I knew that timing my 'awakening' thus would not stop him, for once a man is embedded in a warm quim, only a blow from a club will prevent him finishing what he has started! I gazed up at him as if in wonder as he poised above me, his weight on straight arms, his loins already moving strongly. I reached up for him, wrapped my legs about his, circled my pelvis in that motion I know men love so much, shagging him as I had learned so well to shag my lovers among the tribe.

His weight descended upon me. His loins pumped wildly. His eyes were screwed tight as he fucked me frantically, staying deep, his pubic bone grinding against my swelling cunny-lips as he writhed, rather than pumped. His come, too, was wild as, with gritted teeth and an expression of near-agony, he jerked and gasped and spasmed and flooded my depths, before collapsing onto me as if all life had been driven from him! Despite his weight on my chest, I drifted off into a sleep then, content that I had achieved my goal, and that Hendrick would be mine now.

I awoke alone and went to find Hendrick, not bothering to change out of my sleeping-shirt, for surely Hendrick would not now object to seeing my legs. He was at breakfast, and I entered the room smiling, only to be disconcerted that he seemed once again stiff and withdrawn. How could one possibly deal with such an odd man! What on earth could be the matter now?

Once again (this was becoming tiresome) I came

over all docile and innocent and grateful. He was the strong, worldly man, and I was the fluttering admirer, in awe of him, oh, so deferent! Even so, it was a long time before he unwound and I was able to discover what was the matter. It seemed that Hendrick was shocked by the way I had wriggled and writhed beneath him! 'Good Dutch women', he told me sternly, did not behave so, but kept still as God had intended! I quickly learned that, in Hendrick's lights, the female should be passive and unworldly, should never, ever, make the first move, and indeed should profess entire ignorance, even bafflement, about all matters sexual. Should, in fact, submit to being fucked, but never, ever fuck in return, or show pleasure in the act!

I realised that I must myself adopt this dissembling, nay, hypocritical approach if I was to keep Hendrick sweet and avoid running against his moralistic scruples. Too direct an approach, too open an acceptance of our new carnality, and I would anger him. To manipulate him towards my desire to get back to father, I would have to at least seem to fall in with his own prejudices, however odd.

I began to use the little flirtations I had learned from the girls in the village. I noticed that he continued to take great pleasure in watching me from hiding, and so I turned dressing and undressing into performances, lingering over my choice of garments (which was ridiculous because they were always the same ones!) and deliberately moving slowly back and forth before the knot-hole in the door through which he habitually peeped. At night, he took to making excuses for getting me into his own room. I would take in the water or a glass of schnapps or the book (always The Bible) that he had asked for, and we would go through a pantomime.

He would touch me and I would become still and coy. He would fondle my bosom and I would wriggle and say, 'Oh, Hendrick, don't.' He would lead me 'reluctantly' to his bed and sit me down and fondle me more freely, and I would protest and pretend to try to push his hands away as my clothes came undone. After a while of this silly game I would cease protesting and become more submissive and would let him push me back and pull off my drawers. He was actually not too bad in bed, but what irked me was that I had to keep still, for the game required that I be the innocent victim of his desires; reluctant but made willing by the glory of his manhood. And afterwards I would be blushing and coy and would gather myself and creep shyly off to my own room. Oh! If only he knew what a fool he was!

I permitted myself a smile. So! What I had learned during my time with the tribe applied here, too. Men may have strength, may have the power, even the violence, to dominate their womenfolk, but in the end they are the weaker sex. Their very vanity, their desperate need not only to satisfy their cocks, but to convince themselves that those cocks were regarded with awe by their women, was in fact the seed of their own weakness. All a woman had to do was to pretend worship before the great god Cock and she could twist a man as she willed.

All the while, you may be sure, I was dropping little words and suggestions about how he should try to get me back to father. I had to be very careful and cunning, of course, for Hendrick was one of those men whose pride was such that an open suggestion from a female would have made him bridle. Like so many men, he thought plans and ideas were their province, and females were empty-headed decorations. Such a foolish, but such a useful, notion! But even while I was dropping these hints I realised that a new problem had developed, and a problem I could never have anticipated.

We were going through our little pantomines so that Hendrick could shag me every night now, and he was actually becoming gentler and more relaxed with me during the daytime. At first, I thought this just a pleasant development, for when relaxed Hendrick was really rather nice. Only when, one evening as we were conversing after dinner, he put his arm about my shoulder and kissed me, did I begin to suspect that the changes might mean more than just the relaxing of tensions. And when, after our shag that night, he kept me by him in his bed, rather than packing me off as usual, my suspicions deepened.

For the first time, that night, he held me in his arms as he slept, and awoke and fucked me during the night, and cuddled me again, and had another shag at dawn, for all the world as though I was his good Dutch girl! And, my suspicions aroused, I noticed that when we ate together, and he chatted about the farm or the sermon he would preach next Sunday, his manner seemed more that of a friend or partner than, as heretofore, of a correct Dutchman condescending to an English girl he rather disapproved of. What could the change betoken? My fears were confirmed when he reacted to one of my hints about getting back to father by suggesting that it might be better to remain with him! Oh, Lord! He wanted me for his permanent woman! I must do something! Change his mind!

Just as I had changed my behaviour to entice Hendrick, I now changed it again to persuade him that keeping me was not such a good idea. I asked him

135

about the differences between the Boers and the British, emphasising those differences, and swallowing the many awful things he said about us. I became less submissive, wriggling and writhing during sex; saying those crude things most men like to hear from a woman in her transports, but which I knew would offend Hendrick the preacher; even, once, hinting *during the day* that a shag would be welcome (shocking indeed)! I asked him how his congregation would react when they discovered that he had an English girl in his home.

My aim, which was blessedly achieved in only a few days, was to convince Hendrick that, whereas he desired a good Dutch girl, he would actually be getting a bad English one. And I was successful, for he renewed his efforts to arrange my return to father.

He sent a rider to the nearest town to find out whether there was any circulation asking after me. There was, and not only that, there was a reward posted. It was no longer difficult to persuade Hendrick that he should return me to father, for his eyes lit up at the thought of the reward. Arrangements went on apace.

A much more difficult notion to plant in Hendrick's mind was that he should conceal the fact that I was not 'intact', as he taught me to call it. I persuaded him that if knowledge of my time with the tribe came out, my father might disown me and hold back on the reward. Thus, Hendrick would not only lose money, but would be saddled with a bad reputation for keeping an English mistress. Would it not be wise to concoct some story to conceal my time with the tribe? Make up a tale which would cover the half-year or more that I had been away, yet allay any suspicion that I might be less than pure?

It was such a simple idea. Hendrick would say that he had come upon me wandering alone across the veldt. I had received a blow to the head, and had no memory of what had happened. He had taken me in and cared for me, as was only the duty of a man of God. My memory had only just returned, and as soon as it had, he had set out to restore me to my father. So simple! I only prayed that it would work.

It only struck me later, when I was back with father, that this story made it impossible for me to arrange for Miss Blake's rescue, for how could I know where she was? It has been on my conscience since then, but I console myself with the knowledge that if she could bring herself to accept her situation, she could be happy with the tribe as I had been, for I knew them to be a kind and caring people.

Hendrick's plans for the journey home were coming on, and we were to leave within the week. Much of my time was taken up with sewing, for I was to have a new frock and underthings for my return, which was part of Hendrick's plan to prove that I was still respectable. For myself, after my time with the tribe, I found the heavy skirts and tight sleeves and bodices irksome, and I was made even more hot and uncomfortable by the unnecessary layers of petticoats and the long drawers that reached below my knees. To think that I had regarded these things as normal, even essential, before I had learnt the more sensible and healthy ways of the tribe! But I was able to turn them to good effect, for naturally I showed them to Hendrick as each garment was completed, and took my opportunities to remove them in the undressings that drove him so mad.

I paid close attention and learned every little quirk of his lusts so that I could get my way. I was too humble for words! So shy and so compliant to his wishes that I swear by the time we reached my father's station, Hendrick was almost ready to forego the reward and surrender to his original desire to keep me! I would undress so demurely, for all the world as if he were not there goggling at me from whatever peephole he could find, and then shag him so thoroughly that he was torn between the notion that I adored him and the offence to his morals that I was such a bad girl! And I played his bedroom pantomimes so well that afterwards, while he lay exhausted and I snuggled up against him and caressed his limp cock, he would tell me how the arrangements for my return were progressing.

Just once I forgot his peculiar attitudes towards pleasure. We were lying on his bed after a shagging, and instead of just snuggling and holding his cock I slipped my head down and began sucking it. You would have thought he had been stung! Far from relaxing back and enjoying what I already knew every other man loved having done to them, he reacted as though scalded! Even before my lips could slide fully onto him, he leapt with a bellow, and shoved me so hard I fell right off the bed. He was jumping up and down on the bed in such a rage as struck terror into me. I was the Whore of Babylon! Spawn of the Devil! The disgusting purveyor of ungodly practices! Oh, how I had to weep, and beg, and crawl, and cry that I did not know what I was doing! And oh, how cold and stern he was all the next day. I had actually tried to suck him because I desired to, but if I had planned it to prove to him that I was a 'bad girl' I could not have done better!

Believe it or not, I also managed to convince him that my respectability would be enhanced if I re-

138

turned with a servant. I went through a nice charade of pretending to pick out Tiliu from the other girls who worked on the farm, for it would not have done to let Hendrick know that we were close friends. Tiliu, no mean actress, did not find it hard to pretend surprise and even reluctance when she was chosen.

The morning of our departure came at last. Hendrick drove the cart, and I sat beside him dressed in my new clothes, with Tiliu, as befitted a servant in Hendrick's mind, on the floor in the back of the cart. I had no boxes or bundles of course, for to have them would not have fitted with the story Hendrick thought he had concocted.

The journey from Hendrick's farm to father's station was by cart, then river barge, and finally by train, and took two days and nights. It was not easy for Tiliu and I to maintain our pose as mistress and servant, especially, you may be sure, when Hendrick determined, on the barge and again on the train, that he got some good shagging in before finally giving me up to father, for Tiliu is a ribald minx, and very observant. Manage it we did, though, and at last the happy moment arrived.

Chapter 9

Father's delight when we were reunited was as obvious as my own. His eyes lit up and a great smile of happiness covered his face the moment we saw each other, and he threw his arms about me and swung me around and called me his 'little girl', just as I had longed for him to do. I was bubbling with delight, as you can imagine, but at the same time felt the irony of his greeting after all my experiences.

Father's discussions with Hendrick and the journey by pony and trap, to the house on the edge of the town, all passed in a whirl of delight, and it was only when I was at last alone with father that it struck me how careful I would have to be from now on. I had plumped myself down on his lap, and made to kiss him, just as I always had before my time away, and I was somewhat shocked when he showed every sign of confusion. It was only when I was shown to my room by one of the house-servants, and went to change out of the clothes Hendrick had given me into some of my own things, that I realised the cause of his discomfiture.

During my time with the tribe, and then with Hendrick, not only my experience and outlook had changed. I tried on my favourite green gingham frock. It was too small by far. It was bulging open by several inches at the bodice, and in no way could be buttoned over my breasts! I shucked it off, and stared at my reflection in the looking-glass. I had not seen myself, except reflected in moving water, for more than half a year (the puritanical Hendrick eschewing mirrors as vanities) and the figure which looked back at me was different indeed from that which I remembered.

I pulled off my bodice and drawers and gazed at my naked self, just as I had that time when Jonathan had first made his advances. The reflection was not that of the girl I had seen then, but undeniably that of a ripe and developed young woman. It was almost as though it was not myself but a stranger I was observing. As I looked, I found myself becoming thoughtful, knowing as I did now the things men found delightful in women's bodies, and realising that the figure in the glass amply demonstrated them. I harked back to the time before I went away, before I knew the realities of men's needs of women, and women's of men. Then, I had been innocent. Now I knew. I would need to watch and learn if I was not to lapse into the happy openness of tribal life!

Dragging my gaze away from my reflection, and my mind away from the images which had made my nipples perk, I puzzled over what to wear. Clearly my old clothes were not suitable, and the ones I had worn on the journey were dusty and stale. Then I remembered Miss Blake's clothes. They would do for now, although I thought them a little old and dowdy, and of course they were rather too big. I would get father to find me a dressmaker as soon as I could.

Over the next few days, I reacquainted myself with many of the townspeople, for naturally they were curious to find out what they could about my strange adventure. And the more I mingled with them, the

141

more I found myself seeing them through the filter of my new-found knowingness, and contrasting their ways with those of my friends back in the tribe. The women were all so polite, so mannered towards one another, yet underneath their masks I could detect currents which ran quite contrary to the sentiments they expressed. They would compliment each other on their appearance or on a recipe or some such, while all the time there was a fierce, unspoken rivalry, and a secret delight when *their* gown was more costly than the other's, or *their* tea party had been more successful. The standing of husbands and fathers was of inordinate importance, and Mrs Forster, wife of the bank manager, would subtly queen it over other wives even though their husbands might in fact possess greater wealth, while the daughter of an officer (the dull, catty Felicity, for example) would condescend greatly to she whose father was a farmer.

And the behaviour of single women, or mothers with marriageable daughters, towards any eligible man would have been ludicrous had it not been so hypocritical! Modesty and decorum were the public watchwords. Constraint and demureness were all. To show even an ankle would have been an outrage. Yet the way they manoeuvred for the men's attention: the way they fluttered and acted helplessness; the way the bodices of their frocks and blouses seemed always just a little tighter than they might have been, all showed very clearly that their only ambition was to catch a man. The girls in the tribe were so much more honest.

The men were different, much less concerned with petty social rivalries than the ladies, and punctiliously polite to all members of the fair sex, even servants such as Tiliu now pretended to be. Of course, I only saw them in the company of females, and I soon became quite fascinated by the differences and similarities between them and the men of the tribe. Like them, the gentlemen and officers held themselves aloof from the affairs of the womenfolk, but in contrast to the Africans' simple and honest acceptance of women as partners in life, having different roles, of course, but nevertheless equals, the Europeans insisted on treating females as weak, silly things, capable only of being decorative and empty headed

I thought their condescension rather foolish, but soon realised that the way the women, or at least the younger ones, played up to that image was simply their version of the flirting games we had played in the village. The wide-eyed incomprehension at talk of anything other than tea or servants or such was their version of a tribal girl's sidelong glance and head-bob. The fluttering nervousness at the sight of a mouse their equivalent of the hip-swing. But of course, the resolution of these little manoeuvrings was not the going off together for a nice shag it should have been. Instead, it was only a sort of ritual dance, according only empty little social coups, for any suggesting, any thought even, of actual *physical* contact was too shocking for words! But it was clear to me that the physical was very much in all their minds.

It was as if females were not allowed to be corporeal beings at all, while men's thoughts were entirely lofty and intellectual. Yet beneath all this mannerliness, this artificiality, it was clear – at least to me – that matters sexual were very prominent in people's unspoken thoughts. Why else the constant attention to appearance; the close-fitting bodices; the fluttering when a handsome man was in the offing? Why else

143

the calculating glance with which a man would regard a pretty girl; the preening of the officers in female company; the tightness of their breeches (and some of them were indeed pleasantly tight!)? And why else the horror which greeted the very thought of a man being alone with an unmarried woman lest something indecorous happen!

Of necessity, I played along with all this, and was myself very demure. Indeed, until father's dinner party, the only person, apart from Tiliu and, as shall be seen, our house servants Benjamin and John-John, who came even close to guessing there might be more to me than met the eye was Mrs Barnet, the dressmaker. She was a bustling, matter-of-fact woman, hailing originally from Pimlico in London. The first time I met her she had simply brough some swatches of material and talked to father about various prices. I had hardly come into the conversation, but even so quite liked what I saw of her. She was a buxom woman only an inch or so shorter than father, with very black hair displaying a few grey strands here and there. Her face was strong, with a good nose and dark, widely spaced eyes, relieved by lines around the eyes and mouth that suggested a strong sense of humour. I later learned that she was the widow of a railwayman, whose death of fever had left her needing to make her own way. From her earnings she was saving for her fare back to London and what she called 'real living'.

Mrs Barnet's second visit did not involve father, for it was to do with selecting patterns and measuring up. As I stood there in my room, clad in chemise and drawers, turning, raising my arms, moving this way and that while she wielded her tape-measure, I found myself warming to her. She had begun quite imperso-

144

nally – was I not merely the young daughter of her client? – but as her measuring proceeded she began to cluck to herself and to smile. She walked around me looking me up and down carefully, her eyes very obviously lingering upon my breasts and my hips. She nodded and raised her eyebrows, both amusement and calculation in her expression.

'Hmm,' she said. 'Perhaps we need to look again at our patterns!' You are more grown up than I thought! Perhaps we even need to think in terms of a corset!'

The first sign of possible danger in my new life (for everybody seemed to have swallowed the story about my lost memory) came through my hairstyle. Benjamin knew something of the ways of Tiliu's tribe. Knew, certainly, the significance of the topknot – which I still wore because father had said it was pretty and because my looking-glass told me it suited me, and who could possibly know what it meant! Benjamin could! And when Tiliu told me he had mentioned it to her, even spoken of me in lewd terms, I realised that I was in peril!

The need for action of some kind was reinforced by Benjamin's demeanour towards me when he served my meals, for he looked at me knowingly and with a very unservant-like smile. We determined to act that very afternoon. Tiliu was to entice him into her room before the hour for tea. I would enter upon an excuse, catch them in the act and berate Benjamin with the threat of telling father and getting him dismissed.

The enticement was easy – Tiliu was a considerable expert! – and I hovered by the door between our two rooms for some minutes before girding myself to play the outraged lady of the house. I entered quietly. Tiliu was bent over the end of her cot, her skirts thrown up onto her back. Benjamin stood behind her, gripping her hips, the clenching of his taut buttocks betokening the powerful strokes he was shagging her with. For a moment I was entranced, for it was a delicious scene, but I came to myself and cried out. Instantly the scene became ludicrous! Benjamin leapt back, almost tripping on the trousers which were around his ankles. His face was a picture of shock and fright as he tried to hide his stiff cock in his shirt-tails, hopping from foot to foot, his eyes standing out like hen's eggs. He looked so ridiculous that I was hard put not to burst into giggles!

I gathered myself, though, and launched into a tirade at them, berating them as animals, for bringing shame on the house, and threatening to tell father. The effect on Benjamin was instant. He almost crumpled with fright! I gave him no time to recover. I raged at him and stamped my foot, and when he rushed out of the room, hauling his trousers up over his bare bottom, I collapsed into Tiliu's arms, both of us almost hysterical with mirth! The only trouble was that the sight of Benjamin so heartily shagging Tiliu had excited and frustrated me in equal measure. For more than half a year I had been the beneficiary of a great deal of attention, but now was getting none – a situation made more frustrating by the fact that I well knew Tiliu to be enjoying plentiful sex with both John-John (her favourite) and Benjamin.

Over the next few weeks Mrs Barnet became almost as excited about my new clothes as I was myself, and we sifted eagerly through patterns and materials. She it was who persuaded father to expand from his original idea of 'a couple of frocks', to allow her to outfit me completely. She agreed with me about the discomfort in Africa's heat of the thick clothing Englishwomen habitually wore, and fashioned for me drawers of the finest cambric and chemisettes of muslin and chenille, with bright silk ribbons at waist and neck. My petticoats, too, were of muslin or fine cottons, and the several frocks were of cotton not a great deal heavier, single-coloured (a mid-blue, a pale green and a rose-pink) except for contrasting piping around the neck and waist and buttonholes. They were lovely, and made me feel very grown up. But loveliest of all, so that it made me tingle with delight, were what she called my 'coming out' things.

It was for this outfit that she wanted me to have a corset, and it became clear during the several times I stood naked in my room for the measurings and fittings, that Mrs Barnet was very knowing and down-to-earth. Other than Tiliu, she was the first person to see me unclothed since Hendrick, and she looked me over with frank appraisal and, noticing that my body was tanned from the sun, looked me deep in my eyes, as if showing me she guessed I was not so innocent as I was supposed to be. I found myself blushing, and her face broke into a broad grin. 'Well, Miss Lydia,' she said. 'You have a lovely figure indeed! And one to delight the menfolk if we show it off right!'

And show it off she did indeed, for when the outfit was all made and I tried it on for the first time and looked at myself in the long glass I blushed at how very grown-up, how actually provocative, I looked.

My corset, which Mrs Barnet said was designed to present me, rather than cinch my waist (which was small enough), was of white silk, with black ribbons around the bottom and running in diamonds up the front to my breasts. It was short, reaching from the underswell of my bosom to only a few inches below my waist, and only lightly boned. It did indeed hold me erect when she laced it up, but the most noticeable effect was that it pushed up my breasts, making them stand out and seem fuller.

Over the corset I wore a chemisette, again ribboned at the neckline and hem. It was made of a material new to me, called chiffon, which was so fine and translucent that it did nothing to conceal me. My drawers were of white cambric. They were shorter than usual, reaching only halfway down my thighs, and were loose in the leg, which I found much more comfortable and cooler than the normal ones, which tied with ribbons around the knee. I was also to wear my first ever proper stockings. Silk! White silk, and held up with really pretty jade green garters!

Wearing just these undergarments I turned and twirled before the looking-glass for my own inspection and Tiliu's and Mrs Barnet's. When Tiliu whispered in my ear, 'Ridja look good for fucking!', I am sure Mrs Barnet heard, for she laughed aloud.

The dress itself, my coming-out frock, was wonderful. Of jade green cotton so fine that it was almost like silk, the skirt was straight and plain from waist to toes at the front, so that when I walked it outlined my legs, and gathered into thick folds behind, with a great bow just below my waist at the back. The bodice was cut to resemble a jacket, with tight sleeves set off with white lace at the cuffs, and white frogging around the buttons up the front. It had a square neckline – or should I say bosom-line, for it was the lowest-cut frock I could imagine, clearly showing the cleft between my breasts, pushed up as they were by the corset. The gap left by the bodice, which would otherwise have given father a heart attack, was filled and made to seem modest by a double thickness of figured chenille which rose to a high, lace collar around my throat, overlapping a little so that no gap would appear when I moved or bent. Oh, I so looked forward to the occasion I was to wear it!

As the days passed, and I wore my new clothes, and got to know my way about things more, father began to relax and treat me in a more grown-up manner, allowing me a little more freedom than heretofore and beginning to treat me more as the manager of the household than as his little girl. Now, I was able to go about the house and garden more, involve myself more in its running, go to the town's few shops, with John-John driving the trap and Tiliu in attendance upon me. It was this closer involvement in running the household and closer familiarity with the servants that began to give me the germ of an idea. Benjamin was still afraid after my raging at him when I 'caught' him with Tiliu, and treated me with great deference. Beneath his deference, though, there still seemed a suggestion that he harboured thoughts of me as other than the mistress of the house! We needed to find a way to counter the hazard of gossip, which I realised was a great danger among servants. Besides which, I was beginning to chafe under the lack of a certain activity!

Need is a great spur to invention, and *my* need, both to stop Benjamin's possible gossip and assuage my own yearnings, was serious! Superstition was the key. That and the fact that Benjamin, and thus the others, guessed that I had lived at some time among Tiliu's tribe. What if we, Tiliu and I, could spread among them the notion that I had indeed been with her tribe. Not as a slave though, but as a *witch*? Why, if we could manage that, I would have them entirely within my power. Tiliu squealed with glee at the idea. She dragged up from her memory everything she ever knew about witches and juju, and we began to scheme like the gunpowder plotters.

Putting our scheme into operation was fun indeed, and its effects upon the house-servants were electrifying. Tiliu fashioned some little fetish objects (leaving them uncompleted, for she herself believed in their power) and we secreted them in places the servants would come upon them by chance. I let John-John find me kneeling, chanting over an aromatic fire in a far corner of the garden, and almost laughed aloud as he sneaked backwards, saucer-eyed, and then ran off hoping I had not seen him. I called Benjamin to the parlour and lectured him coldly for taking and eating a piece of cake, telling him in detail how he had pocketed it from the kitchen sideboard and gone off to eat it in the scullery, something I could not possibly have seen, for I was in town with father at the time. Of course, it never occurred to the silly man that Tiliu *had* seen him, and when I admonished him to be careful for I saw all, the poor creature nearly fainted! When they begged Tiliu, after some days of this, to tell them about me she reluctantly confessed that, yes, I had been with the tribe and was indeed a mighty witch, able to give much benefit to my supporters and wreak terrible torment on my enemies. Wide-eyed (she was a wicked actress!), she had told them tales of how I had turned a woman who angered me into a tree-snail, had given the chief boils when he became too haughty and had turned the wind when a storm threatened the village. By the time she had finished with them they would have leapt through fire at my command!

The first benefit of our trick was that never, ever had a body of house-servants striven so hard to please their mistress. Meals were cooked to perfection and served with such exactitude and promptness that even father commented upon my success as a manager. Not a speck of dust was allowed to land. Not a doily or antimacassar was ever an inch out of place. The time came to test the completeness of our victory, and Tiliu became positively Rabelaisian about the fun we would have. For myself, a strange mood crept over me. I was excited at the new power I had and eager to use it for my satisfaction, but there was more. I had been a captive among the tribe and had submitted to serving their pleasures. I had been had in every way be any number of men, deliciously by Talesi and Motallo, less so by Hendrick, and had never really had any choice in the matter. Now, the knowledge that Benjamin, John-John and the other servants thought me a witch and were terrified stirred in me the desire to make them submit to me as I had to all those others. I could verily taste it upon my lips. I called Benjamin to me first.

It was to be a momentous day indeed, for that very night was also to be my first time as hostess to one of father's dinner parties. Father would be out on business all day, and so we had lots of time to carry out our scheme with Benjamin. Having told Benjamin that he was to come to my bedroom an hour after luncheon, Tiliu and I went there ourselves to prepare. We drew the curtains to darken the room, and placed candles upon the floor to make it look mysterious. Tiliu changed her maid's clothing for her tribal gear, kneeling beside my chair ready to bow low and tap the little drum she held when the moment came. I myself donned a voluminous white nightgown and tied a white scarf about my head to make me look ghostly in the low light. We waited. There came a knock upon the door.

Benjamin was astonished when he entered at my command. He looked around him anxiously and his eyes widened as they fell upon me. He positively jumped when I spoke, making my voice low and hollow, and his shoulders twitched as he moved to stand before me, the very picture of submission. I thrilled to my task. Tiliu set up a tapping on her drum and began a low, wordless chant. I stared hard at Benjamin. He trembled even more.

'Do you know who I am?' I demanded in my hollowest voice. His eyes rolled. He spluttered. 'I am Lydia, mistress of this house. But I am also Ridja, great witch of the Nukanna!' He began to perspire. 'It has come to me in my spirit that you have had disrespectful thoughts.' His mouth fell open and he seemed to shrink. 'Do not deny it! I see inside you and I am angry!'

He trembled. I began to enjoy myself. Had he not known the body of my servant Tiliu? Yes, yes but . . .! Had he not looked upon my own self with desire? Please forgive! Had he not desired to know my body as a man a woman? Oh, sorry, missy, so sorry!

I left him to stew for a full minute, then ordered him to stand. Next, I ordered him to strip. He stared at me in shock, but then, when I tutted impatience, he practically tore his clothes off, dropping them in a pile at his feet. Tiliu had been right. His was an excellent body, with thickly muscled arms and shoulders, a deep chest and flat, ribbed belly, long, carved legs, and there, central to my eager gaze, a thick mat of hair from which hung a heavy bag and a member impressive in its dimensions even though limp from fear. I felt my breasts tighten beneath the cotton of my nightgown.

At my signal, Tiliu rose. She pulled Benjamin's

ands behind his back and tied them with a piece of
ord we had prepared. He screwed his eyes around
rying to watch Tiliu as she moved to pick up a black
loth bag (that had been used to carry shoes) and
tood beside him, looking very serious. His eyes
wivelled back to me, wide with fright. I looked at
im with a coldness I certainly did not feel.

'You have transgressed!' I told him. 'But I will be
merciful! You look to be a healthy animal, and I may
ave some use for you!' He looked as puzzled as he
id relieved. 'But I must be sure of your obedience! I
rill summon up a spirit from the world of the dark,
nd we will take your essence, and thereafter if you
ven dream a wrong dream the spirit will turn you
nto a worm at the mouth of a red-ants' nest and you
rill die of a million stings!' His eyes looked to pop
ut of his head! 'Tiliu! The bag!' He gave a moan of
ear as she stepped forward and slipped the bag over
is head.

My emotions were wild, and I wondered at the
pleasure I felt in being thus so cruel to him. But more,
felt such an excitement that one touch would have
xploded me into a come! He looked delicious stand-
ng there, so helpless. Tiliu began to beat her drum
nd wail a wordless chant. Benjamin trembled. I ran
a hand over his belly and thigh, thrilled to feel his
rembling under my fingertips. I reached up and cup-
ed his balls. He gasped, and his cock twitched. I
rircled it with my fingers and rubbed it. He groaned
s he reared in my hand. He was indeed excellent.
Fully as large as my Talesi, and entirely within my
power!

I stroked him for a while longer, delighting in a
tiffness which strained his cock until it almost
touched against his belly. He was like a magnificent

statue in the lamplight, every muscle tense, his glorious cock straining for the ceiling. My cunny was damp and burning, and from the corner of my eye I could see Tiliu positively drooling at the sight.

His cock began to droop just a little. I knelt and, not touching him with my hands, clamped my mouth upon him. He jumped and gave a whimper of fright. For all he knew this was a devil upon him, and his knees shook. I sucked hard, my hands pressed to my lap to hold down my churnings. This was not for his pleasure, but for mine! He was hot and hard and delicious. Oh, how much I had missed this feeling! I was ravenous and licked and sucked greedily, longing for his come to flood my throat. His fright held him back. He did not want the spirit to steal his essence. But come he did at last, exploding with a high-pitched whimper of fright, spurting delicious hotness which I swallowed greedily, sucking hard for more until he groaned as if in pain.

Tiliu, watching the jerking of his hips, increased her wailing and crashed on her drum as he had his unwilling come. I got back into my chair weakly, for I had come myself. I had to delay, recovering myself and I wiped my face and lips upon my scarf. He looked so lovely standing there, his wet cock shrinking, a little dewdrop pearling his plum, that after the frustration of several weeks without a man I almost wanted to leap on him and shag him then and there! But I could not: I must play out the pantomime.

At last, when I was recovered enough, Tiliu's wailing and drumming quietened. I shouted, 'Be gone, spirit! Guard him well!' I clapped my hands and Tiliu whipped the bag from his head. His face almost made me burst with laughter, so frightened was he! I signalled and he fell to his knees. 'So, Benjamin! It is done

154

nd you are mine! Go now, and remember!' He was trembling like a leaf as Tiliu untied his hands. He snatched up his dicarded clothes and positively ran from the room. Tiliu and I hugged and danced with delight.

The dinner party that evening, to celebrate father's birthday, was my coming-out, as it were. I was very excited, for not only was I to be hostess and play the lady of the house among the grown-ups, but I would be able to wear the lovely coming-out clothes Mrs Barnet had made for me. As she helped me dress and brushed my hair, Tiliu was as excited as I, for she too had a new outfit and was to assist Benjamin in waiting at table.

When I was fully dressed and examining myself in the looking-glass, I experienced a moment of nervousness. The corset, which I had only tried on before and not worn for more than a few minutes, did indeed hold me erect. Moreover, the way it lifted my breasts served to attract the eye to that part of me. That my bosom above the low neckline was covered with two layers of cloth did little to conceal me, for the chenille was so fine and lay so softly against me that even though not actually visible, the very shape of my breasts and the cleft between them was clearly suggested. Suppose father objected. Suppose it was *too* grown-up? Father's eyes did indeed widen when I entered the parlour where we were to greet his guests, and for a moment, as his eyes raced all over me, I was afraid he might send me to change. I was quite relieved when he simply told me I looked very pretty.

There were ten to dinner. Myself and father, of course; Mr Forster, the manager of the bank, and his wife; Captain and Mrs Mackay and their daughter Felicity; the vicar, Dr Williams, and Mrs Williams;

and, which gave me pause because of what he had
tried to do to me all those months ago, Lieutenant
Jonathan Andrews, the man who, if all be told, had
started me off on my voyage of sexual discovery.
had met all of them before, and found them variously
likeable. Father dealt with the men while my first duties as hostess were to greet the ladies, supervise
Tiliu's disposal of their cloaks and ensure that they
each had a glass of sherry, and to lead the small talk
as we waited for Benjamin to signal dinner with the
gong.

It is on such occasions that the underlying hypocrisy of polite society is at its most clear. All the ladies
gushed compliments to each other about their gowns
and the way their hair was dressed, and admired a
pretty brooch, while all the time their eyes, and the
twitching of their lips, betrayed that they were calculating costs and making comparisons to their own
advantage, and mentally calculating points they could
later disparage. I myself came in for many sidelong
glances, especially from Felicity. She was several
years older than me and very pretty, with a mass of
red-brown hair and a shapely figure. She had dressed
in her finest for the occasion, wearing a frock of figured yellow silk, with full skirts and a tight bodice
topped with a cravat of fine lace. It set off her colouring and delicate complexion beautifully. She looked
lovely, and knew it, and I took a perverse pleasure in
seeing from her glances and lip-pursings that she
thought me a rival.

During the half-hour before the meal was called,
both Felicity and her mother gushed charm at me,
complimenting me on my frock and my hair (which
was still in its topknot, and which Tiliu had brushed
to a shining veil around my shoulders), whilst all the

time speaking in such a way as to emphasise how young I was – Why, how grown up I looked! How much I must be looking forward to my first proper dinner party – that sort of thing. Had not her glances revealed how she truly felt, had not my looking-glass and father's eyes told me otherwise, I might well have been downcast by her superior manner. As it was, I began to enjoy myself, the more so when, as we mingled just before going to table, even the vicar sought me out. None of the gentlemen looked me much in the eye, always dropping their eyes lower.

It had not been consciously planned, but the seating arrangements could not have given me a greater coup. I, of course, sat opposite father at the big oval table, with Captain Mackay on my right and Jonathan on my left. At first, Jonathan was rather tentative, and regarded me nervously, for this was the first time we had met since that day by the stream. When I let him know, by chatting to him casually, as though nothing had ever happened, that there would be no repercussions, he soon relaxed – and more, as shall be seen. Next to Jonathan sat Felicity, and it was obvious at once that she was setting herself at him. I could not blame her, for he was a handsome man indeed, and the fact that he talked as much to me as to her, indeed more as the evening grew on, really put her nose out of joint.

The meal was delicious, and beautifully served by Benjamin and Tiliu, though Benjamin trembled and almost spilled things whenever he caught my eye. Conversation was lively and I had no difficulty in keeping up my end, for all I had to do was make wide eyes and ask about adventures for Captain Mackay and Jonathan to vie with each other in telling me tales of their experiences. I quickly noticed that whenever

either of them turned to speak to me his eyes would
seek my neckline, and as the evening went on and
wine was drunk (I took only two small glasses), their
glances became bolder. I began to enjoy myself more
and more, though always acting demure and innocent. I also took a perverse pleasure in the way their
attentions seemed to peeve Felicity and her mother!

When, between the fish and the roast, I felt
Jonathan's hand brush my knee, I smiled inwardly.
So! It was not to be all decorum after all! At first it
was just a touch. When I did not move away it became a stroking, very soft and just around my knee.
It was difficult to act as though nothing were occur-
ring, but I managed it. I turned from Jonathan to the
captain, and in leaning to my right was able to move
my knee to my left. Jonathan at once took his opportunity and began to caress the length of my thigh. It
was delicious to sit there, the demure little hostess
above the table while beneath it, unknown to all, a
man's hand was being naughty with me.

And then I felt a touch upon my other knee! It was
the captain! To have two men feeling me up beneath
the table, neither knowing what the other was at,
both thinking they were taking advantage of an innocent child, was exciting indeed. They were both
getting bolder, too, exploring nearly the whole length
of my thighs as I sat with my knees wide apart, both
to assist their touchings and to keep their hands away
from each other.

And then the inevitable happened. Both hands
moved high up my thighs, sneaking towards my lap
itself! They would touch each other and realise what
was afoot unless I acted quickly. If either knew what
I was letting the other do it would be a disaster! I
managed to avert it by knocking over my wine glass.

and leaping to my feet to avoid it splashing my frock. The two men covered their surprise brilliantly, the one reaching out to offer me his napkin, the other instantly dabbing at the puddle of wine. Fortunately, it was time for the ladies to withdraw else I would have disgraced myself by bursting into helpless laughter!

Their cigars finished, the menfolk joined us ladies later in the drawing room. During the half-hour or so before leaving, the two soldiers who had so toyed with me held centre stage. They talked loudly, the captain more than his lieutenant. They preened and twirled their moustaches. They were gallant to all the ladies – Jonathan especially so to Felicity, which made her primp and flutter and improved her mood no end. But the looks they cast upon me were knowing indeed. It was clear that they had each classified me as an ignorant girl they might have their way with. It was delicious! That neither knew of the other's manoeuvrings made it even more fun.

My joy was that they believed they were tricking me, were leading on an innocent little girl. If only they knew! Oh! Men! And when, on bidding father goodnight, they each gained his permission to see me again soon, the captain to give me a tour of his barracks, Jonathan to give me riding lessons, my wide-eyed delight caused them each to preen and give me such smug glances, I almost laughed aloud.

Chapter 10

As I lay abed late the next morning, the events of the last twenty-four hours drifted through my languorous mind. The flirtatiousness of Captain Mackay and Jonathan, the way their naughty hands had explored my thighs beneath the dinner table, and their obvious scheming to take advantage of my naivete, had been nicely exciting.

Afterwards, though, came the voluptuous culmination of a delicious day, for I had summoned Benjamin to my room, taking advantage of my new status as holder of his essence. I confess that the sudden change from frequent activity among the tribe to nothing but posing and manners now I was back home had left me feeling somewhat . . . unsatisfied – a situation not helped by Tiliu's minxish hints that she herself was far from idle – and I would probably have called for Benjamin even had the officers not warmed me up!

At the recollection of poor Benjamin's wide eyes, of the nervous way he leapt to obey my every whim, I cannot but smile to myself. What a change in my circumstances! For half a year and more I had been the common property of Ngossi's tribe, conscripted (albeit willingly!) to satisfy any of the menfolk who called for me. Even after my rescue I had been kept for several weeks by Hendrick, although there was a certain sweetness in the recollection of how I had seduced him to my will. And now. To have a man in *my* power. To have, in fact, my own slave ready to leap to the service of my wishes out of dread of my witchly powers was heady stuff indeed.

When I had summoned him last night, he came trembling, wide-eyed at what the witch might want of him. I had been wearing only the little chemisette and loose drawers made for me by Mrs Barnet, which entirely revealed my figure, and in his terror poor Benjamin did not know where to look. I was warm from the officers' flirtations and my anticipation of Benjamin's arrival, and as he stripped off his clothes at my command I felt my breasts tighten deliciously and my tummy begin to tense. He was indeed an impressive animal! Although his face was not handsome – a broad, flat nose with wide nostrils, deep-set eyes under heavy brows, all set in a square, overlarge face – his body was breathtaking.

Fully a head taller than myself, he was broad shouldered and well-muscled, though not bulky. His chest was deep, with some thin scars across one shoulder which only seemed to emphasise the smoothness of his gleaming skin. His belly was flat and banded with muscle. I walked around him as he stood like a statue. His back fell in a smooth vee from shoulders to narrow hips, the spine a long groove between slabs of muscle. His smooth legs rose to buttocks so tight and firm that it was all I could do not to fondle them in my excitement. I moved to stand in front of him. Even shrunken by his state of fright, the member which hung at the join of his thighs, fringed with its mat of tight curls, was handsome – and I knew it could grow impressively!

The very sight of him, standing like a trembling

statue, so powerful yet so vulnerable, made it hard indeed for me to appear cool, for inwardly I was burning and my breasts felt ready to burst. I stood in front of him, marshalling my composure. His eyes could not help but slide to my bosom, which was clearly revealed through the flimsy chenille. As he jerked his eyes away, fresh fear that he might annoy me widened them. Without taking my eyes from his I reached forward and grasped his cock. He positively twitched with fright. His member actually seemed to shrink in my hand!

I let him go and moved across the room to where I was in the full light of the oil-lamp.

'Benjamin!' I said in the coolest voice I could muster. I used my native name. 'Ridja is not angry with you. She has decided to use you for her pleasure!' Puzzlement joined the fright in his eyes. 'If you are good, and serve her well, she will smile upon you. If you fail her she will be angry. Do you understand, Benjamin?'

He nodded so vigorously it seemed his head would fly off, but his eyes showed only that he was puzzled and fearful. Slowly, I untied the ribbon of my drawers and let them fall to the floor. He caught his breath. I pulled off my chemisette and stood before him naked. His eyes widened, then narrowed, as if he were thinking hard.

I moved close to him again, grasping his cock and pressing myself against him. His hand moved to my hip. 'Be still! You have no permission to touch Ridja!'

He froze, trembling even more than before. His skin was hot against mine. A warm, musky scent filled my head and I could feel his perspiration against my cheek. My breasts were so taut that the very warmth of his skin as I pressed against him brought delicious ache to my nipples. His cock began to stir divinely as I slowly squeezed and rubbed it. I pushed my tummy against the back of his hand, rolling and pressing to ease my growing pleasure cramps. Benjamin remained perfectly still despite what, for him, must have been torment. He was almost shivering and his breathing grew ragged. His cock had become a truncheon, straining up against my hand, the hot skin sliding like silk over the veined hardness within; the ridge between shaft and plum taut and curving; the plum itself filling my palm. My arm was around his waist, my body squirmed against his, and I found myself almost climaxing just standing there touching and smelling him.

I dragged myself off him. This would not do. I had to at least *seem* to maintain control. Even so, the sight of him standing there trembling, his beautiful cock pointing almost at the ceiling, made my tummy lurch and my quim churn. I paused to gather myself and sat upon my bed, glad that Benjamin was staring into my eyes for thus I could avoid looking at his rampant member.

'Benjamin. Do you want to shag with Ridja?'

He jumped. His face rippled with confusion. What should he say? 'Remember, Benjamin, Ridja sees inside your head! Answer! Would you like to fuck Ridja?'

His face struggled with desperate thoughts. His shoulders sagged. His voice was almost a whisper. 'Yes, missy.'

'Good! You do not lie!' His relief was almost tangible. 'Do you want to touch Ridja's *tolli*?' (Tolli is the tribal name for what we females have between our legs.)

Benjamin sighed as if in defeat. 'Yes, missy.'

163

My pulsings were calmer. I was enjoying myself. 'Good!' I said. 'Does Benjamin want to lick Ridja's tolli?'

Benjamin's face wriggled with indecision. I knew from my time with the tribe that although native men universally enjoyed being pleasured with a woman's mouth, except for my beloved Motallo they rarely pleasured a woman thus, feeling it beneath their dignity to bury their heads between a woman's thighs. Then, to my delight for I knew him to be lying out of fear of the witch's anger, he whispered, 'Yes, missy.'

With a flash of inspiration, I leapt from the bed and slapped him fully on his rearing plum, making the delicious cock jerk and sway. 'You lie! You dare to lie to Ridja!'

He yelped. He shrivelled. His eyes moistened with shock. I moved back to my bed, eased close to the edge and parted my knees. I decided to torment Benjamin a little more so I leaned back and parted my knees further. 'Well, Benjamin. You forget that Ridja can see inside your head! But it is only one lie! She will consider your punishment. And while she considers, you will pay homage!' His eyes flicked about the room as if for some escape. There was none. Benjamin knelt between my feet. 'Lick! And be sure to please Ridja lest she be angry!'

Seldom can there have been such a delicious scene in the whole world! Benjamin, huge, powerful, surely a warrior within his tribe, knelt. My thighs parted as his great head dipped forward. I forbade him to use his hands. He tried so hard. His tongue worked almost as if he were some greedy hound. His teeth and lips writhed among my folds. He was desperate to please me. He found my swollen cherry and he lapped it with his rough tongue. Oh! The deliciousness! And

vhat power I had! Why, even when, in my transports,
 gripped his head with both hands and ground my-
elf against his face so that he was like to drown in
ny effusions, the poor man durst not stop his mouth-
ng of me, until I fell back in a glory of coming such
s I had not known since my lovely Motallo had first
hown me this way to pleasure.

It took me a while to recover myself. Benjamin still
nelt at my feet, his head bowed. I bade him lie upon
he floor. I moved to kneel astride him, facing to-
vards his feet so that he could not see my face and
letect the state I was in. His member had softened,
ut stirred at my touch, almost rearing to my belly-
utton as I ran my fingers over it. His belly felt hard
nd slick against my buttocks. I gripped him, lifted
nyself up then rubbed his great plum along the lips
f my oozing cunny. He groaned. I felt him throb.

'Be still!' I cried, pinching his plum with my nails.
I forbid you to come! Not until Ridja gives per-
nission!'

He groaned again and whimpered with mingled
ain and fright. He held himself rigid like a log. I
;uided his plum to my entrance and he gasped and
leld his breath as I began to slide onto him. Oh, how
le filled me. Filled me! I pressed myself down, crush-
ng my folds deliciously against his base, circling
nyself slowly, the rough hairs of his pelvis sending
hock after shock from my greedy cunny-lips to my
hurning insides. My body began to ride him in a
hythm of its own, pressing and circling. Rising a
ittle to press and grind again. My own hands found
ny throbbing breasts. Benjamin was almost sobbing
nd his very toes curled in his efforts to retain con-
rol. My body began to buck, the burning cramps of
a come building their glorious agony.

165

'Now!' I gasped, pressing my hand beneath his tight balls. 'Come now!' He jerked and moaned as I crushed myself onto him, and each spasm of his hotness, so deep inside me, set off burstings in my very being!

Now, in the light of morning, my breasts tingled at the memory of it. Tiliu came in and grinned hugely as her eyes flicked from my face to the damp patch on the sheets where Benjamin's spurtings had oozed out of me while I slept. Tiliu laughed and rolled her eyes. She is such a ribald little minx! But today I did not feel any irritation at her chatter about men and cocks as she helped me with my toilet and dressing. Nor any of those pangs of envy when she told me how this or that gentleman had felt her up and that she had already shagged John-John, our cook, that very morning. I had nothing now to be jealous of, for my own satisfaction was more than assured.

At father's party I had wondered which of the two officers who had flirted so daringly with me, assuming me to be an entire innocent, would be the first to call, and how he would renew his attempts upon my virtue. It was Captain Mackay who won the race, calling the very next morning on the excuse that an exercise was to be held which I would surely find impressive.

From the very first moment when, with a significant look into my eyes, he took my hand and planted a kiss on my fingertips, his purpose was clear. The captain shook hands heartily with father, who was seeing us off, and with great gallantry handed me up into the driving seat of the trap before climbing up himself and flicking the horse into motion with a slap of the reins and a, 'Ho there, boy!'

We bowled along at a merry pace as we journeyed

o the barracks, the harness jingling and the trap
bouncing over the road. The driving seat was narrow
and we were perforce obliged to sit close together – a
closeness the captain only increased by sitting with
his knees apart so that his leg was pressed against
mine. Of course, I feigned not to notice. Nor did I
notice, except to flutter gratefully, that whenever we
hit a rut and the trap bounced he touched his hand
lightly upon my leg 'to make sure I was all right'.
That his hand touched a little higher on my thigh
each time, and remained a little longer, was of course
entirely accidental!

By the time we had gone the mile or so to the barrack gates he was preening happily, convinced of the
naiveté of the commissioner's little daughter, and encouraged by the fluttering admiration with which I
hung upon his every word that here would be an easy
prize. So eager was he to get me alone that he rushed
us through the ceremony of meeting his fellow officers
(though he found time to press upon me two large
glasses of sherry!) and soon hurried us off to see the
exercise, suggesting that we would be able to see it
better from a knoll at the edge of the barracks. We
went there alone, all the other officers having tasks to
do with the exercise.

Since the knoll was some distance off, we rode in
the trap, and the captain's leg was even closer to mine
than it had been on the outward journey. When he
handed me down from the trap I pretended to
stumble and fell against him.

'Oh, sir,' I said, giggling. 'I fear your wine has positively gone to my head!'

He held me for just a little longer than might have
been necessary, his eyes gleaming and a near smirk
upon his face.

The side of the knoll was steep and rocky, and it was necessary for him to assist me frequently, especially since I was deliberately a little more unsteady on my feet than I really needed to be. By the time we reached the vantage point my bottom had been thoroughly explored by his helping hands! The view across the distant parade ground was magnificent indeed. Bands of mounted troopers in perfect lines trotted and wheeled and cantered and charged to the commands of bugles. They looked magnificent. But there was another exercise afoot.

I squealed and clapped and hopped from foot to foot in my girlish excitement. The captain stood close behind me, bending to tell me what this or that manoeuvre signified, holding my waist when I became unsteady. He suggested we step onto a jutting rock for an even better view. He held me, for the place was steep. He stood very close behind me. His arms closed about me for my safety. A hand found my bosom. I leaned back against him and murmured about how hot it was. Both his hands found my breasts. He was breathing noisily. My hands went to his, as if weakly trying to pull them away.

'Oh sir. It is so very hot. Your holding me like that makes me feel strange!' I fluttered and sagged against him. He cupped my breasts more firmly. 'Oh, I do feel odd! Should you really touch me that way? I feel dizzy! I am so hot! Oh, sir, I must sit down!'

The captain's face was very red. His eyes gleamed as he lifted me down from the rock, scooping my legs from under me so that I fell into his arms. He carried me to a grassy space. He lay me down. He knelt above me. 'Poor girl!' he said, his voice thick. 'Perhaps you have a touch of heatstroke. Lie still. I know what to do.'

'Oh, thank you. That feels cool. Sir! Why are you ndoing my buttons? Oh dear! The water feels cool. o much better. Oh captain. Should you be wiping ur handkerchief quite so far down? Oh! It is much oler. But sir, you make me feel most odd!'

He had wet his handkerchief from the water bottle n his belt and damped my forehead. At the same me, and with amazing speed, he unbuttoned my odice with his other hand and pulled it open. He egan wiping my neck with the wet handkerchief, and uickly moved down until his hand was actually in- de my chemise!

I lay there wide-eyed, murmuring protests to main- in my image of innocence while inwardly delighting his excitement at having tricked his way inside my lothing. He was very red of face. He took the hand- erchief out of my chemise. I made to sit up but clined obediently when he pressed me down again, anaging to pull my bodice further open as he did so.

'There, there, my dear,' he said, his eyes riveted pon the breast which was now almost entirely ex- osed. 'Be still! You have a touch of heatstroke, and e wine has not helped. Do not try to move. I have en this many times and know how to treat it. Trust e!'

He knelt upright. I tingled as I glimpsed the im- ressive bulge in his breeches. He told me I was a oor child, and that he would make me feel better. Ie needed to cool me down by loosening my tight lothing. I needed to get air to my body! I murmured urprise and was all shyness as he unbuttoned me fur- her. I protested, but not very vehemently. Oh dear, his was so odd! But I did still feel weak! He unbut- oned me to my waist and then undid my sash. He ugged up my chemise.

'Oh captain! What are you doing!' He pulled th
flimsy cloth up to my neck. I covered my expose
bosom with my hands but he pushed them aside as h
wiped me from neck to tummy with the freshly
wetted handkerchief. I submitted, only looking up a
him wide-eyed and shy.

'There, my dear. Does that not feel cooler?'

'Yes. Thank you, sir. But it does feel odd when yo
do that. Yes, that!' He had begun to caress me with
out even the handkerchief as an excuse. 'Oh captair
Are you sure? It feels most odd! I have never . . .'

His hands were no longer gentle, and he had begu
to openly knead and squeeze me, he even starte
pinching my nipples. I stared up at him all nervou
innocence, and fluttered my hands unavailingly abou
his.

He moved to sit beside me, lifting my shoulders s
that I lay against him, his free hand still cupping m
breast. 'There, there, my child!' he said gruffly. 'W
are friends and you must trust me! You will feel bet
ter very soon.' He cuddled me closer against him.
gazed up at him, trying hard to look trusting an
puzzled as, with the flat of his hand, he teased botl
my nipples. 'See! Does that not feel pleasant?'

I tried to make myself blush, and fluttered my eye
lashes. 'Well, yes. It is odd and nice, but . . .'

'Sshh, my dear! Be still and let Wystan make yo
feel better!

Wystan! The name almost made me giggle, as di
the grave and sympathetic expression on the face o
this man whose only object was to trick his way insid
my drawers! Obediently I sighed and snuggled agains
him. His play on my nipples felt most pleasant.
closed my eyes. Soon he must have thought m
asleep, for his hand slipped down to my tummy, ther

o my thigh. He stroked me very gently through the
material of my skirt. I sighed and, as if making myself
more comfortable in my doze, nestled against him
and raised my knee. For a moment he froze then,
when I remained still, moved his hand again. It was
at my knee. My calf. It was beneath my petticoats,
sliding up my stocking! He reached my garter. Sought
the edge of my drawers. Slipped inside. Explored my
thigh. Moved higher.

His hand covered my cunny. 'Oh sir!' I jerked
awake all startled, clamping my thighs together,
which of course trapped his hand where it was. 'Oh
sir! What are you doing? Oh!'

His arm tightened around my shoulders. The hand
between my legs did not retreat. 'Sshh! Do not be
afraid. You are such a pretty thing and looked so
sweet in your faint.'

'But Captain. Your hand!'

'Sshh! It is to make you feel better after your faint.
There. So. Does that not feel pleasant?' He was moving his fingers just a little. I relaxed my legs. His
fingertips began to play very softly.

'Well, yes, but . . . Oh, sir! What are you doing?
That feels very strange! Oh! Nobody has ever . . . It
feels so . . . Ooh!' His eyes gleamed when my knees
parted, just enough to give him a little room to play.
It was delicious and made the more so by his obvious
delight in seducing me so easily. As his fingertips slipped between my folds, exploring the length of my
crease, finding and even pressing a little against my
opening, I exaggerated my puzzled excitement. I let
my knees fall apart. I sighed and pressed my face
against his shoulder.

He pressed his fingertip in a little. I wriggled. 'Oh,
Captain!' I moved my hand. It fell onto his lap. It

171

fluttered. His finger was half in me. I sighed and moved my hips, my knees now wide flung. Beneath my fingers he was hard to bursting! He lay me down He knelt, removed his hand from my drawers fumbled with his breeches then his member burst out

'Oh sir. What is that? What are you doing? Oh no Not there! What are you doing? It hurts! It is too big Aahh!'

In a trice, he had got between my knees, pulled aside my drawers and was in me to the hilt. What with the pleasure of anticipation and the excitemen of the game I'd played and the captain's mad eager ness, I was already hot and moist when he entered me, and found it hard to pretend shock and fright. H thrust at me wildly. It was delicious. But too quick.

His come was like to have burst the veins in hi forehead, and he gasped and groaned like a buffalo before collapsing and rolling into a heap beside me on the grass. For a long time we both lay there. It had been a good game, letting myself be seduced, bu surely the game could not yet be over! I raised mysel onto an elbow and looked down at his as he lay re covering beside me. His eyes had opened and he wa watching me doubtfully. He had not done up hi breeches. I reached down and touched him. His eye widened.

'Oh captain! What have you done to me? Is this th thing you . . . you put into me? But it cannot be. It i too soft and small, and that was so big and stiff! I felt very strange and frightening, but it was nice at th end. Oh, see! It is twitching! Was it this? Poor thing Have we hurt it?'

Babbling such sillinesses, all wide-eyed innocence, let my hand flutter about the cock which lay limp an defeated against his belly. He told me what a good

172

irl I was, that I was sweet and pretty, that he would
uy me some ribbons. I made myself amazed when he
egan to stiffen. I asked what it was called, whether
 hurt to get so stiff and hard. When he began to tug
t the waist of my drawers I told him that I did not
:el dizzy any longer, that I did not need any more
ir, but I lay back obediently when he bade me and
llowed him to pull the garment from me.

A second time he knelt between my knees. 'Oh sir!'
 begged in my smallest voice. 'It is so big now! Are
ou going to put it in me again? Will it hurt? Oh how
trange. It is too large! Oh!'

He was much more in control of himself this sec-
nd time. Slipping his hands beneath my shoulders
nd pulling me to him, he rested his weight on his
lbows and moved slowly and deeply. Soon I no lon-
er had to feign cries of 'Oh captain!', 'What are you
oing?' and 'Oh! It is so big!', but lay there revelling
 his strength and the mounting warmth and tension
hat radiated out from my deliciously stretched
heath. His breath was hot on my neck. I was glad he
ould not see my face, for I surely no longer looked
he innocent as my body churned and tensed and
urned and expanded into a come so long and deli-
ious it was hard to stop myself crying out aloud.

Afterwards, as I shyly began to button my frock, I
ad an inspiration. All wide-eyed again, I gasped and
rabbed his arm. 'You won't tell, captain! You won't
ll father will you? Please!'

He grinned and preened himself like a cockerel.
Iow great was his success. How complete his con-
uest of the trusting girl. He pulled me to him. He
ouched me under my chin and slipped his hand down
ιy still-unbuttoned bodice.

'Ah no, my dear,' he said, his eyes gleaming, his

thumb rolling my nipple. 'If you are a good girl I wil
not tell a soul!'

I was all simpering gratitude, and promised to be
good girl, as he planted a kiss upon my forehead be
fore releasing me. While I was finishing buttoning m
bodice he bent, picked up my drawers from the gras
and stowed them inside his tunic.

'Perhaps, my dear,' he hurrumphed, primping hi
moustaches. 'Perhaps I may keep these as a souveni
as a token of our little secret!'

Oh dear. They were my nicest drawers, the one
Mrs Barnet had made to go with my coming-ou
dress! Ah well. I could always ask her to make m
some more.

Perhaps it was the fact that he knew I wore n
drawers, perhaps just a natural lasciviousness. What
ever it was, on the ride homeward he suddenly too
my hand and pressed it upon his breeches. He wa
hard again. I went all innocent.

'Oh captain. You poor man. Your thing is all sti
again. How uncomfortable you must be! But we can
not ease you. Not here. Someone might come along.

He steered the trap off the road into some bushe
He pulled open his breeches, placed my hand upo
his hot shaft. 'Oh captain. It must be agony. But w
cannot, there is no room to lie down.'

He leaned back, his cock rearing. He told me ther
was another way. He elicited my pity for his obviou
discomfort. He touched my lips with his finger an
looked down significantly at his stiffness. I becam
amazed. If I kissed it, if I took it into my mouth
sucked it, as he suggested, would that really ease hi
agony? He nodded. Oh, the poor man. I must hel
him. I would do it. I bent, shuffling back on the sea
to give myself room. He rested his hand on my nape

174

parted my lips. If only he knew. He tasted almost
s good as Benjamin. I dared not be too skilful, and
o obeyed the hand that was pressing on my head,
nly beginning to suck when he told me I should,
nce or twice even scraping him with my teeth to
how how clumsy I was. My gagging and coughing
hen he had his come, though, was not acted, for the
illy man pushed my head down so hard that he was
ight to my throat and like to choke me with his
purtings!

He was all grins and smugness and solicitude as he
elped me wipe my eyes, then drove me home and
anded me back to father. Yes, we had had a very
ice day. Yes, father, I was most impressed with the
arracks, and Captain Mackay had been most kind.
es, I would be honoured to visit again soon.

With a cheerful wave the captain went off with
ather towards his study to discuss some business or
ther, and I made my way to my room.

Part of me was irritated that, once again, the little
oman was dismissed when the menfolk talked seri-
us business – women, of course, being far too
inny-headed to understand serious matters! If only
hey knew quite how angry and frustrated this
atronisation made me, and I am sure other women.
)h, the smug self-satisfaction of it! And then I began
o giggle. Had I not today played just such a ninny-
ammer to let Captain Mackay seduce me? Had I not
ust confirmed any assumptions he might have had
bout the silliness of females by my acted gullibility
hile he 'treated my heatstroke,' particularly after the
ay I had fluttered and surrendered when he un-
ressed and shagged me?

Ah, but it had been a nice shag – or at least
he second one had – and the taste of his delicious

member was still fresh upon my tongue, so who was the ninny? The captain, no doubt now talking of important matters and smoking with father while smugly recollecting his success in having his way with me, or myself? At least *I* now knew that I could have him whenever I wished, while *he* would be on hot coals panting for another chance at me! Once again I was convinced that despite their greater physical power and their dominance in society, it was we females who had the real power because of men's weakness against the demands of the great god Cock.

And indeed I had confirmation of this very soon. Although the captain had clearly intended to get me in his clutches again as soon as possible, it was in fact almost a week before we met again, and then it was in the company of father, Mrs Mackay and the catty Felicity. We were at a picnic lunch after morning service at our little church. Dr Williams had preached his usual interminable sermon, but had enlivened it, for me at least, by fulminating against the sinfulness and avarice of the Boers who, it seemed, not only rejected the teachings of the Church in favour of their radical Calvinist creed, but even worse had slighted the name and dignity of our beloved Queen Empress!

My experiences at the hands of Hendrick after my rescue from the tribe arose fresh in my mind. If his pietistical hypocrisy was typical of his kind, I joined the vicar in condemning all and every one of them, and I was eager to find out more of whatever perfidy they had committed. And not least, I wanted to know why it was that they hated we British so. Thus I listened as closely as I could to the two men's conversation as they rode beside the trap which bore we females towards the picnic site. I was frustrated however in being able to catch only the odd word or

hrase here and there. At the picnic site itself, while
iliu and John-John laid out the provisions, I tried to
sk father more about the subject, but he told me not
o worry my pretty head with politics. Men!

During the meal Mrs Mackay and her noodle-headed
aughter dominated the conversation with chit-chat
bout neighbours and forthcoming social gatherings
nd such, and I became so irritated that I confess I was
ess than good company. Thus, when the captain in-
ited me to stroll with him I jumped at the chance to get
way from them, and such was my distraction that at
rst his true purpose did not occur to me. Only as we
alked, and he steered me towards some distant shrubs
nd murmured platitudes in response to my questions
bout the Boers, did I realise what he was upon, and it
tunned me! Normally, I suppose, I would have found
is intentions amusing and perhaps have looked for
ays of helping him to his goal. Now, though, I cursed
yself for having acted the empty-head so well that day
t the barracks, for clearly he thought me too silly to
nderstand anything about politics and just silly
nough to let him get me out of sight of the others.

How foolish a man can be when led by his lust. Did
e not see how dangerous his intentions were? I had
een the cool look Felicity had cast upon me when he
nvited me to stroll and knew of a certainty that she
vould put the worst possible interpretation on the
natter if we were out of sight for more than a mo-
nent – and here he was trying to get me behind the
ushes! As soon as I realised his intentions I began to
dge our path away from the shrubs, and there en-
ued what was almost a tug-o-war, with him pulling
o the left and concealment, and me to the right and
he open grassland.

When we were far enough off to be out of earshot

he began to remind me of our 'little secret', and to tell
me how sweet and pretty I was, and what a good girl.
And how – just look! – he was aching for me. He did
indeed have a considerable bulge in his breeches, and
the expression on his face showed that he would like
to have thrown caution to the winds and leapt upon
me then and there. I protested fiercely, pointing out
the perils: that father would suspect; that his wife and
daughter were near at hand; that even though I knew
his agony and longed to help him, here and now was
far too dangerous. He, though, foolish in his heat,
insisted that we would be safe, that he could not bear
to wait, that it would be quick, that I could suck him
like I had on the way back from the barracks. On and
on he went, becoming wilder and more insistent in the
face of my denial, so that I am sure that had I not
turned and begun to walk back towards the others he
would have thrown me to the ground and fucked me
on the spot!

The rest of the afternoon was awkward indeed, for
though I tried to put off Felicity's obvious suspicions
and lighten the mood by chit-chat and pretended gaiety, the captain made a poor fist of hiding his feelings
and hardly spoke another word all the way home.
The only results of the whole foolish episode was to
strengthen my conviction that men are fools, and to
give Felicity fresh arms in her campaign of cattiness
towards me.

Although I was annoyed with him I was also, I
supposed, somewhat flattered by his eagerness and
his hangdog look when I put him off. Thus when, to
my surprise, I found him loitering in the garden when
I went for a stroll before retiring to bed for the night,
I felt a surge of pity for the poor fool. We could not
be long, for I had told father I would soon return, but

e seemed so steaming and desperate that I had not he heart to put him off again. Besides, in his present nood he would never listen to my exhortations to ake care lest people suspect. Therefore I led him between some shrubs. He was so eager he was like to rip ny very clothes off, but I managed to control him nd as soon as he tore open his breeches I bent my nouth to him. His excitement was such that he gave loud groan and began his come almost the instant ny lips encircled him, and in such volume it near lrowned me!

Afterwards, when he was somewhat calmer, I troked his cock with my hand and let him feel me up s I remonstrated with him about his foolish eagerless, and reassured him that he had no need to worry, or I was just as keen as he to continue our little ;ames. His eyes glowed and I felt his cock twitch in ny hand at this, and he began to tug at my skirts as f wanting a bout then and there. I was able to calm iim, though, and we arranged for him to call on ather the next morning when, I was sure, we would ind a chance to play.

Chapter 11

I had thought that perhaps Jonathan might be more amenable towards telling me about what was happening regarding the Boers. After all, he was much younger than either father or the captain, though perhaps eight or ten years older than myself. determined to question him when I got the chance.

However, let me simply say that from the moment he arrived, the very day after my encounter with the captain at the barracks, to take me for my first riding lesson, it was obvious what was on his mind. Not so glaringly that a casual observer would notice, perhaps, but certainly so from the way he looked into my eyes, and let his glance move over me from top to toe while he smiled and preened. In another mood might have found his smugness irritating, but since his intentions matched my own I simply felt a little thrill of pleasure, for I knew I would enjoy the game almost as much as the prize at the end. Neither of us mentioned his advances of all those months ago, nor his touching me up at the dinner table, but it was obviously on his mind. How would he set about seducing the innocent girl who walked beside him towards the stables? Was she as innocent as she seemed? What would be his tactics? I decided to put my questions about the Dutch to one side for the time being and await developments.

Jonathan is a slender man, a little above medium height, with very dark eyes and a narrow, striking face. Even as we walked the short distance to father's stables, where he had already installed the horses we were to use, there was an easy familiarity in his manner which surprised me. The captain had been very circumspect, and even as he had been undoing my frock would have backed away instantly had I been anything other than 'innocent and gullible'. Perhaps Jonathan was basing his approach on the fact that, since I had not resisted his advances at the dinner, I would not do so now.

He had brought a large bay stallion for himself, which he mounted and pranced about to show me his horsemanship, and for me a very pretty dapple-grey mare which he assured me was as docile as a lamb. Even though she was smaller than the bay, she seemed huge when he took me close to her head and made me pat her neck and scratch between her ears. My evident nervousness seemed to please him, for he held himself taller and deepened his voice the better to show me he was my protector. I became all fluttering breathlessness, and he positively swelled with anticipation.

The mare was already fitted with a side-saddle, and Lieutenant Jonathan was all advice and reassurance as he led her to the mounting block. When one has never done it before, getting square onto a side-saddle and hooking one's leg securely around the thick pommel is awkward and not a little frightening, for one seems very high up. It is also the perfect opportunity for a gallant gentleman to assist a lady! This Jonathan took full advantage of. Of course it was entirely necessary for him to flutter and flap my skirts to ensure my legs had enough room! Of course it was necessary for him to ensure that my knee was securely hooked about the pommel. And obviously I was too naive and nervous to protest that he could do it just as well from *outside* my skirt! Of course it was necessary for him to make sure that my right ankle was firmly clamped behind my left knee, and he made no bones about reaching under my skirts with both hands, even lifting them to see that everything was in order! So, even before the lesson had properly begun, he had thoroughly felt and looked at my legs – and registered the fact that I had not demurred. He was certainly quicker to take his chances than had been the captain!

Talking the while, advising me how to sit, how to hold my back, how to adjust to the swaying of the saddle, he grasped the mare's reins and began to walk us in a circle, casually placing his hand high upon my thigh in order to help keep me steady. Being so high up and feeling so precarious distracted me for a time from the true purpose of this lesson, and I did not need to pretend nervousness. After five minutes of the careful walking, though, I began to grow a little more relaxed and was again able to pay attention to the lieutenant.

He gave the reins over to me, taking the opportunity of my expression of nerves to hold me with both hands, one at the small of my back, the other upon my thigh. We walked all around the edges of the stable yard. He let me ride unsupported a few times, for this was indeed a real riding lesson, but my exaggerated nervousness made sure that he always had to return to holding me again. He kept asking whether I was comfortable, how my seat felt, was my back all right, and after perhaps half an hour I agreed to his suggestion that we return to the stable.

There, I learned that getting down from a horse provides even more opportunities for a daring man than does getting on. It was necessary for Jonathan to put his hands under my skirts to help me unhook myself from the pommel. That the unhooking caused me to slide precipitately from the saddle and fall against him was, of course, entirely accidental! In my flustered state I feigned not to notice that his hands had stayed under my skirts, raising them to my hips, and simply leaned against him, fluttering and gasping my gratitude that he had saved me. He was all solicitude. He held me close, telling me not to be afraid for I was safe now, and he stroked my bottom soothingly. What was I to do? Even such an innocent as I was supposed to be must notice and react!

Back with the tribe it would have been so much easier. I would simply have smiled and wriggled and that would have been that. Now, in our pusillanimous English society, I had to find a way to be flustered while at the same time conveying to him that he might still try for his advantage. I durst not indicate in the slightest way that I knew what he was about, nor seem to encourage him, for a maiden such as I was playing could know nothing of these things. For Jonathan's own part, he had to find a means of getting his way without afrighting me. A puzzle indeed. How on earth could we proceed?

I stepped back from him hurriedly, allowing my skirts to fall without the embarrassment of alluding to where his hands had been.

'Oh, lieutenant! How clumsy of me!' I flustered. 'Please forgive me. It is that I feel weak and the saddle is so high up!'

At once he stepped towards me again. 'No, no! It is I who should apologise!' He put his arm about my shoulder. 'How inconsiderate of me! Come, we will find a place for you to rest.'

He led me through the stable door and we sat upon some bales of straw behind a partition. I exaggerated my weakness and trembling. He was concerned and solicitous. I leaned against him, my hands in my lap. He put his arm around my shoulder and rested his free hand on mine.

'Oh, sir, I do feel odd!'

'Perhaps it will be better if you lie back. There, I will hold you while you recover.' He lay us back. My hands moved away from my lap, but his did not. He began to rub me.

'What are you doing? That feels most odd!'

'Be easy, Lydia. Sometimes the saddle makes one become sore and I am massaging you to make sure that you do not become stiff!' He was rubbing slowly, pressing his hand down between my (naturally) slightly parted thighs. 'There! Does that not feel better?'

'Well . . . I suppose so. It feels rather odd. Are you sure? It is my bottom that feels stiff really!'

'But of course! We must be careful, else you will find walking very uncomfortable for a time. We must be thorough!' He sat up and rolled me onto my side.

'Why, lieutenant, what *are* you doing? Are you sure?'

'Of course, my dear. Trust me. You will soon feel better.' He had thrown up my skirts and was rubbing and squeezing the cheeks of my bottom, his other hand returning to my stomach. I submitted to his attentions with just a little gasp of surprise as he began to get bolder. 'There, Lydia. Does that not begin to feel nice?' His hand was now fully between my legs.

'Well, yes, I suppose so. It is most peculiar. I begin

to feel quite hot and most odd! But, well, yes, it *is* a little nice.' I let him roll me onto my back. He was now massaging me with both hands. I wriggled. 'Oh, sir, do not do that. Please. No. Why are you pulling down my drawers? Surely that is not necessary!'

'Sshh, Lydia! I must check on your little minge!' (Yet another new name for that happy place.)

'Oh, sir. Do not, I beg? You must not look at me there. Oh! Too late! I will die of shame. Do not touch me there. Aah. Please!' My drawers were off. He had thrown my legs apart and his hands were upon my naked quim. I struggled, made to sit up. He pushed me back, knelt above me, tore at his breeches. 'Oh, my God! What are you doing? What is that thing! Is this what one gets from riding horses? What are you doing! No, sir, please do not! You cannot put it there!'

He took no notice, of course. His eyes blazed. His teeth were bared. He was going to shag me whether I was willing or not. I cried out and begged him to desist. Although I had been acting my shock and confusion, I now was actually a little amazed for he was far beyond control. He rammed into me. He rutted frantically. He burst into a come. I pretended to faint – I thought it quite legitimate for a young girl to faint the first time a man fucks her!

He knelt above me. After a long pause while, I supposed, he looked me over and decided what he was to do, I felt him begin to undo the buttons of my bodice. I lay limp. There were a lot of buttons. At last he tugged aside the cloth of my frock and began to feel my breasts through my chemise. He tried to pull it aside, but could not. He decided to remove my frock. It was no easy matter, and I lolled limply in my 'faint' as he rolled me back and forth to remove first

185

one sleeve then the other. He fumbled around to release the buttons at my waist. He grasped my skirt and tugged it downwards. It came off after a struggle. I lay sprawled before him clad only in my shoes and stockings and flimsy chemise. I heard him gasp then felt him tugging my chemise up to uncover my breasts. His hands were sliding all over me. I felt his breath on my skin, his mouth upon my nipple. He began to suck and nibble. It felt delicious! He slid a finger into my quim. It was too much! I could not keep up my pretence! I started up.

'Oh sir! What are you upon? Where are my clothes?' I struggled but he held me down.

'Ah, Lydia!' he said, his voice thick, but triumphant. 'You are so lovely, I could not resist. I have rogered you, and you fainted, and you are delicious, and I am going to roger you again!'

'No, sir. Please let me go. Oh. Help!' I cried in a tiny voice. I struggled, but allowed him to be too strong. I could see, as he knelt above me, that his cock was already stiff again. He lay down upon me. I no longer struggled against his weight. He fumbled between my legs. 'Oh, lieutenant, not again! It is too big! Please do not roger me. You scare me so.'

'Sshh! Be still, Lydia. There. He is in you. Relax. It will soon be nice, you'll see.'

He took a lot longer the second time, pressing me into the straw, taking his weight upon his elbows so that he could look at my face. It felt so good!

'Oh, Jonathan, you are tearing me in half. What is it? It is so big! What are you doing to me?'

'I am rogering you, little Lydia! It is my prick, and I am shoving it up your minge and rogering you!'

'It feels so peculiar. I do not understand. No-one has ever touched me there. I feel so strange. It does not hurt any more. Oh, Jonathan! The way you move so! It does begin to feel strangely nice.'

It did not matter what I said, of course. He had got little Lydia at his mercy and was fucking her to a finish and glorying in his triumph.

He had his second come and I became all weak and shy and submissive. What was it that he had done to me? Why had it felt so peculiar? Why did my private place feel so odd? What was his prick? Why was it now so small, when it had been so very big? Why had he taken my clothes off? Would he have to roger me every time I had a riding lesson? Oh, men are such silly, gullible creatures! Anybody not pumped up with their own illusions would have seen through my shyness and my silly questions in a trice. For Jonathan, though, they were simply proof of my ignorance and naiveté, and of the completeness of his victory.

He talked to me as if I were an idiot child (which, to be fair, I suppose I was pretending to be). He told me that I was pretty. That he had taken off my clothes because I had fainted. That I had a pretty minge. That he would indeed roger me again if I was a good girl. That his prick was the prize given by God to men so that they could reward young girls who were good. It was small now because it was resting but could get big again in a trice. Did I want to look at it properly? Yes, I could touch it if I wished. There, see! It was already growing again. If I was a good girl, he would let me hold it.

I told him how strange and pretty it was. How odd to feel it grow thus in my hand. That it did indeed look pretty, almost kissable. Oh! might I? Oh, see, it was getting even bigger! How could such a thing go right up, what had he called it, my little minge? I was being a good girl, was I not? Might I kiss it again?

Was he going to roger me again? It wouldn't hurt me this time, would it? Would it really feel nice? How stiff it is! How it stretches me! Oh, it is in me to my ribs! It does feel nice when you push so. Oh, lieutenant, am I a good girl? Oh, I feel strange! Do it harder! Please! Harder! Aah! I am bursting! Aah! I am dying!

Afterwards, for I had indeed had a delicious come, I was all softness and gratitude. Jonathan watched me dress, lying back on the bales after helping me shake the straw from my drawers and chemise. He had not done up his breeches but lay there with his cock brazenly exposed to my gaze. He suggested I kiss it again before putting it away and doing his breeches up. As we walked slowly back towards the house he enjoined me not to tell anyone about our little games, and that if I was a very good girl he would find other ways to reward me. I was all gratitude, and told him wide-eyed that I would try very hard to be good, and asked when would my next lesson be?

Outside the house he fondled my bottom lingeringly and said, with a sly grin, 'Perhaps tomorrow, my dear. Yes, I think tomorrow.' And he walked jauntily back towards the stables.

He did indeed arrive the next day, bright and early, and jaunty in the expectation of what he was going to do to me. He chatted with father in his study while I readied myself, putting on a separate skirt and blouse, which both buttoned down the front, some very pretty, loose-legged drawers and one of the new chemises Mrs Barnet had made for me that buttoned down the front. Jonathan would never suspect that I had dressed thus of a purpose, but would be delighted to be able to get at me simply by undoing some buttons rather than the awkward struggle he'd had with my frock yesterday! As soon as we left the house, with father's, 'Take care of her, lieutenant!' ringing in our ears, Jonathan set about his business. He grinned at me lecherously, complimenting me on my appearance and, as soon as we were out of sight, he fondled my bottom lasciviously.

As we approached the stable I asked what the rumours about trouble with the Dutch were about. He looked startled. Clearly, conversation about politics was the last thing on his mind! Like father and the captain, he began to tell me not to bother my pretty head while the hand on my bottom was reinforced by his other on my bosom. I wriggled from his grasp. Insisted that I wanted to know. We were at the stable door. He mumbled something about damned farmers and rebellious villains, but swung me round and pressed me against the doorpost, and was upon me in an instant, kissing me hotly, his hands suddenly everywhere! I struggled and resisted him as best I could. He was wild! He wanted me there and then! He already had my skirt up to my thighs!

Only when I begged him and cried out that father would become suspicious if he did not see us on horseback, did he control himself. Oh, such impetuosity was awkward indeed. I would have to find a means to calm this man if he so lacked control! Besides, in a way it was rather insulting. Did he think all he had to do was grab me in order to get his shags. Did *I* not have any say in the matter? But he had controlled himself now, albeit red-faced and with trembling hands, so all was well for the moment.

He brought my mare to the mounting-block, and was all set to take the same liberties in settling me on the side-saddle as he had yesterday, but I rebuffed him by insisting I could do it myself. Only when I was securely mounted with my legs firmly hooked did I allow him the glimpse up my skirt he so desired – 'Just to be sure, dear Lydia!' – and even then I flicked my skirt down after barely a second. He began to lead me around, his hand on my thigh as before, but I lifted it off and said I wanted to try to ride by myself. He seemed chastened, just as I desired. He watched me walk the mare for a little while, then got his own mount and rode close beside me.

Soon, he mumbled an apology in case he had offended me by becoming so overexcited, but I was a delicious girl and he'd become carried away with the memory of yesterday. I told him that he had indeed shocked me, but that I might forgive him and be a good girl if he was nice to me. At the words good girl he brightened considerably, for he guessed they meant that he might roger me again after our lesson. In the meantime he was on his best behaviour all the while the lesson continued. He even responded to my questions by telling me something about the difficulties with the Dutch, although he was clearly surprised that a little thing like me should want to be bothered with such dry matter. If he'd known about my experiences at the hands of Hendrick he would not have wondered!

I did not really understand much of what he told me – things about a war of sorts before I was even born. Of gold fields and diamond mines, and people called Jameson and Rhodes and Kruger and Botha and such (I found out much more from Mrs Barnet later) – but at least he told me *something*. I tried to get him to clarify, to give me more detail, but his mind was clearly on other things – as mine was beginning to be, not only because he had treated me with at least *some* respect, but because his obvious excitement (and his lack of control earlier) was causing stirrings within my own veins. However, to tease, I extended our ride for quite a long while before allowing myself to be led back to the stable.

Once there, Jonathan leapt from his mount and rushed to help me from mine, his eyes alight. The bulge in his breeches was huge and his hands were ready to fly for my skirts. I was hard put to it to hold him off long enough to reach the hay bales. So excited was he that it was only after the first, very quick, shag that he had enough self-control to readopt his pose of the suave male teaching the little innocent. He had not waited to undress me but had simply thrown up my skirts and pulled aside my drawers in his eagerness. Now he began that cooing and persuasion men adopt when attempting seduction – and it became clear, too, that he was a little nervous that in thus leaping upon me he may have frightened me. He put his arm about me and cuddled me to him. He told me I was a lovely girl. He kissed my forehead. Murmured how nice I was, and what a good girl. His free hand wandered to my breast. I remained silent, looking down shyly. His hand hesitated, only moving a very little, as if testing for my reaction. Then he slid it gently over both my breasts and moved to my buttons.

'Am I really a good girl?' I whispered in a tiny voice. He took this as the signal I had meant it to be. The arm about my shoulders tightened. He kissed my forehead again. My buttons flew open. My blouse and chemise soon gaped. His hands and mouth devoured my exposed breasts. To have a man thus transported by one's charms is a delight indeed!

My skirts were still at my thighs and his hand descended and slid inside the leg of my drawers. He was sucking on my breast, bringing that delicious tingling ache I love so well. I wriggled to help him get my drawers off. His cock was like a truncheon. Our second shag was long and glorious. Yesterday, playing the innocent, I had hidden my come from him. Now I could not, did not even dream of trying, and through my churnings and the light burstings in my head I saw that he was staring down with open-mouthed delight as I writhed and spasmed beneath him.

Afterwards he was smug indeed as I again played the ninny-head, trembling, gasping how nice rogering was, begging to know whether I was a good girl, and what were the strange sensations that had so over-come me. He petted me and cuddled me and told me that, yes, I was a very good girl, and that I had come, which was what happened to good little girls when they were well rogered. He had not done up his breeches, and he moved my hand down. Even soft and slippery as it was after our bout, his member was still impressive. I sighed and wriggled (his hands were roaming again) and murmured how nice it was. My own wrigglings and his crafty manoeuvres soon en-sured that my head came level with his waist. His cock was close before my face. I stroked it, whispered how pretty it was, that it looked positively kissable. He moved his hips, bringing it even closer to me.

'Kiss it then, my dear,' he said, his voice gruff. 'You can suck it if you like. Yes, take it into your pretty mouth, Lydia! You will enjoy it!'

In its part-roused state, the little folds of skin still half covering the rosy plum, it did indeed look pretty. I stroked its length, delighting in the way it twitched and grew. I parted my lips and bobbed my head. He was delicious! He did not hold my head, indeed hard-ly moved save to push slightly to match my rhythm.

His scent was fresh, even a little sweet, and his taste – albeit partly that of my own juices – heady indeed. Somehow he reached around so that his hand slipped between my legs from behind, and he fondled me as I sucked. He was certainly skilled, and the sensations of his fingers exploring my moist folds and teasing my cherry, in combination with the delicious sensations in my mouth, made me pulse and churn, and burst into a second come even before he had his.

For a long while we lay still, my head in his lap, for we were too languorous to move. At last, though, we roused ourselves and dressed ready to return to the house. At the stable door Jonathan grasped my arm and turned me to look into his eyes. He did not speak but just gazed at me. In his eyes was an expression of triumph, calculation and knowingness. I realised with a sudden tightness in my chest that he guessed something, that my comes had been too open, my sucking too skilful. He guessed I was not the innocent I had pretended to be! I could think of nothing to say, nothing to do.

And then suddenly, out of the blue, I got a fit of giggles. Perhaps it came on me through nerves, but the situation *was* ridiculous and soon tears of mirth were streaming down both our faces as we howled and clutched each other for support. How preposterous our charades suddenly seemed; me posing as the wide-eyed ingenue; he striving to bamboozle the little innocent, when all the time our aims had been the same!

I was gasping for breath. Through my giggles and Jonathan's guffaws I heard him splutter, 'Little minx!' and 'Who'd 'a' thought it!'

Each word set me off again, and I verily thought I might actually pee right then and there. At long last we both laughed ourselves to exhaustion and stood facing each other. He wiped his face on his sleeve and I dabbed my streaming cheeks with a handkerchief from my reticule.

Jonathan put his hands on my shoulders and slowly shook his head, his face suffused by a huge grin of friendly astonishment. I smiled and shrugged my shoulders. In a moment we had gone from tricksters in a mutual game to co-conspirators. I felt such relief. Now, with him at least, I would not have to act what I was not!

After that second riding lesson, where we recognised each other as the naughty gamesters we were, we became fast friends. He never asked questions about how or with whom I had gained my experience. Nor did he try to lord it over me or treat me breezily, as so many men do when once they've seduced a girl. If anything, he treated me with greater respect than before, for in his eyes I was no longer a ninny to be seduced but a full partner in the exploration of delights. Thus, as we took tea on the veranda one afternoon, it was easy for me to tease him a little.

Tiliu had served us, and as she moved away from the table I caught him eyeing her appreciatively. I called her back and asked her to pluck a particular flower for me from the climber which festooned the veranda. To do so, she had to stretch up on tip-toes close in front of my lieutenant, and I smiled at the way his eyes raced over her deliciously outlined figure.

'Do you like my little maid?' I asked when she had gone. 'To judge from the way you just looked at her you surely do!'

Jonathan blustered a little and looked around him as if to seek a distraction, but gave himself away.

'Why Jonathan! I do believe you are blushing!'

'What? Eh? No, no! It is the heat!'

'But she *is* very pretty is she not?'

'No, no! Not near so pretty as you, darling Lydia!'

'And you *were* positively devouring her with your eyes!'

He really was blushing now. 'No! What! I never . . .!'

'Why Jonathan, I do believe that you would like to roger her!' He leapt up as though what I had said had been a gunshot, his face amazed and struggling for dignified denial. Then he saw the expression on my own face, and we both burst into giggles.

'Well, well, my lovely Lydia, what an outrageous minx you are to be sure!' he spluttered, wiping his eyes with his handkerchief.

'And what, sir, is so outrageous about a woman noticing when the eyes of her paramour stray to another? Even when that other is a friend and so very pretty as my Tiliu!'

'But, Lydia! I would never . . .!'

'Come now, sir! Do not fib!' I leaned across and tapped him playfully on the cheek with my fingertips. 'Remember that Tiliu is my friend as well as my maid. She tells me *everything*!' I sat back and regarded him with mock severity, hard put not to laugh at his discomfiture. 'Now confess, Jonathan! Confess that you have touched up my little Tiliu's bottom more than once! That you have handled those little titties whenever you had the chance!' Now he really did look uncomfortable, and I came to his rescue. 'And I do not blame you for a moment! I'd do the same if I were a man!'

His mouth had come open in amazement and his eyes searched mine as if to make sure that he had heard aright. 'You mean? You mean . . .?'

'Oh do stop spluttering, you silly man,' I laughed.

'What I mean is, that if you *didn't* find Tiliu desirab[le] I'd think there was something wrong with you. No[w] be a good boy and confess to me. You do find Ti[liu] pretty, don't you?'

'Yes, but . . .'

'No buts. And you have felt her up more th[an] once?'

'Yes,' he said, after a little hesitation.

'And you would roger her if you got half a chance[?]'

A longer pause, and the inevitable, 'Yes!'

I leaned forward and looked mock-solemnly in[to] his face. Before he could begin to squirm again I gi[g]gled and said, 'Well why not ask her then? I know f[or] a fact that she has a fancy for you!'

The shock, doubt and delight that chased them[-] selves across his face were a joy to behold, and the[n] he grabbed my hands and began to kiss them, blur[t]ing, 'Oh, Lydia! You are the most wonderful girl. A[re] you sure? You would not mock me . . .'

I felt such a flush of happiness as I had not felt fo[r] ages. I pulled my hands away. 'Well now, Jonatha[n.] After all that excitement,' I said, 'I feel like a stroll i[n] the garden. No, no! You stay here.' His eyes lit up. [I] turned at the edge of the veranda and frowned at hi[m] fiercely. 'Just so long, you naughty, naughty man, a[nd] you do not start neglecting *me*!'

By the time I had reached the turn in the pat[h] which led to the stables Tiliu had emerged from th[e] house to clear away the tea things. I was too far o[ff] to hear what was said but, stationing myself behind [a] tall bush, I had a clear view of all that transpired [—] and pretty it was, too!

As Tiliu bent to place the cups onto the tra[y] Jonathan said something. She straightened up, clearl[y] startled, and looked quickly about her. Jonatha[n]

196

:ood; she backed away. He spoke again; Tiliu
acked against one of the veranda's posts. He ap-
roached, took her hand. She bowed her head and he
fted her chin with his fingers. He spoke again. She
owed her head again as his hand slipped from her
hin down towards her breast. He took both her
ands in his. She looked up into his face and smiled.
'ogether they turned and moved towards the house.
ust as they were going through the door I saw his
and slide down to fondle her pert bottom.

Oh! My desire to rush back and peep at what was
appening was almost irresistible, but resist I did. At
ast, unable to contain myself, I rushed around to the
ide of the house, thinking to go to my parlour and
ound the piano for distraction. But they had got
here first. As I hurried past my window something
nade me look in, and there they were. I had thought
hey would go up to Tiliu's room, but clearly they
ad been in too much of a hurry and had rushed to
ny parlour as the nearest haven.

Even as I first glimpsed them Jonathan was leaning
Tiliu back across my table. Her bodice was gaping
nd her pretty breasts jiggled as she fell back, an ex-
ression of delight on her face. Jonathan's breeches
vere about his knees. He hauled Tiliu's skirts up to
ier waist. She never wore drawers, and in an instant
ier ankles were locked about Jonathan's waist and he
vas in her to the hilt and pumping like a wild thing.
Ooh, what a delicious sight! My own hand flew to my
tomach as their excitement washed over me, too.

When Jonathan returned to where I sat on the
reranda, he seemed awkward, even though his eyes
gleamed. It seemed neither of us could think of any-
hing to say! Tiliu, too, seemed nervous when she
rought a fresh pot of tea out to us. After all, she

could not know that it was I who had instigated th encounter, and she was anxious I might suspect an become annoyed. All in all, it was very awkward And then, heaven be praised, Jonathan broke the im passe, and in the most direct way.

'I am the luckiest man in the whole of Africa!' h said, suddenly standing and stretching his arms. looked at him in surprise. 'To have a lovely girl as m friend is a joy. To have *two* is very heaven! Ladies, salute you. It may well be my fate to roger myself t death with the two most glorious girls in the world.

I looked at Tiliu, she looked at me, both of us fo the moment amazed by this outrageous speech. The the ridiculousness hit us like a tidal wave and in . moment we were collapsed in each other's arms, al three of us howling with laughter and gasping fo breath. And for a few weeks after that it really wa as if Jonathan was trying to roger himself to death for at any and every opportunity (and the cunning fellow found many!) he would take one or the othe of us aside. Why, the greedy fellow must have worr out the buttonholes on his breeches!

Chapter 12

Despite all my efforts at friendliness, Felicity Mackay became more and more a bane in my life. Although very lovely to look upon, she was astonishingly dull-witted and petty minded. And what is more, had taken a dislike to me because of my easy friendships with Jonathan and her father (although obviously she only knew the surface!). It was common knowledge that she had set her cap at Jonathan long before I arrived in the town, and my advent had clearly put her nose out of joint. Because we were among the very few young ladies of social standing in the town, and because of the close association of her father and mine, we were thrown much together, and no matter how patient and conciliatory I was, I seemed unable to get it into her thick head that I was not a rival or a threat.

It seemed that no matter what I did she would seek to belittle me, finding any way she could to queen it over me. If I wore a new frock, she would find ways of damning with faint praise – oh, it was such a good colour, though perhaps a little bold for one of my complexion; oh, how lovely, and isn't it a pity that such bows are out of the fashion! She was catty where everybody else was sympathetic about the months I had been away with the Dutchmen, making little hints and remarking archly that it was strange the

Boers should have been so kind to me when they were being beastly to the British generally, and she wondered why.

She was an inch or two taller than I, with a full-bosomed figure made all the more noticeable by her erect bearing and admirable dress sense. Her hair, which she always wore beautifully set with combs and ribbons, was a lustrous red-brown. Her large, dark eyes were set off with long lashes and dark, bowed eyebrows which lent added beauty to her flawless, pale complexion. All this plus a heart-shaped face with full, lustrous lips, drew all eyes to her whenever she entered a room, and made her shine in our limited society. That she thought of me as a rival was in fact rather flattering, for I thought she far outshone me. Perhaps the only flaw in her loveliness, and one had to look closely to detect it, was a little downward turn at the corners of her mouth which hinted at meanness of spirit – a feature only I seemed to be aware of.

What finally strained my patience and caused me to feel positive irritation was a series of belittling remarks made when she, Jonathan and I were strolling around the barrack square one evening. Among other pettinesses, these included heavy hints that I was no better than I should be and that perhaps my time with the Dutch was not so innocent as I pretended. Quite how I held myself back from berating her I know not. Even Jonathan was put out by her behaviour and our stroll ended more quickly than we had intended.

Later, as Jonathan drove me home in the trap, he expressed his surprise at Felicity's mood, for usually, with him, she was all gaiety and simper. He seemed genuinely surprised when I explained that she was clearly jealous of our friendship. Oh, he was aware that she had a fancy for him. Indeed, he had a fancy

her, for she was, in his words, 'very toothsome'.
ow silly she was, though for *our* friendship could
t effect her at all. He was not the marrying kind,
d Felicity was the kind of girl to have only that on
r mind. His final remarks on the subject, when we
d drawn the trap behind some shrubs and our
nds had begun to wander deliciously, that she was
tainly too straight-laced and prissy to engage in
s kind of game, set my mind to work.

Was she? Was any girl, when it came down to it?
rely all the social frippery I had become aware of
okened that, although forbidden as an open topic,
ations betwen the sexes, consciousness of physical
ssibilities, was pretty close to the surface? I began
develop a germ of an idea. I watched Felicity more
sely.

As I have said, she was not very bright, and al-
ough tenacious enough to focus and maintain a
mpaign against me, she lacked the subtlety to en-
ely mask those little signs that a watchful
tagonist might pick up on. I had all along suspec-
d, because of her concern for her looks and the cut
her clothes, that Felicity's physicality was not far
neath her surface. Now, as I observed her, my sus-
cions grew to sureties. I noticed that her glance
uld frequently focus, and linger, on gentlemen's
ousers – especially the tight breeches of the soldiery.
aw her become a little flushed one morning when
e came upon a group of Africans splashing in the
er, their bodies only visible above their waists, but
ggesting that they were possibly unclad, and I
iled to myself that she found it hard to drag her
es away, even squinting sidelong as we walked past.
d most of all, I noted with delight the way she
came very flustered and red when, as we sat in her

father's garden, a trooper in the barracks stable ya
led out a stallion and held its bridle while it mount
a pretty roan mare.

Confident in my assessment of Felicity, I put
proposition to Jonathan. At first he demurred b
then, enticed by the prospect I held out to him a
his part in it, and egged on, I have no doubt, by t
fact that he, too, now thought Felicity needed brin
ing down a peg or two, he agreed, and we set out
plot.

During the next week or so, Jonathan paid mu
more gallant attention to Felicity, especially when
three were together. She blossomed. She queened
and simpered and, becoming convinced th
Jonathan would be hers, condescended to me wi
arch graciousness. Jonathan and I played up to h
Soon, she had convinced herself that he was her be
and became just a touch possessive, in the way gi
who have made their conquest do. As well, she b
came nicely relaxed and flirtatious with Jonathan
just enough for him to become a little daring, ev
risqué, without being repulsed.

For his own part, Jonathan kept me up to da
about his progress when I was not with them. I
acted the swain, he said, made eyes, touched h
hand, put his arm about her waist, became red-fac
and excited. That was not difficult, he said, for wh
being flirtatious Felicity was indeed delectab
Luckily, he told me, moving deliciously between n
thighs, there was never any chance for his frustratio
to build up while Tiliu and I were his friends! He ha
even managed, though theirs was not yet an offici
courtship, to steal a few kisses. By the time his birt
day eve arrived, they were on delightfully famili
terms.

Jonathan's birthday was our chosen time. We had ranged to have a celebratory tea at my house, just e three of us. By now, assured of her success, Felty was much more friendly with me, and had not ojected when Jonathan had suggested the location. e had taken great pains with her appearance and oked, I had to admit, lovely indeed. She was wearg a plain skirt of cream cotton, buttoned down the ont, and cut so that it flowed down over her ripe ps to fall to her feet in soft folds which drew atten-on to the length of her legs. Her narrow waist was own off by a sash of brown silk, tied at the side in soft bow. Her short, close-fitting jacket was of the me material as her skirt, with brown frogging about e buttons on the front, and a neckline cut square oove her breasts, from which the flounces of her oile blouse rose to a frilled collar close about her egant throat. Her hair hung in burnished ringlets, opped with a tiny bonnet echoing the colours of her ostume and sash. I had deliberately dressed quite lainly, and Felicity's eyes sparkled with triumph at e constrast between us.

At our little tea party Jonathan fawned on her, ushing over the present she had brought him, whis-ering in her ear that she was the most beautiful oman in the world and touching her hand. On the xcuse of his birthday, we drank some champagne. elicity's objections that it was too early in the day, nd anyway she had never drunk it, were easily over-ome by Jonathan's pleas and his toast 'to our iendship'. They focused more and more on each ther. Felicity simpered, became all eyes for Jonathan nd then drank a second glass of champagne. Even nis small amount of the wine had made her flushed, nd it was a simple matter to persuade her that she

was too hot and should take off her jacket. The vo
of her blouse showed off her delicious figure to adva
tage, and Jonathan's eyes glittered. I absented mys
to put her jacket in the next room – though, natural
not quite closing the connecting door – and po
tioned myself so that I could hear all and see most

Their conversation became animated, droppi
often to whispers. Felicity became giggly. Jonath
held her hand and kissed her lightly. Felicity becar
coy. He kissed her again. Then, feigning a need f
gentlemanly self-control, he went to the window. I
called her across, remarking on the beauty of the eve
ing sky. She went to him and he stood close, pointi
to the glories of the vista. Now was time for the lit
drama we had arranged. Though I could not actual
see it from where I hovered, it was vivid in my mind
I watched and listened for Felicity's reactions.

*Into view, holding hands like lovers the world ove
come John-John and Tiliu. They were walking slow
rapt in each other's company. They pause near a tre
His arm goes around her waist, pulls her close. Th
kiss lingeringly.*

Felicity caught her breath and leaned forward to g
a clearer view. Jonathan put his hand on her waist
he leaned close to her.

*Tiliu leans back against the tree trunk. John-John lif
her chin and kisses her again. As she returns his ki
his hand moves to her breast. She does not demur, b
links her hands around his neck as he fumbles with th
buttons of her simple frock, pulling the material apa
to expose her pert breasts, over which his hand rov
knowingly.*

204

elicity uttered a tiny 'Oh!' and put her hand to her mouth. Jonathan whispered something and held her closer, his hand moving a little so that it was poised in the swell of her hip just beneath the sash.

Tiliu drops her arms to aid John-John in pulling the rock off her shoulders. Naked to the waist, she raises her hands to his nape, her breasts rising to meet the hands which reach for them. As he kisses and fondles her, Tiliu reaches down with one hand and caresses John-John's crotch with slow, lascivious strokes.

Felicity gasped and straightened, as if shocked and anxious to move away from the window. Jonathan held her more tightly, whispered in her ear, kissed her lightly on her cheek. She blushed and dropped her eyes, but remained at the window, pretending not to watch what was happening outside, but her little gasps and tensings revealing that she was observing all, and that my judgement of her sensuality had not been wrong! Jonathan's hand was now fully on her hip, almost, indeed, on her buttock, and he moved his other hand to her upper arm.

Tiliu has undone John-John's shirt and is kissing and stroking the hard muscles of his chest. With both hands, he is raising her skirt. As his hand slips between her parted thighs, Tiliu is caressing his groin more and more actively. They sink to the ground and lie back together. Tiliu's skirt is at her waist, her thighs together, hiding the place he is fondling but not concealing the way his hand is moving upon her. Tiliu's arms are above her head, her body abandoned to John-John's caresses, her breasts pointing to the sky. John-John kisses them, begins to nibble and suck.

205

At the window Felicity, her face flushed, tried to move away, muttering protests. Jonathan seized his opportunity to hold her more closely, hushed her protests, kissed her, persuaded her not to go. The effects of the champagne added to Felicity's fluster, and she seemed not to notice that the hand had moved from her arm and was now resting lightly on the underswell of her breast.

John-John is kneeling beside Tiliu. She smiles up at him, and spreads her thighs as he fumbles with the buttons of his fly.

At the instant his engorged cock leapt into view, Felicity gasped, and fell against Jonathan in a faint.

I was sure it was one of those faints young ladies use as a ploy, Jonathan possibly less so, for her collapse was sudden and her gasp heartrending. He scooped her up in his arms and carried her across to the couch. We had not planned on a faint. We had assumed that getting Felicity a little tipsy, exciting her somewhat by the lascivious scenes outside the window, and some ardent courting from Jonathan would win our day. Now, we had a brilliant opportunity and Jonathan did not fail to seize it!

Expressing dismay at her collapse, Jonathan touched Felicity's forehead, rubbed her wrists, checked her pulse and then the beat of her heart. She stirred at that, for in doing so he placed his hand full upon her breast. She struggled up, all fluster and confusion. He threw his arm about her shoulders, cried in relief at her recovery, kissed her and pressed another glass of champagne upon her 'to make her feel better'. Felicity drank it down. She leaned against him on the couch, his arm about her shoulders as he dabbed her brow with his handkerchief.

Jonathan lifted Felicity's chin, murmuring how lovely she was, and kissed her upon her lips. Without hesitation, she returned his kiss. He covered her with kisses, her eyes, cheeks and throat. As he moved back to claim her lips again, they sank against the back of the couch, and his hand went to her breast. She did not protest, indeed returned his kiss with equal passion. When his hand slipped between the buttons of her blouse to cup and squeeze the breast within, Felicity gave a muffled squeal, and her hand fluttered to cover his. She gripped his wrist and tried to pull his hand away. He would not be denied. He kissed her with greater passion still, and leaning so that she was now half-reclined upon the couch, pressed himself against her. Her hand ceased to pull at his, and went to the front of his shoulder as though to push him away, though she did not.

When Jonathan broke off his wild kissing, Felicity did not protest at the hand which was freely exploring inside her blouse. She gazed up at him, her face flushed.

'Oh, Jonathan!' she said, her voice small. 'Please Jonathan, don't!' But she did not move to stop him. He groaned his passion for her and kissed her again. Her blouse was now fully undone. Her hands were on his neck as he kissed her, surrendering her delicious breasts to his touches. When his hand went to her lap, Felicity stiffened and murmured a protest and tried to push it away. She could not prevail in the face of his ardour.

His mouth moved to nuzzle her breasts. His hand ran over her clamped thighs, and found her vee, and pressed and rubbed. Felicity rolled her head from side to side, her face flushed.

'No, please. Please don't!' she repeated and repeated

in breathless gasps, at first with tones showing some panic, but slowly dying to querulous pleadings as his mouth and hands worked on her.

Whether it was a submission to his greater strength, or the stirrings of her own passion I could not tell, but I knew, with a flush of delighted excitement which made my already warm cunny lurch and tense, the moment of her surrender. She gave a shuddering sigh. She murmured, 'Do you love me? Tell me you love me, Jonathan!' Her eyes rolled and slowly closed. The tension in her thighs disappeared. Jonathan sensed it also and his fondlings became gentler. He kissed her mouth and whispered that she was so lovely she could drive a man to madness.

Felicity slumped, fully reclined upon the couch now, and only murmured something as Jonathan's hand explored the length of her thighs, reached down, slipped beneath her hem then rose again, bringing the skirt with it. She trembled and covered her face with her hands as Jonathan's moved slowly up, above her garter, onto the cambric of her drawers, up and inward to cup her vee. Her thighs clamped, then suddenly relaxed as he fondled her.

I could not breathe, and found myself pressing a hand to my own quim as Jonathan explored Felicity's. She gasped another, 'No. Please don't!', as he tugged at the waist ties of her drawers and began to pull them down. Oh, she was delicious. I could not help but rub my cunny against the doorhandle for relief as Jonathan pulled off Felicity's drawers and folded her skirt up onto her waist, revealing wonderful, marble thighs above the black of her stockingtops. How he could contain himself when confronted with such glorious feminine charms I know not, and for sure the bulge in Jonathan's breeches was huge!

Contain himself he did, though, and instead of leaping upon her then and there, he set himself to working her up even more.

Kneeling beside her as she reclined on the couch, he kissed her softly upon her lips while his fingers gently traced the line of her thighs, ran lightly over her stomach and hips, and eased down into the reddish fuzz of her vee. He slipped his fingers down, seeking her folds. Her thighs were still closed, but not so much as to prevent access. His fingertips moved. She gasped as he found her cherry, then she whispered some kind of protest. She covered her flushed face with her hands again as Jonathan moved to kiss her breast, her stomach and her thighs.

I had to cram my hand to my mouth to stifle a groan as, grinding myself against the doorknob, I throbbed towards a come at the sight of Felicity's lovely thighs responding to Jonathan's kisses and gentle nudges, slowly moving apart, exposing the most delicious of cunnies to Jonathan's fingertips and tongue. She gave a shuddering gasp as he parted her soft folds, his tongue at once lapping at her cherry. His fingertips explored the length of her glistening crease, down to the cleft between her round buttocks and back again, to tease her moist nether lips. Her face still clasped in trembling hands, Felicity was no longer dissembling surrender, for her breathing was ragged and the muscles of her stomach and thighs were bunching and straining in reaction to Jonathan's touches – touches I well knew to be capable of driving a girl wild!

That she was far gone was amply shown when Jonathan ceased his lickings and touchings, and moved to undo his breeches, for she did not move. Did not close her legs. With a smile of triumph,

Jonathan looked to where he knew I was hiding. His cock reared with fierce pride as he parted Felicity's knees further, and moved to kneel between them. As he leaned down, Felicity's hands flew to his shoulders as if to hold him off, but then, as his engorged plum found her folds, slipped back and forth along them then ultimately found her opening, she gave a sobbing gasp. Her eyes were hooded and her mouth slack as Jonathan moved. Her thighs tensed and her hips lifted as he pressed against her glistening entrance, as if her body was instinctively helping him to find the right place. He found; he pushed. Her eyes flew open and she gave a cry as he thrust into her, tearing through her virginity in one movement. For an instant, Felicity was rigid, her mouth agape, as he thrust to her depths. Then, in a change that had me coming at the recollection of how it felt, surprise flickered across her brow, her mouth slackened, her eyes rolled and slowly closed, as Jonathan began to move in her, his hips rising and circling, his hard body tensing and flexing.

So rapt was I by the voluptuous sight that for a while I forgot what I was supposed to do. Felicity's arms had fallen above her head in abandonment of control. Her chest was flushed. Her feet had hooked themselves behind Jonathan's knees. Her pelvis was circling, pressing against him. Did I look thus transported when Jonathan fucked me? Oh! I wanted to rush in, to throw myself upon them, to join in, to share the glory they were feeling! With difficulty I gathered myself, took quick breaths to calm my sensations and mopped the cleft between my breasts in an effort to cool myself.

I waited, composing myself. Jonathan's body bucked and writhed as he burst into his come. Felicity whimpered, her eyes and mouth wide, as he pumped his all into her. His body slackened then ceased to move on her. He looked down at her flushed face, her eyes now closed. He kissed her then moved from between her limp thighs to sit on the couch, resting her head on his lap. He stroked her damp brow.

'Do you love me, Jonathan?' she murmured, touching his hand with her own. She moved her body a little to accommodate his other hand, which now sought her breast, pulling her clothing further apart so that her pale, flushed orbs were fully bared. 'I love you. I love you, Jonathan. Say you love me!'

I watched the delicious tableau for a minute or two. Her surrender was complete, absolute, as he gentled her, murmuring wordlessly, caressing her brow and temples, teasing with a fingertip the proud nubs perking from her areolas. She had not moved to lower her skirt, which still lay above her creamy, parted thighs. She was as if in a dream, her breathing soft, her hands limp upon the couch. I crept into the room.

Jonathan smiled at me triumphantly as I lowered myself silently into an armchair close by the end of the couch where Felicity's parted feet lay. Those feet twitched, and Felicity mewed softly as Jonathan's hand moved to cup her moist cunny. Her knees closed a little for an instant, then fell apart as Jonathan began to work on her. Her eyes remained closed and her breathing quickened as his fingertips explored her folds, parted them, teased her swollen cherry then slipped into her glistening opening. Her eyes stayed closed as he moved to kneel beside her again, close by her head. His hand still gently fondling between her thighs, he eased her head towards the edge of the couch, her face close against his half-slumbering cock.

'Do you love me, Felicity?' he whispered, edging closer at her murmured yeses. His swelling plum was a hair's breadth from her red, full-lipped mouth. 'Kiss me, Felicity, kiss me!' Without looking, she moved to kiss, then pulled a little back, surprised that it was not his lips she met. She looked up at him, her eyes now wide with surprise and doubt. Jonathan's hand was caressing her nape, and gently holding her head still. He moved his hips a little, touching his plum again to her mouth.

'Kiss me, my darling Felicity! Kiss me to show you love me!' She blushed, her eyes flicking from his face to the cock which now reared so close. Doubt, perhaps even a little fright flickered across her lovely features. She closed her eyes and with a tiny sigh, she moved her face and kissed him full upon the tip of his erection.

He remained at her lips. 'Love me, Felicity! Honour me with your beautiful mouth!' he whispered gruffly, pressing himself against her. The hand between her thighs circled and pressed knowingly. Slowly, oh, so slowly, her trembling lips parted. Gently, he nudged. Her mouth opened, the tip of her pink tongue showed for an instant as he slid between her lips. He did not push, merely rocked a little, not even the whole of his plum in her, though a little more each time, as she began to suck like a baby at a breast. As the curved ridge between his plum and shaft slipped into her soft mouth, her hand moved to grip his base, to press gently against his thigh. She, too, was moving now, adopting his slow rhythm, moving her mouth onto him then slipping back in a cadence which took my breath away. Oh, if Felicity was beautiful under normal circumstances, she was loveliness personified now as, with eyes closed and eyebrows arched beatifically, with her ivory thighs

212

nd tummy writhing slowly, lasciviously, beneath his
and, her breasts flushed and naked, she pleasured
onathan with her delicious mouth!

I had long thought Felicity had a sensual nature
oncealed beneath her mannerly surface. Now that
urface was abandoned and she became a complete
oluptuary as her mouth moved upon Jonathan's
ock and her hips circled beneath the hand in her
uim. I could hardly contain myself at the sight of her
bandonment, and felt my own quim writhing in
ympathy with hers.

Jonathan did not come. Instead, after long minutes
f her delicious sucking, he pulled out, and bent to
iss her upon her flushed cheek. Lifting her in his
rms, he moved to sit beside her on the couch. Felic-
ty leaned against him, her face resting on his chest,
er hand remaining on his deflating cock. I sat un-
noving and silent, and for a long while she was
nconscious of my presence. When she saw me, she
creamed.

All was suddenly panic! She sobbed then scrambled
o throw down her disarranged skirts, close her blouse
ver her breasts and beat her fists on Jonathan's
hest, all at once. She screamed that he was a mon-
ter, a ravisher, a destroyer of innocence. On and on
he went, and I thought she would truly go into a fit
f hysterics. Jonathan grasped her with both arms,
olding her tight to calm her struggles. I had meant to
emain when our scheme reached this stage, to join in
elling Felicity about her new situation in life. Instead,
eeing how her wild eyes regarded me, I thought it
est to leave them alone until her raging had ceased.

I did not know what Jonathan said to her or how
e calmed her, but when I returned an hour later
he change in Felicity was dramatic indeed. She was

sitting next to him on the couch, her clothing nea
and correct, looking chastened, flushed and rathe
timorous. Her hands were clasped in her lap and he
eyes were lowered. Jonathan sat relaxed, and the only
sign that anything out of the ordinary might have
occurred was that his left hand rested lightly upon
Felicity's right thigh. He smiled and welcomed me
when I re-entered the room, but Felicity seemed to
flinch a little, her eyes flicking in my direction before
lowering again, her blush deepening.

'Felicity and I have had a long talk, haven't we my
dear,' said Jonathan, his hand moving a little on the
cream cotton of her skirt. 'We are all good friends
now, and dear Felicity is sorry for her outburst
Aren't you, my sweet!'

She did not look at me this time, but nodded almos
imperceptibly. Whatever it was that Jonathan had said
to her, whatever the persuasions he had used, the effec
was wonderful, for she seemed humility personified.

As if to demonstrate there and then the completeness of Felicity's surrender, Jonathan suggested that
I ordered some tea and, while we waited for Tiliu to
bring it, he told me that Felicity had 'given him his
birthday present', though naturally he did not say
what it had been. He had no need to, for even as he
spoke Felicity darted a glance at me, gave a sigh almost like a whimper, and blushed again even more
deeply. He slipped his arm around her and, talking
about how nice it would be now that we three were
true friends, moved to openly cup her voluptuous
breast in his hand. Felicity gasped and shuffled in her
seat, looking anxiously from him to me, and made as
if to push the hand away.

'Now, now, my sweet,' Jonathan said, almost as if
he were addressing a naughty infant. 'Don't be silly

We are all friends here, and anyway . . .' He bent and whispered in her ear. Felicity paled then flushed, cast a timorous glance at me, and dropped her hand. For the rest of the time before they left to take Felicity home, she said nothing, nor did she resist or protest as Jonathan continued to toy with her breasts, even while Tiliu was serving us our tea. She did not look at me either except once, when they were leaving, a glance of such nervous pleading that I verily felt a lump in my throat.

Though desperate to know how Jonathan had worked the miracle of chastening Felicity so, I had to contain myself until the next afternoon, when he came to ride with me (both with and without horses, of course!). What he told me made me laugh aloud with delight! It seemed that he had simply slapped her face (but only lightly) to shock her from her hysteria, then rolled her across his knee and spanked her bottom as if she were a naughty child! The effect had been instant. Though squealing and begging him to stop, she had hardly struggled at all, and when, in mid-spank as it were, he had slipped his hand between her thighs to feel what he called 'her irresistible cunt', she had stopped squealing and begging, and even, he swore, parted her legs a little.

Afterwards, although she had wept a little, she had told him she loved him, apologised for being a bad girl and begged him not to be cruel to her. She had sworn that she would be good if only he would tell her he loved her. Ah, she had been so sweet and humble, he told me, so grateful when he kissed and fondled her. It was as if the very thought that he loved her had opened all doors (and buttons) for him. Why, she had hardly hesitated at all when he allowed her to give his cock a few more sucks!

215

Chapter 13

I was able to witness for myself Felicity's new-found complaisance only a couple of days later, for Jonathan had arranged for us to drive out for a picnic by the river. He told me, with a smile, that Felicity had wanted to go alone with him. He had squashed the idea and, being now delightfully obedient, she had accepted his decision.

Jonathan drove the trap, for we had brought no servant with us. Felicity sat very quiet and with her head bowed as we drove but, from where I sat opposite her, I noticed that several times her eyes flicked to where Jonathan sat in the driving seat, whereupon she would blush and give a little sigh.

She did not look in my direction at all and so I was able to observe her closely. She wore a very pretty green hat with a narrow brim. It was fastened with large silver pins, which nicely set off the red-brown tresses which flowed about her shoulders. The hat matched her gloves and full skirt, and the richness of their colour was set off by the white, pleated, high collared blouse which completed her outfit. Whether she had calculated her effect I cannot know, but she looked so fresh and demure that one could not have dreamed how she had behaved so recently, albeit under the influence of a little champagne, Jonathan's persuasiveness and a little spanking.

When Jonathan had lifted the picnic things down from the trap, Felicity hurried to start unpacking, but I was ahead of her. With my sweetest smile, I suggested that she and Jonathan should go for a walk beside the river while I set out the rugs and foodstuffs. Felicity hesitated, looked at me questioningly, then blushed delicately and turned to go with him. My smile broadened as they walked away from me. We would soon know how complete her surrender was.

They returned after about half an hour. Jonathan was smiling broadly and almost strutting, his thumbs hooked in his belt. Felicity was rather red of face and could only look at the ground. I could see that the front of her skirt was quite creased. She said nothing at all and did not even glance at me as I told them where to sit and began serving out the food. Nor did she respond save with the occasional sigh as Jonathan and I chatted lightly about the niceness of the day and the prettiness of the country, and invited her comments.

Her first real reaction came when I remarked that her back was covered in grass, and chided Jonathan that a gentleman really ought to brush his lady down afterwards. A tear trickled down her delicate cheek. We both 'come, come'd and 'there, there'd, and Jonathan moved around to sit beside her and put his arm about her shoulder. She sank against him, her head bowed, tears pouring down her cheeks and dripping from her dimpled chin unchecked.

'Come now, Felicity,' I said. 'Come now. Do not be upset. You are not a bad girl at all. It is not wrong to enjoy what you did with dear Jonathan!'

From her downcast expression, she would clearly need some convincing. Could it be that what really upset Felicity were the sensations she had felt, the desires, the welcomings, when Jonathan had so aroused her? Could it be she felt that in surrendering herself to him thus, she had become immoral? In our society, as well I knew, the loose woman was the object of contempt. Was despised. Did Felicity feel that by reacting as she had, she was such a creature? Certainly there was in her eyes something shadowy. Was it shame, or was I imputing to her from my own guesses? Since she had sagged back against him, Jonathan had begun fondling both her breasts, and the way she shuddered and reddened suggested that might be right.

Or was it just that she was uncomfortable being handled thus in front of me? Certainly, she had always pretended to be better than me, a pretence she could in no way now maintain.

'Do not be a ninny, Felicity,' I said. 'We all enjoy such feelings!' She looked at me with surprise and doubt, a tear still in her eye. 'Come. We are friends here. We all know that you enjoy it. Is that not so Jonathan?' He laughed softly and squeezed her breasts a little more firmly, making her blush even more. 'There! Jonathan says you enjoy it, so you might as well confess. I know that *I* enjoy it.'

Her eyes widened with surprise, and suddenly I understood. Why, the silly little numbskull thought that she alone had 'fallen' (as she became wont to call it). It had not occurred to her dull imagination that other girls, least of all myself, could experience and enjoy such games.

I had moved closer to them as I spoke, and now reached out and began to rub my hand on Jonathan's lap. Felicity's eyes widened as I unbuttoned his breeches, and they widened further when I parted them and his cock, half-stiff, lolled out. She gasped

d turned her face, but I noticed that she did not
rn so far as to be unable to see what was happening
om the corner of her eye! Jonathan parted his legs
d I eased his hairy balls out of the breeches. I be-
n to stoke him and he reared stiffly. I cooed and
urmured how pretty his cock was, and tried to put
r hand upon it but she snatched away. She was
tually trembling, but I noticed that her gaze had
t shifted!

It was a delicious situation. Here was Felicity, torn
her and thither by what Jonathan was doing to her
som and her shame at her own sensations, and yet
cinated about what I was saying and doing. Here
s Jonathan, who must have been in seventh heaven
ndling one young woman and being fondled by an-
er. And here was I determining the course of what
uld happen! I enjoyed the sense of power even
ore that I enjoyed the feeling of Jonathan throbbing
my hands.

The piquancy of the situation struck me as I
oked the length of his lovely rod. What had begun
ply as a plot to bring this girl down a peg or two,
d have some fun with her, had changed so that now
as giving her a lesson in how to give, and to admit
eiving, the pleasures of sex! To be sure, getting
licity to admit that she felt pleasure was unlikely,
though she had amply demonstrated it, and would
so again, in our society for a girl to admit such a
ng would be truly shocking. And in fact, Felicity
vays pretended reluctance at the beginning of any
ne, as though in doing so she could maintain her
f-image as a good girl being led astray.

Although I was enjoying the activity as much as I
vays did, I did not caress Jonathan for very long,
t stopped while he was very stiff. Felicity was still

219

pretending not to look. Her face was flushed and her
eyes half-closed as Jonathan's hands caressed her
breasts, one of them inside her now unbuttoned
blouse.

'There,' I said. 'Is Jonathan's member not delicious? I like it as much as you do.' She blushed and
dropped her eyes. 'Come on, Felicity. You touch him
now!' Her eyes flashed wide again. She squirmed and
flushed deeper. 'Don't be a goose,' I said. 'You know
you want to really.'

I held Jonathan's shaft in my hand again and was
stroking it slowly. Felicity's gaze moved from my eyes
to what was in my hand. She blushed deeper and took
a trembling inward breath. Tentatively, as though
fearing she might be burnt, she reached out a hand.
There! She was holding him, moving her hand as
was mine, her eyes gazing fixedly at Jonathan's cock
like a rabbit at a stoat.

For long, silent moments, Felicity stroked him.
Then Jonathan gently kissed her cheek and whispered, loud enough for me to hear, 'Gobble me,
darling. Take me in your pretty mouth!'

Felicity gasped and snatched her hand away,
blushed furiously. Jonathan moved one of his hands
to her nape, still kissing her, and from the way Felicity stiffened I guessed that he was gently pressing her
forward.

'Go on,' I said, 'you know you want to. You know
you enjoyed it last time.'

Slowly, with Jonathan's hand on her neck all the
while Felicity bent forward. A few inches above her
target she stopped. She glanced up at me briefly, her
eyes puzzled and appealing. I smiled and nodded.
Felicity sighed deeply, and licked her lips. Jonathan
pressed. Only when she was right upon him did she

220

rt her lips. I felt a surge of tingling warmth as her soft
ɔuth slid onto him. Jonathan's hand rested lightly on
r head, not influencing the way she bobbed slowly up
d down. I could see from the movements of her cheeks
d throat that she was sucking actively, as I had known
e would. I reached up and removed Jonathan's hand
ɔm her neck. Her movements continued as before and
ɛw, if anything, a little deeper, more voluptuous. Her
uctance having been conquered by our joint persua-
ɔns, Felicity surrendered to the act, and thoroughly
ijoyed the cock her tongue was rolling around.

Jonathan's hips began to move. With a glance I
ɪrned him to be still. I wanted Felicity to do this
rself, to know that she had done so and to be un-
le afterwards to tell herself she had been forced.
nathan kept still. Felicity's cheeks puffed as she
ɔved down and sucked in as she pulled back. For
ɪg minutes the licentious tableau continued, and I
ɛw hot indeed, my bosom tense to bursting.

At last Jonathan could contain himself no longer.
s eyes closed, his loins jerked and with a gasp he
gan his come. Here was my proof, for Felicity did
t pause in her efforts! If anything, she sank deeper
to him, and the movements of her throat showed
ɪt she was swallowing all. She continued even after
nathan sagged back at the end of his come. At last
e released him and for a moment rested her fore-
ɪd upon his thigh before slowly rising, her head
wed. On an impulse I threw my arms about her
d hugged her to me.

'Good girl!' I cried. She leant against me, her head
on my shoulder. I lifted her chin and smiled into
r eyes. 'There! Was that not delicious? Was it not a
light?' I could not resist giving her a little kiss on
e forehead.

221

She dropped her eyes and gave a sigh. She cou
not bring herself to agree but she had not denied
and that was good enough for now.

The afternoon continued its happy course witho
cloud. Although Felicity said almost nothing and a
ted entirely passively, she no longer made even ha
hearted protests and seemed to accept, rather th:
just submit to, our attentions. We continued our p
nic and although she did not eat very much, Felici
accepted several glasses of wine. Jonathan spent m
of the time fondling her in various ways, and :
though she blushed at each new intrusion s
accepted the undoing of her blouse and the exposu
of her glorious breasts to the daylight. She welcom
his hands and mouth, and the raising of her skirts a1
the insinuation of his hand inside her drawers. T
parting of her knees and the bright red patches on h
neck and cheeks were better confirmation than wor
would have been of her body's surrender to the se
sations he was stirring. She even lifted her bottom
assist him when he began to tug off her drawers, :
though as he got them to her knees she glanced at 1
apprehensively, as though I might be disapproving
her.

The sight of Felicity' deshabille and her submissi\
ness in the face of Jonathan's fondlings had raised 1
to a pitch, and at last I could no longer bear the sig
of Felicity lying back against Jonathan, her hard-ni
pled bosom lolling, his hand moving purposefu
between her thighs, without some satisfaction for 1
own arousal. I moved close beside Jonathan. Kiss
him. Whispered in his ear. He looked surprised fo1
moment as Felicity panted quietly and moved up
his hand, then he grinned hugely. What man wo1
not!

He lay back, Felicity reclining with him, her beau-
ful breasts trembling as she did so. Her knees lolled
 allow freedom to the hand moving sensuously be-
een her thighs. Jonathan had not done up his
eeches after Felicity had caressed him with her
outh, and I moved forward to touch and fondle his
mbering member, delighting in the way it slowly,
en more quickly, roused in my hands. I lifted the
nt of my skirts. I pulled off my drawers and moved
 straddle Jonathan's recumbent body, my leg be-
een his hip and Felicity's raised knee. The twill of
nathan's breeches scratched oh, so delicately
ainst my inner thighs, sending shivers through me
 I moved above him.
He was ready now, stiff and handsome, but no
ore ready than I! I lifted myself, guided him then
nk down with a shudder of joyous fulfilment. I
essed myself onto him and circled my pelvis upon
s, my lips and cherry rioting against the hardness of
 loins. Through the fiery mist of my passion, the
ght of Felicity lying so wantonly held my gaze. I
uld not help myself. I reached down and smoothed
y hand over her naked breast. She stirred slightly,
d placed her hand on mine, but not to push me
vay. I caressed her with more and more abandon as
ode Jonathan's glorious member, the very lining of
y sheath writhing greedily about him. Felicity
uealed as I churned into a wonderful come in per-
ct synchronicity with Jonathan's spasms, because in
y transport I had unwittingly pinched her erect
pple too hard. Afterwards, as Jonathan subsided
thin my oozing sheath, I leaned down to kiss the
licious breast, more for my own pleasure than by
y of apology, and felt another sweet lurch in my
mmy as the nipple perked against my tongue.

223

Poor Jonathan was, in his rather coarse expressio[n] 'shagged out' and needed a rest, so Felicity and [I] packed away the remains of the picnic and went f[or] a walk beside the river until it was time to dri[ve] home. The afternoon had been a triumph and I w[as] very happy as the trap rattled along. But then th[e] impish part of me prompted a new thought. I whi[s]pered it to Jonathan. His face lit up with surprise a[nd] delight, and he nodded eagerly. He drove the trap [to] a clump of shrubs and stopped. He whispered to F[el]icity. Her eyes widened. He spoke again. She blush[ed] and glanced at me. My thought had been for t[he] thing she had not had this afternoon, the joy of [the] shag – which would not only give her pleasure, b[ut] establish that she surrendered because she wanted [it] rather than because she was obliged or coerced.

I remained in the trap as Felicity and Jonath[an] climbed out. Jonathan kissed her, whispered agai[n] and Felicity turned and bent forward. She raised h[er] own skirts behind, pulled her own drawers down [to] her knees, and grasped the side of the trap, her fe[et] apart. Jonathan undid his breeches. How well a vi[g]orous man can recover! Although only an hour a[go] he had professed to being exhausted, his lovely co[ck] rose pround and rampant. He stepped forward. F[el]icity gasped and stiffened as he moved close. She ga[ve] a low moan as he slid the bulb of his member alo[ng] her exposed charms, bending his knees to reach b[e]neath, exploring the length of her moist folds and t[he] cleft between her gorgeous buttocks. Then he sl[id] down again to find her warm entrance. She gaspe[d] and gave a little cry as he entered her. Her pale, bea[u]tiful bottom trembled at each audible slap of his loi[ns] against her, and she was gasping and panting all t[he] while he ploughed her. His hands grasped her hips

id his thrusts. She groaned aloud as he burst into his
ome, then straightened slowly after he pulled out, as
 she had been carrying a heavy weight, and stared
t the ground as she pulled up her drawers and
traightened her skirts.

The only words she spoke during the rest of the
rive and when we deposited her at her house were in
 tiny whisper to Jonathan when, just before parting,
e fondled her bottom. I could hardly hear her, but
rilled with pleasure at the words. 'You hurt me a
ttle. That last time.'

Jonathan smiled and patted her bottom. 'Don't
orry, my dear,' he said. 'It will get nicer every time!'
nd with those words, not even pausing to say good-
ye, Felicity went into the house.

Over the next weeks I saw Jonathan a little less
ten than the almost daily visits of heretofore, which
as only natural I suppose and did not worry me. He
ave me what amounted to progress reports on Fel-
ity's development, and professed himself to be the
ckiest man alive in having not one but three deli-
ous girls to frolic with. Because of the proximity of
s own bachelor quarters to the captain's house, and
 the closeness of his friendship with his superior
ficer, and most of all because Mrs Mackay looked
vourably upon him as a suitor for her daughter's
nd, he found plentiful opportunities to be with her.
deed, both the captain and his wife actively encour-
ed their daughter to walk out with him. If only they
d known!

And it seemed that Felicity was no less eager than
r parents. Gone, it seemed, were her prissyness and
r inhibitions, at least when they were alone to-
ther. She did sometimes pretend reluctance, he told
, and once or twice he'd had to spank her. At my

protest, for I have always had a horror of such thin
and could not approve of anyone being thus cha
tised, he astonished me by saying that she seemed
get pleasure from it, and was always even more r
sponsive than usual after her bottom had be
tanned! I could hardly believe that anyone could d
rive pleasure from being spanked, but have be
assured since that such people really do exist. Ama
ing! One would never have guessed that Felicity w
one such from the maidenly dignity she pretend
whenever we were in company.

Pretending to be what one was not seemed to
the normal traffic among the people of the town.
all the gentlemen of my father's acquaintance, t
most pompous and pretentious of all was Dr Wi
iams, the vicar. He was the most sanctimonio
creature one could ever dread to meet. Had it n
been so comic, I would have found the pious wor
he spoke to me whenever we met decidedly unco
fortable, given the lie as they were by the way his ey
would crawl over me, and his little tongue would da
to wet his lips, quite as if he were undressing me
his head while he talked of God and morality! I kne
too, from Mrs Barnet's gossip, that Dr Williams w
not averse to becoming less than entirely spiritual
his dealings with his parishioners, for it seemed th
there had been a number of most unusual penan
imposed on the more naive girls of his congregatio
and several of his erstwhile servant-girls had tales
tell. Even Tiliu had been subject to a number of le
than fatherly pats and touches.

You can imagine, then, my thoughts when
learned that father had arranged an interview 'for r
spiritual well-being'! One would have thought th
even father might notice the oily smugness with whi

226

he vicar behaved around me, his lip-licking and
and-rubbing; they way he preened and leered. But
o. How blind can otherwise intelligent men be. I
ried hard to avert the interview but then, since father
vas insistent, consoled myself with the thought that
t least I might get some amusement from it.

I prepared for the visit by donning some of the
rettiest clothes I possessed – a brown skirt of light
otton, with only two muslin petticoats, and a high-
ollared, cream voile blouse with many tiny buttons,
ver a chemise cunningly darted to suggest the figure
rithin. Because I intended to tease the pompous little
nan, but wanted to ensure that matters would not get
ut of hand – or perhaps I should say *into* hand – I
ad suggested the parlour as the best place to meet.
is close to father's study and opens onto the en-
ance hall, and thus somebody or other would
lways be close by to act as a deterrent if the vicar
ot carried away. Unfortunately, father thought I
neant *my* parlour, my pretty little room at the very
ack of the house, and sent Dr Williams straight
rough to me.

My parlour was not large, and was made smaller
y my little upright piano and the table I used to take
a at and used as my writing desk. Apart from the
ngle upright chair at the table, the only seating was
small settee. Far from being able to keep off from
m I was to be thrust into the closest proximity, and
as well out of earshot of father.

The vicar sat upon my settee, smiling and looking
e up and down. I greeted him with my brightest
nile, even bobbed a tiny curtsey, and allowed my
nd to be taken by his rather pudgy one. A flicker
disappointment crossed his face when I sat on the
pright chair, instead of next to him on the settee, but

227

he soon began his sermonising. As I had guessed, railed against the Boers, telling me how evil th were, how disrespectful they were of our belov Queen Empress, how greedy and treacherous th were. They were devious and cowardly and ungrat ful, and oh, poor child (at this point he put his ha on my knee for the first time) I had been in th clutches for so long. And at such a tender age!

His face was glowing with his outrage and wi compassion for me. He took my hand and pulled n towards him. Ah! I must tell him of my sufferings, said. He would comfort me. He looked like a frog his earnestness, and had I not been so wary I wou have laughed aloud. I got my hand away from hi on the excuse of pouring some tea, and eased as f away as my chair would allow. He changed tac talking now of their lack of religion, of their hypo risy in daring to call themselves Christians wh refusing to accept 'God's own Church of Englar and Empire', of the ranting mumbo-jumbo of t 'so-called services' they held in their 'barbarian linge

'Oh, you poor child,' he said, leaning forward a laying his hand upon my knee again. 'To be dragg off to their so-called churches and exposed to th heresy, and all the while out of possession of yo critical faculties and the protection of your ov people.'

He was positively kneading my thigh in his passio though I feigned not to notice. He was becoming d liciously excited. He shuffled forward awkwardly his seat as he preached, his hand sliding further my leg. I gazed at him wide-eyed then, as if on sudden thought, reached for the bell to ring for sor more tea, moving just out of his reach to do so. I rose and would have paced had the room been larg at instead he walked to the window. After looking at for a little while he turned, and came to stand behind me.

I was a poor child who had suffered terribly, he said. I had experienced an attack by savages; had lost my faculties; had fallen into the hands of the heathen Dutch. They had held me at their mercy for long months. He stepped up behind me, his round belly close beside my head. He placed his hands upon my shoulders. They were hot, and he was breathing quickly.

'Ah, child,' he croaked. 'Who knows what terrible things they may have done to you.'

'They did nothing terrible, sir,' I replied, looking up at him and fluttering my eyelashes. 'They cared for me and brought me back home.'

'But only after months and months. And then only for money.'

He had moved closer beside me, one hand still on my shoulder, the other resting on my upper arm. 'They are our enemies, my child. They could have taken advantage of your innocence. Done anything!' I fluttered, and wondered aloud what he could mean. 'But how can we tell? You had no memory. And you are so innocent and lovely.'

Ah! Now we came to it! He bent towards me, his fat face red and glistening. The fingers that were on my arm stretched to touch the side of my breast. I gazed up at him in innocent puzzlement. 'They are our enemies. They would not hesitate to take advantage of an English girl in their clutches.' He was pulling me towards him. His hand was now almost fully on my breast.

I let him enjoy it for a moment or two, then said, 'Oh, sir, what can you mean?'

229

I got up from my chair and moved to the other si[de] of the table, not registering any reaction to the wa[y] he had been touching me. I gazed at him wide-eye[d] 'I do not understand what you mean when you sa[y] they took advantage of my innocence.'

'Ah! Exactly so!' he said, advancing around th[e] table. I did not yet retreat. He came close and lift[ed] my chin with a rather sweaty finger. 'How could o[ne] so sweet, so ignorant of the ways of the world, kno[w] what I mean?' His eyes were burning, and there w[as] a gleam of perspiration on his nose. His eyes fell [on] my bosom. I breathed deeply, and fluttered. Ha[d] Tiliu not entered with the tea things I am sure [he] would have touched it again.

Innocent that any such thing could be on his min[d] I offered him another cup of tea, and moved out [of] reach again. I could almost feel his frustration. Pee[r]ing under my eyelashes as I poured, I was hard p[ut] not to giggle at the frown on his reddened face, a[nd] the way he chewed his lip trying to think of his ne[xt] move in what was becoming a game of tag. I near[ly] did laugh at the way his features became sudden[ly] beaming and condescending when I looked up a[nd] held his cup out to him.

I went and stood at the window, half-turned awa[y] from the vicar, knowing that, thus, the brightne[ss] outside would make a shadow-show of my blouse. [I] reached up as if to tidy my hair, aware of the way m[y] breast lifted as I raised my arm. Dr Williams clear[ed] his throat loudly. When I turned back to him, his ey[es] were on stalks!

He recovered himself brilliantly. He buttoned h[is] frock coat, as much, I am sure, to conceal the bu[lge] I descried in his trousers as to give himself time [to] think.

'Well, well, my child,' he said, his voice a little
ick. 'Of course, one such as yourself cannot know
' the things of the flesh, things sanctioned only by
e marriage vows of our Church. How could you?
nd yet, as your spiritual guardian it is my duty to
sure that you have not been taken advantage of in
ur innocence.'

'In what way do you mean, sir?' I replied in my
yest manner.

He approached the window and stood close behind
e, a little to one side. His eyes were gleaming again
ith his new idea. 'My child,' he said, his voice deep
d almost liturgical. He placed a hand upon my
oulder. 'My sweet child, as your friend as well as
ur confessor,' (a liberty this, for I had never gone
 him for confession!) 'it is my duty to enquire into
ur time among those evil Boers. For who knows
ow they might have taken advantage of your inno-
:nce – such innocence, indeed, as might have left you
norant that their advances were less than honour-
ble.' He was quite close to me now and I could feel
is breath hot on my neck. 'Regard this room as the
onfessional, my child. Tell me all, as guardian of
ur soul. It cannot go further than our own ears.'

I turned towards him, allowing the hand to slip
om my shoulder to my waist. 'But, sir,' I simpered.
f I do not know what it is you mean, and know not
hat are the "advantages" to which you refer, how
an I possibly tell you?'

He held my forearm, and I allowed myself to be
uided to the settee. We sat, of necessity very close.
lis arm remained about my waist, the other hand
till on my upper arm, his face aglow with sincerity.

'My dear,' he said. Clearly I was no longer his
hild! 'Permit me to guide you in this difficult matter.

231

Did they, did they, for example,' he cleared his thro[at] noisily, 'kiss you?'

'Oh, yes. Every day, in my bedroom . . .' I blurte[d] turning eagerly towards him, not noticing that on[ce] again his tubby fingers were touching the side of [my] breast. His eyes lit, and he positively glowed at wh[at] I was about to reveal. 'Miss Henrietta would kiss [me] goodnight!'

I nearly burst into a giggle at his disappointmen[t]

'Miss Henrietta. I see,' he muttered, his regret th[at] my revelation had not been more salacious almo[st] palpable. He gathered himself for a fresh tack. 'P[er]haps, though, perhaps such a pretty thing as you a[re] attracted the attention of the men? Perhaps th[ey] made advances upon your person?'

'Advances, sir? What kind of advances can y[ou] mean?'

'This!' he croaked, suddenly seeming to lose co[n]trol. He pulled me to him, grabbed my breast a[nd] smeared a sloppy kiss upon my cheek. Oh! His s[elf] control had collapsed more suddenly than I had ba[r]gained for. He was surprisingly strong, and I had [to] struggle hard to push off the hands that seemed [to] move all over me and harder to get away from t[he] settee. As I struggled up and backed against the tab[le] his face was a picture of frustrated desire struggli[ng] with attempts to regain dignity.

I leant back against the table, staring at him [in] puzzled surprise. I pressed my hands to my breast[s] incidentally lifting them. 'Oh, sir,' I gasped tremulou[s]ly. 'No-one has ever touched me thus! I know that [it] would be very naughty to let a gentleman kiss me a[nd] touch my chest.' His eyes were flicking from my fac[e] down to the hands which were holding my breast[s] 'Even such a respectable gentleman as yourself, sir.[']

'Lydia! Lydia!' he spluttered, levering himself up from the settee. 'You must understand that it was not my intention to . . . I was merely . . . I wished only to demonstrate what those heathen might have done.' His features were working, and I detected not a little fright in his eyes lest he had gone too far, moved too fast.

'Oh, no, sir!' I fluttered, becoming all soft and simpering again. 'I do quite understand that you could never be anything but honourable and would only ever seek for my welfare.'

His relief was almost comic, as was the way he smiled as he moved to stand close to me again. I looked up into his eyes and said, 'It is just that I was a little surprised.'

He visibly relaxed, becoming more sure of himself. I decided to turn the screw a little. 'Mind you,' I murmured thoughtfully, 'there was one . . . but no, that was only a game. And he did give me sweets.'

Dr Williams started like a pointer at a quail. I could almost hear him thinking, 'Ahah!' He took my hand and looked seriously into my wide eyes, 'Now Lydia, you must tell me of this game. What was only a game to a naive girl such as you might not be so innocent in the eyes of the world. Come, my dear,' he said, pulling me down beside him on the settee again, his voice solicitous. 'Tell me about this game!'

I hesitated, for I needed time to think. I had not planned this excursion in my teasing of him. Ah, well, might as well give the silly man something to get really excited over!

'Well, sir, it was only a game, and he didn't take advantage of me to be sure. He never even tried to touch my chest.' Dr Williams was staring at me, the hand that held mine hot and rather damp. 'It was in

233

the barn one day. Peter, that is one of the men wh
worked on the farm, was showing me a new foal tha
had just been born. Oh, it was so pretty. Have yo
ever seen a newborn foal, sir? They are so weak an
lovely, and have such soft eyes, and . . .'

'Yes, yes, my dear. But what of this Peter?'

'Oh. Well Peter was ever so nice. He used to tell m
all about the farm and the animals, and so on. I reall
liked Peter.'

'The game, child. Tell me about this game.' Poo
Dr Williams was clearly put out by my shillyshally
ing!

'Well, as I said, we were in the barn with this prett
little colt, and Peter let me rub its little nose, and
was ever so happy, and so was Peter. And he said
was pretty, and if I was a good girl he would let m
see his sausage.'

'Ah,' said the priest. 'Now we come to the nub.
The hand which had been holding mine all the whil
now lay in a fatherly fashion near the top of m
thigh, and felt hot through the material of my skirts

'Oh, no, sir. It wasn't a nub, it was a sausage.' Th
vicar was actually licking his plump lips as I glance
coyly at him. 'I was surprised at what a strange plac
he kept it in. Well, you would think he would have i
in his pocket, or somewhere, and wrapped in paper t
keep it clean before he cooked it! I said as much, and
Peter laughed and said it was a special kind of saus
age, and I could hold it if I liked.' Dr William
coughed, and ran a finger round inside his collar be
fore returning his hand to my skirt – a little highe
now, I was sure. 'It was most surprising, becaus
when I held it, it sort of grew a bit, and . . . Oh, look
You have one too, vicar, and just like Peter's. And hi
went just like yours when I rubbed it! Do all gentle

234

en have sausages, sir?' I was almost squirming with
elight, and had difficulty maintaining my thread, for
e vicar had taken out his own sausage (though I
ever even saw him undoing his buttons!) and was
aning back pop-eyed as I innocently rubbed it for
im. I confess it was quite a handsome member, too!
'Does it feel nice when it goes all stiff like that, sir?
eter said it did. I think yours is a little larger than
is, though. Ooh, and his did that, too! But his
lashed onto the ground, and yours has gone all over
our trousers. Oh dear. Shall I get a cloth for you to
ipe it up? Will you give me some sweeties too?'

The poor vicar was in quite a case, you may be
ure! Under my 'innocent' caresses, he had come
opiously, and his pearly effusions had splashed all
ver his trousers and waistcoat, as well as my hand.
Oh, I could have hugged myself in delight at his dis-
omposure! I jumped up from the settee and hurried
ut to fetch a cloth to wipe him. Outside the door,
iliu – who had naturally been spying on my little
ame – had her hands stuffed in her mouth, and tears
f laughter coursing down her cheeks. I gave her a
ap on the wrist, and gestured mock-sternly for since, for I was almost bursting myself!

Back in the parlour, Dr Williams had buttoned
imself up, and was dabbing at his clothes with his
andkerchief. I fussed about, and wiped him down
he reddened even more when I rubbed the cloth firm-
y over his trousers) and clucked over the mess, and
oped it would not stain too badly. I asked him
where my sweets were. He had none. I pretended to
e upset, even a little petulant. I really ought to be
given some sweets for playing with his sausage! Never
mind, perhaps my father would give me some when I
old him.

235

If I had slapped him in the face, the poor ma[n] could not have been more startled. 'Oh, no! No nee[d] for that, my dear girl!' He was almost gabbling. 'N[o] need to mention it to anyone. I will bring you som[e] sweets myself. No need to tell a soul!' He leapt u[p] from the settee, fumbling with his coat then hurrie[d] from the room. Only when I heard him stumblin[g] along the passage did I allow myself to fall back an[d] give vent to the hilarity that had been bubbling insid[e] me.

After our little contest in my parlour the vicar be[-] haved with much more circumspection towards m[e] obviously terrified that I might tell father of ou[r] game. He did indeed bring sweets for me, and tried t[o] get me in my parlour again, but when I dropped hint[s] about 'sausages' and 'asking father', he became con[-] vinced that I was silly enough to actually do so, an[d] he gave up his attempts. He even, I learned late[r] stopped touching up Tiliu, and so both of us ha[d] much to be grateful for.

236

Chapter 14

he thing I became determined to do, as the weeks
w past, was to pay another visit to the Ambroses.
was not that I was dissatisfied, for I was enjoying
gular and frequent dalliances with both Jonathan
d Captain Mackay, and could always call upon the
rvices of Benjamin at need. No, it was rather that
e image of Richard's dark, lustrous eyes, and of
at lovely cock I had so innocently rubbed and rub-
d, played on my imagination. How naive I had
en then.

Had I really curled with embarrassment at the sight
Albert's chest revealed by his open shirt? Had I
uly been so shocked and scared when Richard had
ssed me and fondled my breasts? Foolish child!
ow much more entertaining it could be now; now
at I knew how to flirt and tease, and what delights
expect when I surrendered!

It was not difficult to arrange. I convinced father
at a little holiday in the highlands would be good
r my health. A squad of troopers, led by one Ser-
ant Roberts, happened to be journeying in the
irection of the farm, and would serve well as escorts,
oth outwards and on the return. Tiliu would accom-
any me as my maid, and Mrs Ambrose would be my
haperon at the farm. All was as well as could be –
nd was made even better when Captain Mackay

himself suggested that Felicity, too, would bene[]
from a holiday. At first she was dubious, but h[]
father and Jonathan were persuasive, and Felic[]
consented to come along. I was delighted, because h[]
experience so far had been confined to Jonathan, a[]
who knows what chances I might find to arrange []
extension.

Our welcome at the farm was effusive. Mr Ambr[]
se loomed and laughed and greeted us like so[]
amiable bear. Mrs Ambrose flittered and fussed li[]
a lively sparrow. Albert and Richard held themselv[]
very erect and eyed us, especially Felicity, with ca[]
tious calculation. Richard seemed even more han[]
some than I remembered, and I felt a little thrill []
happy anticipation at the questioning, rather hopef[]
way he looked into my eyes across the supper tab[]
that first evening, as if checking whether I remen[]
bered our encounter in the barn – and whether []
might be repeated.

Felicity and I were, of course, completely demur[]
and it was great fun to watch the way Albert an[]
Richard (and even their father with respect to Feli[]
ity) chatted and preened and strove to impress. A[]
boded well when I awoke refreshed for my first fu[]
day of holiday. And that very day, confirming to m[]
that their intentions were far from chaste, the tw[]
young men arranged to take us girls for a drive to s[]
the native village. Remembering my own naive fluste[]
all those months ago on seeing the half-naked villag[]
girls, and the flirtatiousness that ensued, I watche[]
Felicity carefully.

As I had expected, she became embarrassed an[]
fluttering, for she – like me that first time – had neve[]
seen Africans not togged out like Europeans. And []
am sure that Albert and Richard were as aware as []

of the difficulty she had in dragging her eyes away from the display of naked breasts and handsome male torsos all around us. It had certainly made her hot, for she continued to blush and fluster whenever she caught one of the men's eyes, long after we had left the village.

I had wondered how Richard would make his approach to me, for of course an innocent girl, such as I was supposed to be, could never make the first move. With a little help, for I followed him about admiringly, he managed to get me alone in the barn. He was a little awkward and hesitant, obviously wanting to try matters with me but unable to think how. I took the initiative. I reminisced about how pretty it had been at the lake, and wondered whether he would take me there again. He became very still, gazing at me and blushing. He had taken my hand to help me over some hay strewn on the floor, and still held it. I looked up at him wide-eyed. 'Oh, Richard,' I whispered. 'You are not going to kiss me again, are you?'

He did, instantly. I fluttered and protested, but allowed his hot kisses, and the hands which flew at once to my breasts. 'Oh, Richard, Richard! Do not!'

A hand had slid to my cunny, and was pressing through my skirt. At a second protest, he stopped and stood back breathing rapidly. I do believe he would actually have left off had I not taken the initiative again!

'Oh, Richard, I am sorry. You fluster me so. And oh, dear, you have that nasty pain back again!' I placed an innocent hand upon the bulge in his trousers. At once he stepped close again, and kissed me on my forehead. 'Do you need me to rub it again? I am sorry!'

He did indeed want me to rub it, and more. Ve
quickly, as I caressed his handsome cock slowly, f
I did not want to bring him off too soon, his han
were all over me, and he had hauled up my skirts a
was rummaging to get inside my drawers. Of cour:
I was all concern and confusion, but was entirely u
able to prevent him getting me down onto the ha
and pulling my drawers down, and getting betwe
my legs! It was delicious. He had his first come ev
as he slid into me, but stayed in. He hardly shrank
all before firming again, and gave me a long, love
shagging. Naturally, when he had his second com
and climbed off me, I was all innocent wonder. H
was so proud of his conquest! I became shy and a
miring; he became caring and masterful. I made su
that he had it firmly in his mind that he would get
shag this innocent girl quite a lot before her holid;
was over.

As for Felicity, she relaxed and blossomed in th
relatively informal atmosphere of the farm. She r
sponded to the easy manner of the menfolk with
lightness and gaiety which made her even more desi
able than usual, and the effect upon the males w;
very obvious. Nevertheless, she effected not to notic
or perhaps she genuinely did not, for she was entirel
fixated upon Jonathan. It was only when, one evenin
after about a week, she came rushing into my roon
outraged because Albert had got her into a corne
and kissed her, and even touched her bosom, that
was able to plant a seed into her slow mind.

I calmed her, and sat her down, and echoed he
own distress at such a shocking thing, but then bega
to profess a little pity for Albert, for she was so ver
beautiful, and he was a handsome young man no
often in the company of such lovely creatures as she

ow could he have resisted her? Her beauty and re-
nement were as a fine rose set in the roughness of
he farm! And really, she was fortunate, for he was a
ery nice, and handsome, young man. She really
hould forgive him.

How much was born of my hintings and how much
of the innate sensuality I knew to be in Felicity's nature I cannot guess, but to all outward appearances
she did forgive him, and remained easy with him, not
protesting when he placed a hand upon her shoulder
or waist while showing her about the place, nor when,
in helping her down from the trap, he held her under
the arms and surely got a surreptitious feel of her
lovely breasts. But no other progress was made, and
I became almost as frustrated as Albert, for I dearly
wished to unlock Felicity's delights to men other than
Jonathan.

As for myself, after that first exciting bout with
Richard in the barn, I got plenty of satisfaction! He
was a vigorous young man, plentifully endowed in his
trousers, and clever at arranging opportunities. Of
course, being a man it would never occur to him that
I was as keen as he, and so he always had the joy of
getting me somewhere, unbuttoning me and seducing
me. He was so proud of the success of his frequent
essays upon the naive girl he managed to fuck so
thoroughly. Nevertheless, being such a small commu-
nity, it was not long before the inevitable happened.

We were in the barn. Richard was in a fever, and
had got me bending over some bales of hay. My skirt
was thrown up onto my back, my drawers were
round my ankles, and Richard was in me from the
rear, holding me by my hips and shagging me deliciously. Suddenly, there was a cough and a gasp. I
turned my head. It was Albert! When a man is in

mid-shag it would take a gunshot to distract him, a
so Richard had not noticed anything amiss. I cou
do nothing save stare at Albert's astonished face
his younger brother ground and thrust at me befo
bursting into his come.

When Richard finally noticed his brother there w
pandemonium. He leapt back from me, whipping n
skirts down, hauling at his trousers, blustering a
protesting. For his part, Albert stood like a statue f
a long minute, then began to bluster in his turn. Th
railed at each other, the one attacked for sneaki
about so, the other for dishonouring the family.
was so ridiculous I almost laughed aloud! Wh
might have happened had I not interposed I dread
think. As it was, I seized an opportunity I had be
hoping for, for I had long had a fancy for Albert.

I got between them as they ranted at each othe
though it was only when I stamped my foot and crie
out that they stopped their silly wrangling. Albe
stared at me. I smiled. For a long moment both
them were frozen with surprise, then their expressio
changed as they realised I was not averse to playin
with both of them. I smiled at Albert again, an
glanced towards the bales of hay. His face lit up in
grin of delight as he stepped towards me.

I was still moist from Richard. My drawers we
still around my ankles. Albert was in me in one lon
delicious thrust. You may be sure that energet
games ensued, for they were both vigorous males, an
each seemed sparked off by the lust of the other. B
the time I got out of the barn that afternoon I ha
been very thoroughly shagged indeed, and Albert an
Richard were well nigh exhausted! For the remainin
couple of weeks I was at the farm, the lads seeme
hardly able to get enough of me, and I could have n

242

mplaints about lack of satisfaction. There were
me pleasant surprises, too. Neither Albert nor
chard had ever seen a girl entirely naked, and I
sked in the admiration they paid to my body when-
er I stripped for them. Nor had either of them even
eamed that they could be pleasured by a girl's
outh, and were weak with delight when I insisted on
ating them. Both my bedroom and the lakeside
w any number of delicious naked romps.

In the midst of my own gratifying activities one
ought nagged at me. Felicity was adopting her old
perior airs. She surely guessed at my own romps
th the two lads, for I made little secret of them,
om her at least, but she said little, save to go on
out Jonathan, as if devotion to her beau made her
tter than I. Yet I knew she had a strong lascivious
reak; that she found Albert attractive and that he
ncied her. How could I push matters to a con-
usion and show the silly girl that she was not
mune from the calls of the flesh? In her dull-witted
oddle she had convinced herself that her pleasures
uld only be found with Jonathan. How could I
anage to show her otherwise?

It struck me that the fluttering complaisance she
monstrated whenever in male company was my
ue. Was Felicity not entirely submissive to Jon-
han? Did she not cleave to the belief that a man's
le was to dominate, to demand, and a girl's to sur-
nder? Did she not even submit, nay respond, to
ing spanked? Perhaps a little dominance from Al-
ert might do the trick?

When I put it to him, Albert was reluctant. What
I was wrong? What if she resisted, told his father?
here would be hell to pay. His father would horse-
hip him! By dint of persuasion: by telling him about

243

Jonathan; by insisting I knew her well, even by assu
ing him that I would stand alibi if she tried to tel
at last persuaded him. In the event, I was proved e
tirely right, and was able to witness a delicious lit
drama into the bargain.

Mr and Mrs Ambrose, with Richard, had gone
a neighbouring farm, and would not be back un
late evening. Felicity, Albert and I took tea togeth
in the parlour, and then I left them alone in the roo
and watched through the window. They sat togeth
on a sofa. They chatted. Albert told Felicity she w
beautiful. She simpered. He held her hand. He kiss
her. She squealed a protest. He threw his arms abo
her and crushed her to him. He kissed her hotly, to
her she was lovely, told her he was mad for her. S
struggled and squirmed, but not very effectually. S
failed to push his hand from her breast, though s
begged him to desist between avid kisses.

His hand went up her skirt. Her protests becar
weaker, her struggles less vehement. Soon, he w
pressing her back on the seat, tugging at her drawe
and rummaging between her legs. Her hands we
covering her face, and she was still murmuring pr
tests, but I noticed that her thighs parted themselv
at only a nudge of his knee. And once he was firm
mounted, she ceased her struggles altogether and la
unprotesting as he rode her. She even, towards th
end, showed by the lascivious circling of her pelvi
that she was far from unresponsive.

Afterwards, as Albert kissed her fervently, held h
close and fondled her breasts, she became the yield
ing, submissive creature I so well knew her to be.
could amost read her mind! He had made love to he
had got carried away by her beauty. She had tried
stop him, but he was too strong. He had got carrie

ay with his passion. She could not help but let him
ve his way. This was how men were. A poor girl
uld only submit to such extremes of passion for her
arms.

And from then on, until we left to return home, her
ttering coyness was a great source of amusement to
:. She became entirely obedient to Albert's wishes,
t as she had with Jonathan. She pretended all the
ile, of course, that she had no choice in the matter,
t showed only token hesitations at his requirements
d even, I noticed, manufactured occasions to be
ailable to him!

Quite how she could maintain her silly self-decep-
n I can only put down to her dullness of mind, but
aintain it she did. Why, when I teased her one day
out the fun she was having with Albert, she even
otested that it was not her fault, that he made her
 it, that she did not enjoy it, that she loved only
nathan. And yet I had just seen her, half-naked and
nting and writhing in a vast come on the lake
ore!

Always afterwards, and I know she had many
otic experiences before we finally arrived back in
igland, she convinced herself – and tried to con-
nce me – that they 'did it to her', that she was a
or victim of men's lust for her beauty! Even when,
 the journey back home with Sergeant Roberts and
s troop, I saw her, simpering and mock-reluctant,
ing shepherded away from the campfire towards
me bushes by several troopers, she tried to tell me
first that nothing had happened, and then that they
d got carried away, and she'd had to let them.
learly, all it needed was for a man to be a little
rceful for Felicity to fall back and surrender.

When we arrived back home we were greeted with

245

wonderful news. There was to be a ball! For so
weeks now the barracks had been busy with the a
val of companies of troops and officers becau
apparently, the situation with the Boers had been g
ting more and more difficult and it was thought w
to reinforce our garrison. Now a whole battalion w
assembled and a ball was to be held to acquaint t
townspeople with the new officers.

I had never been to a ball, indeed had only re
about them in the journals which arrived from ti
to time from England. I was very excited and gr
frustrated with father, who seemed reluctant to adr
that I was grown-up enough to attend, even thoug
was now past seventeen years of age. Of course
pressed and nagged and wheedled and at last he ga
in, and I rushed to engage Mrs Barnet in the planni
of an outfit and for advice on what to expect.

Dear Mrs Barnett was twinkle-eyed at my exci
ment, and together we thumbed through patte
books looking for the perfect gown. She told me
and who was I to doubt in the face of her vast expe
ence – that the purpose of any ball was very simp
For the menfolk it was to confirm contacts and stat
and to survey the fillies, as they called us you
ladies. For us, it was to outshine our rivals in dre
and deportment, to flirt discreetly with the office
and, finally to make a catch.

Behind that, though, were many subtleties. In fli
ing, for example, a girl was required to appear passi
and ingenuous while somehow managing to conv
to one's partner the degree to which one would w
come, or otherwise, further attention. Too passi
and one would be passed over for somebody mo
interesting. Too responsive and one was disrespecte
and considered as being of easy virtue.

Mrs Barnet had a wealth of patterns for ballgowns
d she was as excited as I at the prospect. As she
mplained good-humouredly, she rarely got the
ance to make such things in 'this benighted town'
d was now snowed under with orders. She was de-
rmined that my own gown should make me the
lle of the evening. And not just the gown but the
derthings too, for, as she said with a chuckle and
arch look, 'Who knows but that someone might
mpse them!'

Naturally, there was to be a corset. Not because I
eded cinching in, she told me, but because any
ficer who danced with me and did not feel the regu-
tion boning when he placed his hand upon my waist
ould instantly think me a strumpet and my reputa-
on would be shot. She surprised me by suggesting
at it should be black, because it would set off my
in colouring. It had never occured to me that
derwear could be anything except white or pale
stel shades, with perhaps trimmings in bolder reds
greens, but when she held the heavy silk against me
that I could see myself in the glass I had to agree
at it did indeed look very fetching. Like my first
rset, this one stopped at my bosom and had that
nning little shelf arrangement which lifted my
easts so as to emphasise the cleft between them.
he effect of having my bosom thus offered up, as it
ere, was made more startling in that the corset was
pped with a wisp of a new material I'd not seen
efore called chiffon which, although it covered my
easts, was no more than a black shadow upon them
nd was entirely translucent!

I was also to wear full-length black stockings, and
r contrast my garters and drawers were of pure
hite silk. The drawers, naturally, were of the short,

loose-legged style Mrs Barnet made so well, wh
looked so pretty, and felt so comfortable.

When I first saw myself in the glass even I thoug
I looked enticing, and dear Mrs Barnet chuckled a
said, 'Heaven help any lucky man who sees you
these!'

The gown itself was of black and pale cream. It h
a panelled skirt, short, gathered sleeves which w
set off with elbow-length gloves, and a fitted bod
with a square neckline. A chiffon panel rising to
high ruched collar was encircled by a black s
choker. The neckline came just above the cleft of r
bosom and at first glance the gown looked qu
prim. Such was Mrs Barnet's genius though, that t
bodice was made of lighter silk than the rest of t
gown, and was cut so cunningly that when I mov
at anything more than a sedate walk the trembling
my breasts beneath it could be easily detected.

Oh, my darling Mrs Barnet was so clever! To a
casual onlooker, and to any ladies I might sit a
converse with, my gown would look entirely proper
but any gentleman I should dance with would be i
stantly aware that there might be more to me th
met the eye!

As well as working upon my outfit (and those
many other ladies) sweet Mrs Barnet found time
give me some rudimentary dancing lessons, for whi
I had a sore need. She teased away my doubts abo
my clumsiness by assuring me that any officer
danced with would be far too concerned with n
looks, and his chances, to worry about the occasion
slip. And anyway, she told me, all I needed to kno
were the waltz and the polka, which were simple, ar
how to allow my partner to lead.

Finally everything was ready, and the great da

ived. Mrs Barnet and Tiliu fussed about dressing
and doing my hair, which I was to wear up for the
t time since I had stopped wearing the tribal top-
ot. I confess that seeing myself in the glass, clad in
underthings, made me quite excited, and Tiliu
ghed and made round eyes at the way the corset
ed my breasts. The gown itself was a dream and I
like a veritable princess.

was delighted at father's reaction when I descend-
the stairs to where he waited to accompany me. He
s obviously impressed, and I guessed that for the
t time he realised that his little girl was actually
ite a grown woman! John-John, in his finest uni-
m, drove the trap, and father sat close beside me
neath the canopy which had been rigged to cover

To my delight, for father was never demonstra-
e, he not only held my hand but put his arm
und me and actually kissed me on the cheek as
ll as telling me several times that I looked very
tty and he was proud of me.

Since there was no hall of sufficient size, the troops
d erected a huge marquee in one corner of the par-
e ground, with several supper, refreshment and
tiring-tents linked to its sides. From somewhere
ey had brought, or perhaps manufactured, a
lished wooden floor for dancing upon, which was
d straight upon the ground and served its purpose
imirably. There was already a throng when father
d I arrived and made our way to a refreshment-
nt, for it seemed the whole town had turned out.
he band was already playing some light music, and
en as father handed me a glass of fruit cup both
nathan and the Captain arrived to claim places on
y dance card.

The dance proper had not yet begun and, standing

249

by the entrance to the refreshment tent, I was able
drink in the glittering scene. The officers of our
garrison were all there, resplendent in their blue a
white dress uniforms, their medals gleaming. Th
were, though, almost put in the shade by the n
arrivals, whose bright scarlet tunics, with black a
gold epaulets and black cross-belts, outshone ev
some of the ladies' gowns. Already, I could see Fe
ity surrounded by several of them. She look
ravishing in a green silk gown. This and her r
brown hair set off to perfection her flawless skin.
was not long before I, too, had attracted a covey
officers, and my dance card was soon full, much
my relief I confess!

As Mrs Barnet had told me, most of the dan
were to be waltzes or polkas, but I was a little app
hensive to see something called a Schottisc
featured, and towards the end of the card the na
'Galop', each appearing several times. I had no id
what they were, and was relieved when the capta
claimed the first Schottische and Jonathan the fi
Galop, for at least I would be able to try them c
with someone safe, and not with one of the ma
strange faces I saw milling about me.

Naturally, father took my first dance – fortunat
a slow one, for I am sure he would have sent n
straight home were he to have seen my bosom jigg
within the cunning gown! Thereafter, I found mys
in a whirl of partners. Captain Mackay, of cour
was among the first and complimented me and su
gested straight away that, perhaps a little later, v
could take the evening air. Trust him to get in ear
I danced several times with Jonathan, who con
mented amusingly upon the fluttering of some of t
townswomen, and told me he fully intended to ta

250

icity aside later, as well, of course, as myself! Most
my partners, though, were from among the new
cers, and a raffish lot they were.

The very first one set the tone all the others were
follow. He was tall, with large and handsome
ustaches, and as he spun me around to a waltz he
ed me all about myself, and told me I was very
tty, and that I was wasted in such a dead little
vn. He made it very obvious that he had noticed
figure, glancing quite openly at my bosom and
ck to my eyes, his own twinkling roguishly. At the
d of the set, as he handed me towards the refresh-
nts and got me some fruit cup, he made it clear he
ended to see more of me. And compared to one or
o of his colleagues he was quite subtle, for they
tually went so far as to suggest taking me outside
n and there! Mrs Barnet's warnings about coquet-
hness rang in my mind, so of course I was shy and
mure, but I confess that these gentlemen's flirta-
ns were very pleasant indeed.

The dances came in sets of four, with a short break
tween to catch one's breath. Since I had not one
nce free, and it was a warm evening, I seized the
portunity of one such break, fairly late in the even-
g, to take my glass outside to get a breath of fresh
r. After a moment I was joined by the fusilier officer
ho had been my first dance partner. He was jovial
d glitter-eyed. He clearly had high hopes for him-
lf, and preened at me. These new officers, I had
ready discovered, were much more forward than the
sident garrison, possibly because they were new
re, and would not be around for long. This one
rtainly wasted little time, and I confess I was
nused by the way he straight off took my elbow and
ered me away from the marquee, chatting about

how lovely the night was and how clear the mo
and suggesting that, since he had booked the n
four dances, we might as well take the air instead

As we walked, passing among a small shrubb
he talked of England, and the trouble with the Bo
and how much he was looking forward to teach
them a lesson. It seemed that there had been so
kind of conference in May, which had broken do
in acrimony. You may be sure I listened eagerly to
this, for so few of the men in my life would answ
my questions on the subject. So concerned was I w
what he was telling me about Kruger and Lord M
ner and the Bloemfontain Conference that I w
hardly aware that Lieutenant Phipps, though he t
me to call him Arthur, was leading me well aw
from the ball, and actually into a small copse beh
the officers' quarters.

Only when he stopped and manoeuvred me agai
a tree did my mind snap back to what I knew w
his real intentions. His arm had stolen around
waist as we walked, and now he pulled me to him a
kissed me hotly. I was quite genuinely surprised, a
he took my reaction for naivete. He held me clo
kissed me, murmured that I was a lovely girl and th
he was mad for me. His hand was already fondli
my breast, and he pressed himself against me. I l
came concerned for my gown. He was very hot, a
it would not do to return to the ball rumpled. I tr
to push him off, struggling with him. He would bro
no denial. A hand was grasping at my bottom, a se
ond rubbing my skirt at my thighs. He was pressi
his loins against my hip.

I managed to extricate my mouth from his l
kisses, begged him to desist – he would muss m
crumple my gown, someone might see. He told m

s irresistible, was beautiful, that he had to have me. ddenly, and I did not know how he managed it so ickly, his cock was out and he was pressing my nd to it. He was scrabbling at my skirts, trying to se them, trying, even, to pull me to the ground. I d to do something. If he got me to the ground my wn would be ruined for all to see! I gripped his npant member in my hand and told him to wait. ait! I bent and took him between my lips. I heard 'Gosh, what a girl!' as my mouth closed over him. : kept still, not even holding my head as I sucked him, anxious to bring him off quickly in case we re missed at the marquee.

He was almost there, just starting those twitches d gaspings which signal the onset of a come, when eard, 'By gosh, Arthur has a filly!' Next, my skirts re thrown up over my back. At the very moment rthur began to spurt onto my tongue, my drawers re hauled down to my knees and hands gripped my ttom. What could I do? We had been discovered, d whoever it was had leapt at his chance! I almost t Arthur as a rampant member thrust into me. Be-g ploughed from the rear, whilst standing up, by mebody taller than oneself is awkward to say the ast, and whoever it was that had thrust into me was o concerned with his own intentions to worry about e fact the I had to go on tiptoes, and clutch Ar-ur's coat-tail for support. I could actually hear, as ell as feel, his loins slapping against my bare but-cks as he rutted!

You may well believe that I squealed in surprise at is sudden invasion, only to have my cry greeted with w laughter. 'Why Arthur!' I heard, over the grunts f whoever was shagging me. 'You've got that pretty irhead with the bouncing titties! Well done, old boy!'

253

I was being bounced quite thoroughly, as you c
imagine, and knew that, had I not been grasped
my hips, I would have tumbled inelegantly to
ground. Shining black boots appeared on the gra
My shoulder was gripped. I turned my head. Tig
white breeches stood like columns close by my ey
At their join, a hand was fumbling with buttons.
cock bounced forth. My head was lifted. A red-pur
plum bumped against my nose.

For all this trio knew, I might have been the m
innocent damsel possible, but that did not stop th
enjoying their ruts, accompanied by quite the lewd
of comments – though with one man shagging
heartily and another plugging for my throat I w
hardly in a position to listen closely.

They did not take long, fortunately, but I was
little put out when, after the fuck had finished, and
the man in my mouth was spurting onto my tong
I felt a hand rubbing firmly over my bottom a
heard, 'Pretty arse, Arthur! Pretty arse, you old do

At least Arthur, unlike the others, who wander
off as soon as they had done their deed, was gent
man enough to wait while I pulled up my drawers a
adjusted my skirts before leaving me with a qui
kiss. 'Best not go back together, my dear. Mig
make people talk,' he said. But at least they had n
creased my gown!

As I walked back towards the ball I was not su
whether to be amused at the episode, or annoyed
the men's rather cavalier behaviour towards a passi
girl. On the whole, though, I thought, their attitude
rather like that in the tribe in its way – was rather le
mealy-mouthed than I had become used to lately.

Back at the marquee, I discovered that the who
episode had taken only about ten minutes. Even s

nathan was seeking me anxiously. Knowing me as
did, he looked me up and down quizzically then
ughed, guessing what I had been up to. 'Come,
inx,' he said, leading me towards a refreshment
nt. 'Perhaps you need a drink and a rest more than
lother dance!'

The ball had really warmed up now, and conversa-
on and laughter competed with the music to which
uples whirled and spun. Ladies with flushed faces
miled gaily at their partners as they whirled about
e floor. Even Mrs Forster, usually so concerned
ith appearances, was laughing happily in the arms
f a senior officer. For myself, I seemed to spin from
e arms of one officer to another with hardly a
oment's pause. It was divine! And all the more so
ecause pretty well all of them wanted me to promise
see them again soon, and prospects for future fun
oked very rosy.

When I did go outside, it was with Captain Mack-
y, for after all I had promised him. He was hot for
e, but even so, controlled himself enough to take me
a little hut near the stables, for which, naturally,
e had the key. I was still concerned lest my gown
ecome creased, but luckily there was a trestle affair
pon which I could park my bottom. The captain's
yes gleamed in the moonlight that shimmered
rough the little window as I took off my drawers
nd perched myself on the trestle. He was very ready
or me. It was a lovely shag, even though I was a little
istracted by my need to hang well back to prevent
e captain crushing the skirt I held bundled above
ly waist. He had both his hands under the cheeks of
ly bottom, and my ankles were clamped around his
aist as he pumped vigorously into me. I rose quickly
voluptuous spirals, and burst into a delicious come

255

at the very moment the captain jerked and spurted the very nicest kind of come a girl can have.

We did not stay until the end of the ball, for father wished to return home, it being after midnight, and he had much work to do on the morrow. Though I was a little disappointed, I confess I was quite exhausted by my evening's activities, and not unhappy to accompany him.

Chapter 15

ather's days became busy indeed thereafter, and I
en heard rumours of the possibility of warfare.
'hat concerned me much more, though (perhaps I
n an empty-head after all) was the constant toing
d froing of a great many officers. Many of them
ere rather senior, and weighty with important busi-
ss. Quite a few of them, though, were dashing
ung subalterns, with the time and inclination to
lly with the District Commissioner's pretty daugh-
r. Many were the opportunities for chatting and
ild flirtation, and there were quite a few more or
ss subtle offers of further dalliance. The offers of
vo young lieutenants in particular were not very
btle at all, and I soon realised that these were the
vo who had taken advantage of me when they
ught me with Arthur Phipps at the ball. And of
urse, Arthur himself soon found an opportunity for
acquaintance.

Quite how my adventures of those weeks did not
ecome common knowledge I cannot imagine. Nor
ose of Felicity, for that matter. Perhaps it was some
rt of officers' code. Who knows? Not only was I
ntinuing my liaison with dear Jonathan, but Arthur
hipps and the two lieutenants were also active in
eir games with me – and they knew about each
ther, too, as was proved when all four took me for

a day out to see some strange ruins in the bush, and ensured that before we returned in the evening the had got me naked, and I had been very thoroughl and very deliciously, fucked in every way they cou invent.

Only Captain Mackay did not know about th others, for on the occasions he sought me out it wa clear he still thought of me as the naive girl he ha seduced. Neither did he know about the activities his delicious daughter. If he had, it would surely ha given him an apoplexy!

Although Felicity still put on her airs of reluctanc and helplessness in the face of men's lusts, I knew h to be at least as active as myself. Indeed, I becam something of a confessor to her, for she had nobod else to turn to with her little puzzles and worries. A well as Jonathan, she was being had regularly by se eral of the junior officers and, in particular, by th commanding colonel.

This last liaison was at first announced to me wit considerable pride, but soon became a worry to he for his demands were, she said, rather odd. I had t reassure her that there was nothing especially wron with the fact that he seemed to prefer her bottom to, i her words, the proper place. That he liked having he in exposed and rather risky places was of great concer to her, and I found it vastly amusing that it seeme never to occur to her that she might resist occasionall Why, even when he'd got her to her knees in her ow parlour, and made her suck him off when, at an moment, her mother might have walked in, she ha complied. I confess that the image of her kneelin there, gobbling him like mad, her eyes screwed toward the door in case someone came in, gave me the giggl which put Felicity into quite a pet you can be sure.

And then, amid these pleasant – and very satisfying
activities, came the bombshell. Father had decided
send me home to England! Oh, you can be sure I
gued and begged and pleaded, even cried, but he
as adamant. There would be a war, he said. The
ers had proved themselves to be dangerous and
vious opponents in the past. Oh, Her Majesty's for-
s were certain to prevail, but in the meantime there
uld be dangers. He would not rest content until I
as safe and well away from any risks. That those
ks were serious was betokened by the fact that Felty, too, was to be evacuated, and in fact would
company me.

He would not be moved. None of my pleas and
guments had any effect. Everything was arranged. I
as to travel with a small escort to East London, a
rt to the south of our town, and there embark
on a steamer for England. Once there, I was to
dge with an aunt in Brighton. The only real light in
is unhappy plan was that I would be allowed to
ke Tiliu, who would act as maid to Felicity as well
myself, and we were to be chaperoned by Mrs Bar-
t. Had it not been for the latter's cheerful bustling,
e next few days of packing and goodbyes would
ve been unhappy indeed.

She it was who pointed out that Brighton was a
retty town with lots of lively society, especially in
mmer. And she it was who suggested, archly, that
rhaps the voyage itself might hold pleasant pros-
cts, for we would see many exotic sights, and who
nows what adventures might occur in the enclosed
mmunity on shipboard.

I confess that my goodbyes to my gentlemen were
quant. Lovemaking in those last few days was in-
riably gentle and fulfilling, despite – or possibly

because of – the underlying sense of sadness at [n]
departure. Many were the tokens of regard and affe[c]
tion I was given, and many the tokens I gave [in]
return, usually items of my underwear, of which, [by]
the time we left, my supply was sadly depleted.

Actually, Jonathan cheated, for only after I ha[d]
shagged him very thoroughly by way of goodbye d[id]
he tell me that he was to lead my escort!

Everything was ready, but the evening before we we[re]
due to leave Tiliu came to me looking very serious. [It]
seemed that Benjamin was very afraid and unhappy. T[he]
witch Ridja was in possession of his essence, and now s[he]
was taking it across the sea. He would die if she did n[ot]
give it back. As she revealed this to me with saucer eye[s]
Tiliu suddenly burst into fits of giggles. I, too, could n[ot]
help laughing at the pathetic image of poor Benjamin [a]
atremble with terror, but he was a nice man, and ha[d]
given me a great deal of pleasure, and I soon began [to]
feel sorry for him. We would have to think of somethin[g]

Again it was Tiliu who had the idea – she seems [to]
be the source of most of my juicier notions. We pr[e]
pared my rooms as we had the night I had 'take[n]
away his essence', and I dressed as I had then. Tili[u]
crouched with her little drum as she had before, an[d]
Benjamin looked just as terrified as he had the fir[st]
time I ordered him to strip. Even though I was [by]
now very familiar with it, I still felt a flush of warmt[h]
at the sight of his magnificent body.

'Ridja has sent for you,' I said in my hollowe[r]
voice, while Tiliu tapped upon her drum, 'because s[he]
is going over the sea.' Benjamin was trembling an[d]
his eyes were huge. 'Ridja is pleased with Benjami[n]
He has been a good servant. Because he has been [a]
good servant, Ridja has chosen to return to Benjami[n]
his essence, for which she has cared for so long.'

260

His gasp of pent tension was loud, and he almost gged with relief. 'But,' he stiffened again with ght. 'But, it is a rare gift she gives. It is here, in this ulet.' I held out a thong which I had kept hidden the folds of my nightgown, from which dangled a all leather bag. Benjamin's eyes fixed on the bag as ough he would draw it from my grasp by desire one. Oh, how lovely it felt to be able to use a man's perstitions for such a voluptuous purpose as I had mind. My nipples were already straining.

'In this amulet lies Benjamin's essence,' I intoned. o return Benjamin's essence, Ridja must release me of her own. Benjamin must swear an oath. He ust swear never to speak of Ridja and never to re- ove this amulet from his body. Nor open it lest his irit fly away. Does Benjamin swear?'

He nodded eagerly, his eyes starting. I looked at m sternly, and he stammered, 'Yes! Yes! I swear, iss Ridja!'

I stood, and shucked my night gown from my oulders. Naked except for my headscarf, I stepped wards him, holding the amulet before me. I touched to his forehead. 'No. Do not close your eyes,' I id. He stared into mine as I trailed the little leather g down from his forehead along his jawline, his ck, the firm, plate-like muscles of his chest, the rd corrugations of his stomach. At my order, he uffled his feet apart. I slid the bag along his hip, wn his thigh to the knee then returned up his inner igh between his tense legs and found the cleft of his ut buttocks. His balls brushed warmly along my rearm. I smoothed the leather gently up, lifting his ck, smoothing around his tufts, delighting in the ay his balls tightened and his lovely cock twitched my touch.

261

His eyes were staring, and stared even more as
moved back and dropped to my knees. Slowly, fixin
his eyes, I moved the bag to my cunny and slid it ba
and forth along my folds. His eyes veritably bulg
at the sight. I moved the leather back and forth, e
suring that is was thoroughly soaked in my juic
Benjamin's delicious cock twitched. I stood, rais
the bag to my lips, then moved close and placed tl
loop of the thong about Benjamin's neck. So close d
I stand that my nipples brushed his chest, and I f
his cock bump against my tummy. Delicious!

Standing thus close, I looked up into the eyes th
were staring into mine. He looked less frighten
now. I went on tiptoes and kissed him. 'There,'
whispered, my lips brushing his. 'It is done. Benjam
has his essence back.'

As I kissed him again, more lingeringly, holding h
head in my hands, I felt his cock rear like a trunched
against my tummy. His eyes were not frightened no
but burning. I reached down and grasped his thro
bing cock. I smiled up at him, and sidled towards n
little day bed, the very couch upon which Jonathc
had seduced Felicity. He followed me, doubt ar
hope flickering across his features. As I lay back ar
he loomed hotly over me, Tiliu increased the pace
her drumming.

Ah, it was glorious! Benjamin was no longer a serva
submitting to a great witch, but a man in full possessic
of his vigour. Held back a little, perhaps, by a lingerir
doubt about the danger of thus fucking his master
daughter, Benjamin was nevertheless very much
charge, his adorable prick surely bigger and stiffer tha
ever. I began rising towards a come almost as he ease
into me, and was soon in a rapture of red-gold throl
bings as his loins ground against mine in his passio

262

Now that he thought himself a whole man again, Benjamin blossomed. For hardly five minutes after ocking me to a pulsating finish, he had Tiliu up against the wall, her legs clinging about his waist, the muscles of his thighs and buttocks tensing and bunching as he shafted her heartily. It was an exhausted but happy Benjamin who crept out of my room not long before dawn, and two very satisfied young women who sought soap and water to wash their sticky, glowing bodies ready for the day of departure.

The train journey to East London was uneventful, though Tiliu was very excited, and kept us amused with her wide-eyed enthusiasm at all she saw. This was of course only her second ever train journey. Jonathan, who was commanding our escort, Mrs Garnet, Felicity and myself shared one compartment, and the sergeant and four troopers and Tiliu another, though there was enough room for them in ours. According to Jonathan, it was not done for ladies and officers to travel cheek by jowl with other ranks and servants, which I thought rather silly, for Tiliu had been anything but a servant lately, and anyway were they not people like us?

The dockside appeared to be a pandemonium of boxes, crates, shouting porters and debarking troops. Even though I was tired, for evening was drawing on and we had been travelling all day, I found my excitement rising almost as high as Tiliu's. To the obvious surprise of the sergeant and escort, Jonathon kissed me goodbye very thoroughly, before handing us females over to a smart young officer from the vessel we were to sail on. He led us up the gangplank. The trimness of his figure in its neat white ducks caught my eye. Oh, Lydia! How flighty you are, and only just having said goodbye to Jonathan!

263

But I was not the only flighty one. Mrs Barn
looking from the young officer, to me, to a group
bare-chested Laskars working on the deck nearb
then back to me again, grinned and winked an ey
Ah, Lydia, she seemed to be thinking. Perhaps o
voyage need not be uneventful, after all!

Looking about me, from the waiting officer to t
glistening torsos of the labouring seamen, to t
group of other officers who stood on the bridge,
considered. Our voyage was to last a number
weeks. There would surely be many secluded noo
and crannies aboard the vessel. We were four fema
among who knew how many lonely sailors. Yes i
deed, there were surely prospects for entertainme
here. That Felicity was having similar thoughts b
came obvious from the way she blushed and look
down when I whispered to her that the young offic
looked rather handsome.

As we were led below decks to our cabins, M
Barnet and I smiled at each other conspiratorial
Leaving Africa, though sad, might not after all
without its compensations. Had I even dreamed wh
adventures would befall us, I would not have been
sanguine.

NEW BOOKS

Coming up from Nexus and Black Lace

Nexus

gering Lessons by Sarah Veitch
ril 1995   Price: £4.99   ISBN: 0 352 32990 4

nne has just inherited an old boarding school, but she has
hare it with the mysterious Adam Howard. Only one thing
ertain about her new partner: he is a true devotee of cor-
al punishment. The last thing Leanne expects is to be
wn into his sordid yet exciting world, but the temptation
ves irresistible.

e Awakening of Lydia by Philippa Masters
ril 1995   Price: £4.99   ISBN: 0 352 33002 3

the daughter of a district commissioner during the Boer
r, Lydia has plenty of opportunity for excitement – and
nty of sex-starved men to pleasure her. But their skills are
thing compared to the voracious sexual appetites of the lo-
tribesmen, who waste no time in taking the stunning six-
n-year-old captive.

errie by Evelyn Culber
y 1995   Price: £4.99   ISBN: 0 352 32996 3

airman of an important but ailing company, Sir James is
ving trouble relaxing. But in Sherrie, seductive hostess on
business flight, he has found someone who might be able
help. After one of her eye-opening spanking stories and a
le practical demonstration, money worries are the last thing
Sir James's mind.

use of Angels by Yvonne Strickland
y 1995   Price: £4.99   ISBN: 0 352 32995 5

a sumptuous villa in the south of France, Sonia runs a very
lusive service. With her troupe of gorgeous and highly
lled girls, and rooms fitted out to cater for every taste, she
fils sexual fantasies. Sonia finds herself in need of a new
ruit, and the beautiful Karen seems ideal – providing she
shed a few of her inhibitions.

BLACK
lace

Crimson Buccaneer by Cleo Cordell
April 1995 Price: £4.99 ISBN: 0 352 32987 4

Cheated out of her inheritance, Carlotta Mendoza wants venge; and with her exquisite looks and feminine wiles, th is no shortage of men willing to offer her help. She takes to seas with a rugged buccaneer and begins systematically boa ing, robbing and sexually humiliating her enemies.

La Basquaise by Angel Strand
April 1995 Price: £4.99 ISBN: 0 352 32988 2

Oruela is a modern young woman of 1920s Biarritz who se to join the bohemian set. Her lover, Jean, is helping her achieve her social aspirations. But an unfortunate accident volving her father brings her under suspicion, and a sinis game of sexual blackmail throws her life into turmoil . . .

The Devil Inside by Portia da Costa
May 1995 Price: £4.99 ISBN: 0 352 32993 9

Psychic sexual intuition is a very special gift. Those w possess it can perceive other people's sexual fantasies – a are usually keen to indulge them. But as Alexa Lavelle c covers, it is a power that needs help to master. Fortunately, doctors at her exclusive medical practice are more than will to offer their services.

The Lure of Satyria by Cheryl Mildenhall
May 1995 Price: £4.99 ISBN: 0 352 32994 7

Welcome to Satyria: a land of debauchery and excess, wh few men bother with courtship and fewer maidens deserve But even here, none is so bold as Princess Hedra, whose qu for sexual gratification takes her beyond the confines of castle and deep into the wild, enchanted forest . . .

NEXUS BACKLIST

books are priced £4.99 unless another price is given. If a date
applied, the book in question will not be available until that
th in 1995.

NTEMPORARY EROTICA

ACADEMY	Arabella Knight	
DUCT UNBECOMING	Arabella Knight	Jul
TOURS OF DARKNESS	Marco Vassi	
DEVIL'S ADVOCATE	Anonymous	
FERENT STROKES	Sarah Veitch	Aug
DOMINO TATTOO	Cyrian Amberlake	
DOMINO ENIGMA	Cyrian Amberlake	
DOMINO QUEEN	Cyrian Amberlake	
INE	Stephen Ferris	
MA'S SECRET WORLD	Hilary James	
MA ENSLAVED	Hilary James	
MA'S SECRET DIARIES	Hilary James	
LEN ANGELS	Kendal Grahame	
FANTASIES OF	Josephine Scott	
SEPHINE SCOTT		
GENTLE DEGENERATES	Marco Vassi	
RT OF DESIRE	Maria del Rey	
EN – A MODERN	Larry Stern	
DALISQUE		
MISTRESS'S VOICE	G. C. Scott	
USE OF ANGELS	Yvonne Strickland	May
HOUSE OF MALDONA	Yolanda Celbridge	
IMAGE	Jean de Berg	Jul
INSTITUTE	Maria del Rey	
TERHOOD OF THE	Maria del Rey	
NSTITUTE		

EROTIC SCIENCE FICTION

BLUE ANGEL SECRETS	Margarete von Falkensee	☐
CONFESSIONS OF AN ENGLISH MAID	Anonymous	☐
PLAISIR D'AMOUR	Anne-Marie Villefranche	☐
FOLIES D'AMOUR	Anne-Marie Villefranche	☐
JOIE D'AMOUR	Anne-Marie Villefranche	☐
MYSTERE D'AMOUR	Anne-Marie Villefranche	☐
SECRETS D'AMOUR	Anne-Marie Villefranche	☐
SOUVENIR D'AMOUR	Anne-Marie Villefranche	☐

SAMPLERS & COLLECTIONS

EROTICON 1	ed. J-P Spencer	☐
EROTICON 2	ed. J-P Spencer	☐
EROTICON 3	ed. J-P Spencer	☐
EROTICON 4	ed. J-P Spencer	☐
NEW EROTICA 1	ed. Esme Ombreux	☐
NEW EROTICA 2	ed. Esme Ombreux	☐
THE FIESTA LETTERS	ed. Chris Lloyd	£4.50

NON-FICTION

HOW TO DRIVE YOUR MAN WILD IN BED	Graham Masterton	☐
HOW TO DRIVE YOUR WOMAN WILD IN BED	Graham Masterton	☐
LETTERS TO LINZI	Linzi Drew	☐
LINZI DREW'S PLEASURE GUIDE	Linzi Drew	

Please send me the books I have ticked above.

Name   ....

Address   ....

....

....

.... Post code ....

Send to: **Cash Sales, Nexus Books, 332 Ladbroke Grove, London W10 5AH.**

Please enclose a cheque or postal order, made payable to **Nexus Books**, to the value of the books you have ordered plus postage and packing costs as follows:

UK and BFPO – £1.00 for the first book, 50p for each subsequent book.

Overseas (including Republic of Ireland) – £2.00 for the first book, £1.00 for the second book, and 50p for each subsequent book.

If you would prefer to pay by VISA or ACCESS/MASTER-CARD, please write your card number and expiry date here:

....

Please allow up to 28 days for delivery.

Signature ....